FOUR-SIDED
TRIANGLE

FOUR-SIDED TRIANGLE

WILLIAM F. TEMPLE

With an Introduction by
MIKE ASHLEY

This edition published 2018 by
The British Library
96 Euston Road
London NW1 2DB

Originally published in 1949 by John Long

Cataloguing in Publication Data
A catalogue record for this book is available
from the British Library

ISBN 978 0 7123 5231 4

Frontispiece artwork by Harold W. McCauley,
from *Amazing Stories* November 1939
Photo: Chronicle/Alamy Stock Photo

Typeset by Tetragon, London
Printed in England by CPI Group
(UK) Ltd, Croydon CR0 4YY

FOUR-SIDED
TRIANGLE

INTRODUCTION

The term "science fiction" was little known in Britain until the late 1930s and then only among groups of devotees who had started fan clubs in a number of cities. The phrase itself had been coined in the United States in 1929 by the entrepreneur, inventor and publisher Hugo Gernsback, but it took a while to catch on. In Britain the standard phrase had been scientific romance, when applied to the works of Jules Verne and H. G. Wells, and occasionally scientific fiction.

It was quite common for both terms to be used disparagingly. As far back as 1876 the noted astronomer Richard Proctor had remarked that Verne's *From the Earth to the Moon* had several scientific inaccuracies and was, in any case, based on the spurious idea that you could ever reach the Moon. Verne's fiction was aimed at younger readers, both in France and Britain—many were serialized in translation, in the British *Boy's Own Paper*—and, as a consequence, these wild scientific adventures became associated with boys' fiction. No surprise, then, that the first British science-fiction magazine, *Scoops*, in 1934, was a juvenile story-paper which helped consolidate the image.

If British writers wanted to sell more serious science fiction it was necessary to try the American science-fiction magazine market, which had grown significantly during the 1930s. So it was that John Beynon Harris (better known later as John Wyndham), John Russell Fearn and William F. Temple began to establish their names.

Temple was fortunate in that his dogged persistence meant he did find the occasional British outlet, including the first adult

British science-fiction pulp, *Tales of Wonder*, which began in 1937 and managed to survive into the early years of the War before paper rationing and the fate of its conscientious-objector editor, Walter Gillings, put paid to the magazine after sixteen issues.

Temple (1914–1989) had been born in Woolwich in South London and had entered the London Stock Exchange as a clerk in 1930, but his interests were of a different speculative nature, thinking of journeys to the planets. He had joined both the newly formed Science Fiction Association (SFA) and the British Interplanetary Society (BIS). He became active in both organizations, chairing the Writers' Circle of the SFA and joining the editorial teams of the SFA's *Nova Terrae* (the forerunner of Britain's later leading British sf magazine, *New Worlds*) and of the BIS's *Journal*. At this time he became firm friends with Arthur C. Clarke and for a while the two shared a flat in London which became the centre of various sf fan activities.

Meanwhile Temple's writing was progressing slowly. He had sold a horror story about an intelligent plant, "The Kosso", to *Thrills*, one of the Creeps series of anthologies in 1934, and "Another Chance" to Gernsback's magazine, *Wonder Stories*, in 1935. Unfortunately, that magazine was sold on to a new publisher and his story was abandoned but he soon resold it to *Amazing Stories* in the USA in 1938 where it was published as "Mr. Craddock's Life-Line". "Lunar Lilliput", which has the BIS succeed in the first manned moon flight, appeared in *Tales of Wonder* in 1938.*

Temple had long been dating his girl-friend, Joan, and they married in September 1939, just after the start of the Second World War.

---

* That story is included in the British Library anthology *Moonrise*, edited by Mike Ashley.

During their courtship Temple had considered the problem of the Eternal Triangle, and what if there was a rival for Joan's affections. Science fiction, of course, had the answer—matter duplication (this was long before the concept of cloning)—and Temple used that as the starting point for exploring the consequences. He developed the idea as a short story, "The 4-Sided Triangle", which his agent sold to *Amazing Stories* (November 1939 issue) but he knew there was more potential.

Unfortunately, Temple had first to serve king and country. He was conscripted in September 1940 and assigned as a field artillery signaller. His wife, Joan, and young baby Anne, were evacuated to Cornwall which was fortunate as, soon after, their home in Wembley was bombed.

In December 1942 Temple set off on a troopship heading for Egypt via South Africa, a 10,000 mile trip that gave him plenty of time to work on expanding the original story into a novel. He continued it as the Army marched through North Africa to Tunisia, engaging Rommel's troops. He had completed about half the novel when his satchel, holding the manuscript, fell from his truck during the battle of Takrouna in April 1943, and vanished into the desert.

From Africa, Temple was involved in the invasion of Sicily in July and while there he was spurred on by the news of the birth of a son, Peter, in September 1943. He started the novel all over again. From Sicily, Temple's battalion fought through the Italian mainland, and was involved in the fiercely contested battle of Anzio which raged from January to May 1944. Temple had again reached the half-way point in the novel when his jeep got bogged down in the mud. When he tried to extricate it, he found the manuscript had vanished again!

Temple was out of communication with home so it was months before he learned that his son had died of a viral infection when only seven months old. Devastated, it was not until he was on leave in Rome that he returned to the novel and saw it almost to its conclusion. He finished it in snowbound barracks in the Alps. Once home in October 1945 he typed the final copy. Though rejected by four publishers, the novel was accepted by John Long in August 1946 and eventually published in July 1949, nearly seven years after he had started.

Reviews were encouraging. "An outstanding first novel," wrote Eileen Bigland whilst John Keir Cross, reviewing it for BBC Radio, felt that it may well be "a better book even than the author altogether intended…" Certainly it made Temple's reputation and he went on to become one of the most popular British sf writers of the 1950s. The book was filmed in 1953 by Hammer Films, starring Stephen Murray and Barbara Payton. It remains Temple's best known and most resilient novel.

MIKE ASHLEY

CHAPTER ONE

THE IDEA WAS TOO BIG FOR THE MIND TO GRASP IN ALL ITS implications at the first attempt. But when you did get a grip on it, just to let the imagination rove with the possibilities…!

There were only six known genuine signatures of William Shakespeare in the world. And now there might be sixteen, sixty-six, six thousand and six.

There was only one Mona Lisa. One Venus de Milo. But now the Gioconda smile was in peril of losing its uniqueness. "Unique" was a word that had been suddenly bereft of its essential meaning during the last five minutes.

There could be fifty Mona Lisas, a hundred Venuses—in fact, no limit to the multiplicity of either interesting female—and each Mona Lisa and each Venus could claim to be as genuine as the one which had felt the brush of Leonardo or the chisel of an unknown Greek. The very same canvas and paint, the identical stone, just as the six thousand and six signatures could claim to be of the ink which had flowed from the poet's quill.

I turned from the solid result of the miracle I had just seen worked before my eyes and said in a voice croaky with awe and uncertainty, "I suppose—suppose it would even be possible to bring into existence another Sistine Chapel this way?"

"Complete to the last hair of the last beard of the last prophet, if we went about it in a big enough way," said Rob, with a smile from which he tried to keep the indulgence.

"Myself, no longer being a student of anatomy nor a believer in the Pearly Gates, I prefer the decorations of the local super-cinema," remarked Bill. "But if you want something like that for a birthday present, we'll see what we can do."

Oh, this incurable English habit of pretending to treat as a joke the strange and the new, whether idea or fact; and the more important the subject the lighter the treatment! No doubt a laugh is better than a bawl of rage and fear prophesying calamity and downfall, but it is no more helpful a reception, and lord knows how much genuine inspiration has wilted, withered and died under gentle but wearing Anglo-Saxon laughter. There is one thing forgivable about it: it is just as often disarmingly self-deprecating, if no more reasonable. And in this case the people who mocked were the same who had produced this miracle from brain and labour, the same who held the power to match Michelangelo and create a new Sistine Chapel.

To mount this miracle in its proper place in the strange story of the four-sided triangle it is necessary to go back a dozen years, to that rainy afternoon when a small red-headed schoolboy presented himself at my surgery, quite calmly bearing his broken left wrist in his right hand.

He wore an abominably frayed and darned green jersey, his socks were around his ankles, his trousers had been cut down clumsily from a secondhand larger pair, and the violence of the hue of his hair was equalled only by the violence of its disarray. (Even at twenty-six, when he began working these miracles, his hair was never anything but an unholy tangle, due to his habit of running his fingers through it continually in all directions whilst thinking—which was most of the time.)

I thought then, on that wet afternoon, that either his mother was a careless and thoughtless woman or else he had no mother. And then, placing the boy as the son of the unpleasant Fred Leggett from the poorer end of the village, I remembered that Mrs. Leggett was a patient who, some ten years previously, had faded rapidly from my grasp into complete non-existence. A pale little woman to begin with, some inexplicable anaemia drained her as though invisible leeches clung to her body, and before one could really think out the best course to take about it her paleness had become the ultimate pallor.

This boy had the same white face, although I judged from his condition, and from some knowledge of the character of his father, that malnutrition had more to do with it than anaemia. Though, as I was to find, he certainly did not lack life.

"Hullo, sonny," I said. "What have you been doing with your wrist?"

"I was doing an experiment, Doctor."

"Experiment?" I echoed, examining his wrist. "Trying a double somersault or something?"

"No, Doctor, I was testing the breaking strain of a rope. I had slung it from a tree and I had loaded more weights on it than should've snapped it, 'cording to the sums I'd worked out. Mechanics, you know. But it wouldn't break. So I got wild and went and swung on it myself. Then it broke. So did my wrist."

"I don't think it's broken, lad. Maybe only a sprain."

"No, a sprain would've swelled up more than that. I believe it's just a simple fracture. Prob'ly a Colles' fracture. Don't think it'll even need setting."

I looked at him pretty sharply at that. It was scarcely the line of talk to expect from a fourteen-year-old of the elementary school class. His pallid face was quite serious. There was no smirk of self-conscious precocity. I guessed that he must have been poking about in First Aid handbooks.

"Well," I said, "I'll run you along to the Cottage Hospital and we'll see what the X-rays say it is."

He was fascinated by the idea of being X-rayed. During that journey in the car I found there was more to this child than poking about in First Aid books. Because I was a doctor, quite an old doctor with greying hair, the boy thought I must know all about X-rays, their history and nature, and tried to get information from me.

Now, I was never of a technical turn of mind. I could not even do running repairs to my car, and was fleeced terribly by garage hands. I knew I was fleeced, but I would rather accept that than waste hours messing about hopelessly with spanners and wires and getting nowhere but into worsening mental and physical confusion. Electrical apparatus particularly baffled me. I could no more get an electrical circuit to stick in my mind than memorize a volume of *The Dutch Republic*.

Similarly with anything to do with physics or anything but elementary chemistry. People have to have a kink that way. I certainly hadn't got it. The steady progress of the ordinary G.P. from a simple administrator of castor oil and sedatives towards becoming a skilled operator of the most complicated clinical gadgets was the most unsettling realization that haunted my mind. I saw myself fumbling and blundering and perpetrating shambles of degrees that not even a lifetime's practice of the bedside manner could hope to cover or atone for. I was glad that my retirement was near enough within reach for me to have a fair chance of departing with a still intact reputation, even if in no blaze of glory.

So the boy's persistent questions were embarrassing. At first I tried to pass it off with the suggestion that it was all very difficult and hard to explain, and that the boy wouldn't understand anyway.

But the boy made it quite clear that he *would* understand. He said he had studied the pioneer work of Röntgen and the Curies and other people whose names were less familiar, and generously "reminded" me of it in some detail. I wasn't certain about Röntgen, but I happened just recently to have read a magazine article about the Curies, so I was able to keep up a façade of knowledge there. For a time. Then the boy smashed through it with the mathematics of the radiation of energy, trampled all over me with the Quantum Theory, and was wielding the Special Theory of Relativity like a bludgeon when I finally pulled up at the hospital with globules of sweat starting on my brow.

A Prodigy had come into my life.

While the boy was having his wrist photographed and taking one of the nurses on radiotherapy at the same time, I had a quiet word with the resident doctor, my old friend Hake, who was also a surgeon of no mean ability.

"That boy should be watched," I told him. "He should go a long way—and the quicker the better. He's nearly driven me crazy this afternoon."

"A short drive, in any case," said Hake (my old friend). "But just how?"

"Just listen to that patter for a bit," I said.

Radiotherapy had been neatly parcelled up and disposed of. The awestruck nurse was having the benefit of a discourse on the psychological side of nursing, which broadened into psychoanalysis, and Freud, Jung and Adler were tossed around like so many handballs.

"I think I see what you mean," said Hake after a time.

"He's fourteen. A boy at that age shouldn't even know he's got an unconscious mind!"

"He's obviously got one, anyway. And plenty of the conscious sort. What's his name?"

"Er—Leggett," I said. "Can't remember his christian name. He's the son of the notorious Fred Leggett—"

"Oh, that D.T.s case! Pity. The kid can't have much of a life. Let's see—" He pondered. "I'm sure his son was named Richard. Or was it Claude—?"

"Possibly another name that sounds like those," I suggested, just a bit too heavily.

My friend Hake glowered.

The nurse had finished with the boy but the boy hadn't finished with the nurse. Hake earned her long-lasting gratitude by calling him off. He came over, his arm in a smart white sling now.

"Sir?"

"What's your christian name, my boy?" asked Hake.

"Bill."

"William?"

"No—just Bill."

I have often noticed that in significant, historical and therefore presumably serious events, some incongruous factor generally pops up and twists things away towards the ludicrous. Hamlet, after the performance of the year, has fallen dead, but in that death holds the audience in an iron grip—and the theatre cat strolls up and licks his face. William the Conqueror, come with all his Normans to subdue England, leaps ashore at Pevensey from the leading boat, and falls flat on his face before his interested men. After a long and impressive ceremony of intricate ritual faultlessly performed, the climax of the Coronation comes: in a breathless hush, the aged archbishop, with slow and infinitely majestic dignity, goes to set the crown upon the King's head—and almost places it there back to front.

So here. A momentous discovery is made. A youthful Newton, possibly an embryo Galileo or Archimedes, is introduced to the world. And his name turns out to be Bill—just Bill.

"Come along, Bill," I said, taking his hand. "You must come and see me every day now, and we'll continue our chats."

The boy had every right to kick me there and then for the presumptuousness of that "our", but apparently grey hairs still draw a certain amount of respect from extreme youth, for he did not.

When I got the negative and report from the hospital, the case turned out to be a Colles' fracture. I told myself it wasn't worth mentioning to the boy, and anyway, he never asked about it. But there was precious little else that he did not ask about.

Risking the mental suffering it might cause me, I encouraged his curiosity. I gave him the run of my library. It was textbooks he wanted most, and it was hardly that sort of library. Some necessary medical reference works, some volumes on optics (purchased when I was dreaming of becoming a specialist—it remained a dream), Wells' and Huxley's *Science of Life* and other less popular biological publications, a few books of the "everyday science" sort, and an *Advanced Mathematics* (much too *Advanced* for me) were the best the shelves could supply.

Bill accepted the offer with real gratitude, which didn't prevent him from being critical. Sir Ray Lankester was dismissed as "childishly self-contradictory" and Sir Oliver Lodge got off with "outdated, and substituting wishful thinking for straight thinking".

Fiction, unless you included Shakespeare's plays in that category, was almost wholly ignored by Bill. He said you could say everything you wanted to say about life in essay form without jigging about demonstratively with puppets. The best prose appealed to him, though, and poetry very strongly.

Here at least, in the realm of the arts, I was able to introduce Bill to some things he didn't know too much about already. It wasn't that he hadn't been able to get at the facts. Howdean Village Library is, and was at that time, an excellent one. It was the main source of Bill's extraordinary knowledge of many things, although he had about exhausted its technical books at the time of our meeting. But I taught him appreciation.

In the sort of home—as far as it could be called a home—in which the boy was unfortunate enough to have spent the beginnings of life there was no appreciation of anything but alcohol. Nor was that a poetic appreciation in the manner of Omar. I had never met anyone more unpoetic than Bill's father. His bad language was not even colourful, only wearisomely repetitious. He chose to harp on an epithet for Bill which denied his own legal parentage of him, though he was probably too out-and-out ignorant to realize that.

It is said that alcohol affects people in different ways. It does not. It merely releases their inhibitions, and they blossom forth into a queer imitation of the sort of person they secretly wish to be. I myself probably wish to be a saint: when alcohol takes me beyond care of the opinion of others, I become a most generous, big-hearted and benevolent fellow, kindly disposed towards every living soul, seeing no faults and incapable of hatred. This *alter ego* also has bottomless depths of sympathy and pity, and a desire to bestow all his worldly goods upon anyone who appears to have even the slightest need of them.

But Mr. Leggett had distinct leanings towards power by force and threat, and (perhaps because of the frustration brought about by the early departure of his wife) a desire to possess women in abundance.

Poor Bill was the main lever by which Mr. Leggett achieved his illusion of power. Cuffs, boots, even punches came the boy's way at whim, and if he tried to escape, the superman would drag him back into the kingdom by his hair or his ear. This latter exhibition of the inexorable arm of justice in action would bring gratifying, if not very musical, laughter from the kind of women whom Mr. Leggett from time to time "possessed", on loan. There was, too, a certain Uncle Joe, a pervert, whose occasional appearance brought a grotesque strain into this symphony of existence.

On the whole, a more promising breeding-ground for subjects for the case books of Freud and Adler than the Leggett homestead could scarcely be visualized. In such hells the madman and the genius are wrought by stress. If Bill escaped with his sanity it was because of the happily-to-hand refuge of books, the doorways to other men's minds and dreams. And science was the most stable and sound structure in an unstable world, a haven of quiet verities found away from the harshness of loud lies and senseless mouthings.

The Howdean Village Library became Bill's real home, his school, his place of worship. He sat there reading until closing-time as often as he could. He dared not borrow books and take them home. Twice he had done that. The first book went into the fire. ("How dare you sit there reading when *I* am talking to you!") The second, on one of Mr. Leggett's peaks of power, was rent into scrap paper. ("Think because you can read you're cleverer than me, eh? Well, you *ain't*!") Trying to get together the money to pay the library for replacement was one of the most racking and anxious tasks Bill ever had thrust upon him.

It was a long time before I heard the real details of these things that had gone into the making of Bill. Those revelations came on the memorable night when Bill got drunk for the first time in my experience, the night on which perhaps it can be said that the first paragraph of the extraordinary sequence of the four-sided triangle was written.

For this is as yet the introduction, as necessary as a programme for a play.

But even a programme can be overburdened with detail, and there are other players to introduce yet. So the story of Bill and his progress after I had taken him under my wing must be taken in brief.

I was able to manage my protégé much more satisfactorily after the night when Mr. Leggett's will to power rivalled in strength and amount the Irish whisky he had poured into himself, and gave him the illusion that he was able to use it physically and with impunity on a fourteen-stone quarryman. It was his last illusion, and it was shattered together with his skull as he grounded after a flight backwards down the ten stone steps that mounted to the public bar of the "Lamb and Unicorn".

I became Bill's guardian. His odious Uncle Joe was at this time in the second week of the first year of a long sojourn in Parkhurst Prison.

I shall never forget those evenings we pored together over books. Bill opened up more wonderlands for me than ever I could for him.

Heaven lies about us in our infancy not solely because of our clinging trails of glory, nor because of the novelties we encounter here, but because of the *possibilities* of things yet to be discovered and explored, and the eager, excited anticipation of the imagination. The dullness of maturity only thickens upon us after a long succession of disappointments. When school turns out to be an affair of impositions, caning, things learned by rote, threats and misunderstandings. When the sea turns out to be grey, and not blue as in the advertising posters and the pirate books. When one's school hero in unguarded moments unveils a petty temper and a strong streak of selfishness, and makes impossible of realization certain fancied noble adventures for two. When Stonehenge is revealed as much smaller than the immense and mighty temple of the imagination and is, moreover, found to be caged in unromantic wire fences.

In the long run cynicism is unavoidable. We note at first with knowing amusement, then with impatience and boredom, and at last with drab acceptance the hack behind the pen, the calculation behind the advertisements, the vacuum behind the politician's speech. Then enthusiasm is blunted, and becomes more and more reluctant to respond to appeals because everything is suspect, even the genuinely worthwhile, and we are tired of breaking through into the same old world of vanity and self-interest, posing, pretence, smallness and snobbery. Continually one comes at last through the ideals of the art, religious, dramatic or political societies to just that same tangle of human weaknesses. A genuine enthusiast is a rarity. Generally speaking, only the very young are that.

Bill's enthusiasm was so vital, boosted by an alert imagination, that my own semi-dormant imagination was stirred into movement. The magic of the stars and the lure of pioneer trails caught me again, nature again was mysterious and not merely a stupid and purposeless process, and philosophy once more the old wonderful region of speculation and not a vaporous wasteland.

I became more young-minded as Bill matured, and when the boy mounted over examinations and scholarships to depart at last for Cambridge, it was as if he had taken all the colour in his train and left the village of Howdean in grey monochrome.

It was in the Cavendish Laboratory that Bill became acquainted with Robin Heath.

Probably this was primarily because they both came from Howdean. They had to go their various ways to Cambridge to meet and talk on common ground. For Robin was the elder son of Sir Walter Heath, and the Heaths had owned most of the land and property around Howdean for generations, and they lived a life apart in the big country house out of the village. In any case, Robin was only in Howdean for portions of his vacations from Eton, and later, Cambridge, and it is doubtful whether he ever noticed the red-headed boy who walked the remoter lanes and sprawled in the more secluded nooks in a perpetual reverie.

Now Robin had an unusually receptive mind and rather more than the general quantity of imagination for his type, but the fact remains that he was a type. He had had little chance to be anything else. His father had inserted him in the public school machine, designed to produce English gentlemen, at an age when the normal boy has neither the status nor the judgment to agree or disagree.

I imagine that Bill at the same age (in point of fact, he was a year younger than Rob) might have had some comments to make about the system, and would have propounded his own ideas about his education. But all the Heaths of the past, or all of the past that the Heaths cared to remember, had gone unprotestingly and apparently with benefit through the process, so who was Robin Heath that he must be different? Rob didn't want to be different then, nor did he now. It was not the thing to be "different". That pointed to immodesty at best and cheap vanity at worst. The gentleman does his job quietly in the ranks, and never on any account dashes out from them to cut capers and strike poses to draw the attention of his fellows to himself.

With which attitude I agree in the main, though I think much original knowledge and potential expression has been inhibited and thus lost to the human race through it, and consciously blind eyes have been turned upon new truths because the eyes of the ranks were still blind and could not, or would not, perceive their emergence.

Being the Heaths' family doctor, I knew Rob since he was born, and was aware of him as a living being before he was born. I saw him through measles and chickenpox and, once, pneumonia, and took his measure long before Bill walked into my surgery and my life. Yet, until the final racking stages of the four-sided triangle, I did not know what went on inside him half as well as I understood that crazy tangle of conflicts which was Bill's nature.

It was that hard-grown armour of reserve which defeated me, the chain-mail suit of behaviour wrought and tailored for each individual at the big public schools. His visible reactions were as conditioned as Pavlov's dog.

The non-committal tolerance towards violent expressions of opinion. The silent, compressed-lipped aggressiveness towards obstacles and chains of things that would go wrong. The "Well tried, old man!" comradely pats on the back to the failures. The half-pretence that sticky and uncomfortable positions were things to be desired as promising sport and fun. The stubborn and unreasonable loyalties, and incapability of going back on one's word. The mannered behaviour in the presence of the ladies. The reluctance to talk of self or analyse others. The genuine fondness for the English countryside, the farms, estates and villages, their historical background and the traditions that went with that background.

All those things went to make up Rob, a typical member of his class, and one doubted that he ever had a private opinion. He always sounded as though he said what he was expected to say.

With all that he was neither dull nor stupid. And he was ever the optimist. People like optimists, and seek their company. For the duration of that company their own doubts and hesitancies are pushed out of thought by the calm radiating faith of he who knows that everything is for the best in the end, and who is not daunted by the possibility of any catastrophes, and, in fact, does not believe in catastrophes.

"Don't worry, push on," was Rob's philosophy in four words. People, catching something of his buoyancy of mind, were often surprised to find themselves floating quite lightly over the diminished presentations of feared obstacles that yesterday loomed up before them as precipitous cliffs scored and scored again with chances of slips and falls.

But he was not foolhardy. He was merely methodical, and all the time his clear mind, reaching ahead of him, was planning his path with cool logic, and what may have looked like a bold risk to others was actually a step along a track already probed and tested and found firm.

This orderly mind could have fitted itself into many professions other than that of scientific research. It was more or less chance that it came into the laboratory at all. It could have been at home in the lawyer's chambers, at the manager's desk in any big business organization, over the architect's drawing-board or among the paper mazes of the Treasury or the Foreign Office.

But Sir Walter Heath had sat next to a famous research chemist at a dinner. The chemist had given him some idea of the possibilities of the future of plastics, particularly the financial possibilities.

Instead of buying shares, as he would normally have done, on a whim, Sir Walter set up his own manufacturing and research plant. It prospered. So Sir Walter thought it would be a good idea for his son to take over the managership of it. Thus Rob avoided the Classic side of the University, and studied commerce and chemistry.

And there one day he met Bill, the scholarship boy from his native Howdean. Bill was carrying out private experiments to verify certain revolutionary theories in atomic physics which he had built up. The experiments were successful. Bill explained his theories, and Rob, after thinking them over, perceived in them a far greater future than any plastics could have. They joined forces.

It was not an unequal partnership. Rob's unfailing patience and persistence balanced Bill's butterfly type of approach. Bill's attention jumped from problem to problem, and either solved them at once or threw them aside when the end was not in reasonable prospect of being disentangled. He was easily lured on to the possibly quicker reward of the next puzzle. On the other hand, his brilliant mind often leapt by something like intuition to the solution of a problem which would have taken Rob months to reach by his steady, planned path of trial and error and re-trial, the true scientific method.

How often have I seen that contrast in the rough laboratory, known to us as the "Dump", where they came at last to the fruition of their work!

"Damn and blast the thing!" Bill would exclaim, and suddenly, with a noise like "Grrr!", would rend across the papers on which he had been trying, in vain, to bring to some manifest sense the unearthly collection of symbols and brackets and signs he had scribbled furiously upon them.

Rob would look up and smile faintly.

"No go?" he would ask. "Here, pass me that original data. And the log book. How far did you get?"

Bill would tell him or not, according to his degree of irritability and self-disgust, but it would make no difference to Rob. He'd fill his pipe and get that going properly, and then sharpen his pencil with deliberation and start the whole thing again from the beginning, setting everything down neatly on numbered sheets, checking again and again with Bill's violently-scrawled-upon and disordered scraps of paper.

He might be still writing and pondering when everybody else had gone to bed, but next morning he would not only produce the indubitable answer but also point out where Bill had gone off the rails. This was generally a simple slip through sheer haste and carelessness. Bill was never wrong in his general prognosis. If it were possible to do everything in the mind, that is the way Bill would always have done it. It was the abstract that fascinated him. To have to demonstrate theories by mundane methods often irritated and bored him: physical activities prevented his mind from juggling with further mysteries.

Let me come now to the last of the *dramatis personae,* and, I suppose, the strangest of the trio.

Lena.

I can explain something of her, but nothing like all. One can only form his opinion of her from this record of what she said and what she did. I am only certain that she was the most generous, courageous, spirited and lovable character I ever met.

This meeting took place shortly after Bill and Rob left Cambridge and came back to Howdean and took over a small abandoned brick factory at the far end of the valley from the village and made it their place of experiment.

"What a dump!" I said, on my first sight of it, and thereafter they called it the "Dump".

They did not waste any time in beautifying it, but merely made a lab of the largest room, and made another room rainproof to sleep in. They were in haste and excitement (or Bill was, at least) to push on with their work.

Bill hinted to me of great discoveries and imminent results. Sir Walter Heath had put up something of a struggle for his son to take up the plastic factory management, but Rob had opposed it with quiet obstinacy. He had set his heart on this work, he said. Eventually Sir Walter gave in, and said he would invest a thousand pounds in this research—whatever it was—but not a penny more until a substantial profit in hard cash could be shown him, not as a prospect, but as an accomplished fact. Rob took the money, and the two adventurers got started.

I returned from my first visit to the Dump in the making to find a Mrs. Wilson waiting for me in a state of agitation. She was an aging woman of the village, but originally from Hackney, who lived by taking in laundry, taking out other people's babies, and helping with the neighbours' housework.

"What's wrong, Mrs. Wilson?" I said.

"Oh, Doctor, it's Miss Maitland—I dunno whether you know 'er—she took the old Martins' cottage abaht a month back. She's a nartist or somethink. She's bin took queer. She's in a bad way. Oh, Doctor, 'urry!"—breathlessly.

Without removing my hat I steered her straight out into my car.

As we rounded the corner of the by-lane leading down to the one-time cottage of the Martins, Mrs. Wilson vouchsafed: "She was lying on the floor. She'd bin sick. I lifted 'er on the bed and tried to give 'er water. She couldn't take it."

"Was she unconscious?"

"Not at first. But she was goin'."

"How did you happen to find her?"

"I scrub the cottage out for 'er on Friday afternoons. But I got to look after Mrs. Arnott's twins this afternoon—she's got to go to London. So I come round this morning instead. And the door was open and there she was, on the floor."

"I see."

We stopped at the cottage. I walked in, Mrs. Wilson scuffling at my heels.

I stopped just inside the door in sheer surprise. The cottage was not as it had been. The worn and age-rickety early-Victorian furniture of the Martins' had gone and left not a wrack behind. Original canvases in staring colours, framed and unframed, covered the walls, and etchings filled the odd spaces. At first glance it was like walking into a room in the Tate Gallery. Except for the fact that heaps of books lay about on the brown carpet and a third of the room was taken up by a baby grand piano. I had to step over a cascade of volumes still in their dust-jackets to reach the door of the small bedroom at the rear.

This was a bare place. There was nothing in it but a kitchen chair and a single bed with cheap stained plywood ends. And hanging down over the edge of the bed was a long mop of shining brown hair with golden threads running through it as though it were in parts sun-bleached. One white arm hung down and the hand lay limply on the floor. The owner of these things had too obviously been very sick.

I lifted her up and laid her on her back and pulled the coverlet off. Scarlet-and-white pyjamas leapt to my eye. Her eyes were shut, her mouth open, her lips bluish, and her skin grey. She was breathing, not very strongly, but with little jerky intakes. I rolled back her eyelid and examined her pupil.

As if that action had caused it, she tried again to be sick. She choked and nearly suffocated. I turned her over on her stomach again, which relieved her. Then I darted out quickly to the car and returned with a stomach pump.

When that messy business was over, and Mrs. Wilson, on my orders, was concocting some hot sweet tea, I tucked the patient up warmly, checked her temperature and pulse, found neither too good but improving.

I looked curiously at her face.

It was obviously no time for it to be appearing at its best. But no discrepancies of colour could offset the perfection of its modelling: the small, straight nose, just the slightest bit tip-tilted; an unusually firm little chin, against which weighed that faint curl and indentation at the corners of the lips which means a high sensitivity; the lips parted to show the two even edges of very white teeth. In contrast to the indeterminate hair (spread by mere chance across the pillow in an appealing abandon) the eyelashes were thick, long, and black, and lay upon her pale cheek like the strokes of a sketcher's pen on paper.

It is not so easy to judge the age of a person who has her eyes shut. Somehow the eyes are the greatest indicative. But I put her age at about twenty-two. As it happened, I was right on the mark.

While Mrs. Wilson fought with the oil-stove in the little scullery-cum-kitchen, I wandered inquisitively around the room which contained the books, the pictures and the piano. Many—too many, I thought—of the paintings were unfinished. They were mostly in the garish, slapdash style of Gauguin. But even those that were completed, although they showed originality of grouping, did not in some way "come off" as Gauguin's unfailingly did. The wielder of the brush had tried to be bold, but, I judged, was over-bold, with a sort of desperate, unfounded confidence, and things had lost cohesion. The colours had not been too well mixed, either: there were inconsistencies. I admired the artist's enterprise and ambition, though—nudes, landscapes, still life, symbolism, patterns—everything had been attempted, and not one was a particularly good example of its class.

The etchings were, if anything, worse. Even the ones which weren't out of drawing were blotched.

Poor Miss Maitland, I thought. If she thought she had a future in art, she had a sad realization yet to come.

There was music on the piano. All the Chopin preludes. Schumann's *Aufschwung*. Debussy duets. Scarlatti studies. Brahms sonatas. Whole books of Bach and Beethoven. Much Rachmaninov and Ravel. And an amount of blank staved sheets, some with a few pencilled bars scored across again and again by an obliterating indelible.

It was a piano of renowned manufacture, and not very old.

I turned my attention to the books. Dame Laura Knight's *Oil Paint and Grease Paint*, Vasari's *Lives of the Painters*, Berlioz' *Autobiography*, Sitwell's *Liszt*, J. W. N. Sullivan on Beethoven—a whole section of such works on painting and music, some elaborately technical.

Apart from these, I thought them a pretty mixed lot. But then I noticed one unifying quality. They were almost all by or about writers who sought, or sometimes produced without seeking, the perfect prose: Walter Pater, Virginia Woolf, Henry James, Robert Graves, James Joyce, Katherine Mansfield, Stephen Crane, H. M. Tomlinson, Joseph Conrad, and, in French, Flaubert and Julien Green—all deliberate stylists.

There were gems by less careful people, picked out by an aware, critical mind. And all the short stories of Tchekov, Wells, A. E. Coppard, and Stacy Aumonier. All the essays of Hazlitt, C. E. Montague, Max Beerbohm. *Arabia Deserta*. More's *Utopia*. The cream of literature.

There was scarcely a poet, lyrical or modern, unrepresented.

Half concealed behind Flecker's *Hassan* and Housman's *Last Poems* on a shelf was a green tin. For a moment I thought it was tobacco. The lid was loose, half off, lying askew. I picked the tin up, merely to replace the lid. I have a certain tidiness about such things.

Strangely, only little things like that jarred on me. Large untidiness, like everything about Bill, or this room, did not affect me. In fact, the general dishevelment of this room rather appealed to me. There was something unconsciously artistic in its disarrangement, like Miss Maitland's hair on the pillow.

I was putting the tin back when a word on it caught my eye. I examined the label carefully, and then the tin's contents. It was concentrated weed-killer.

I replaced the tin thoughtfully.

Mrs. Wilson called from the kitchen that the tea was ready. I went out and tasted it.

"Another teaspoonful of sugar, please, Mrs. Wilson," I said.

As she reached for the bowl I noticed an unwashed cup and saucer standing on the drain-board by the small sink. There were dregs in the cup. I took a sip of them and spat ungraciously into the sink. The tea was still very slightly warm. It could not have been made so very long ago.

Taking the cup of fresh, hot tea from Mrs. Wilson, I returned to the bedroom. Miss Maitland had not changed her position, but she was breathing more easily. I lifted her into a sitting attitude. She gave a little sigh. I teaspooned the tea between her teeth. At first it merely dribbled out again, and then, without volition it seemed, she began to swallow.

When the cup was half empty I laid her back, and sat on the edge of the bed, waiting.

There was a heap of small objects on the kitchen chair beside the bed: a powder compact, a lipstick, nail scissors, a cigarette-case, a booklet of matches, and a phial of tablets. I examined the phial. Veronal tablets. And the phial was completely full.

Mrs. Wilson stood hesitating at the door.

"'Ow is she, Doctor?"

"She seems to be doing nicely. I don't think she'll get any worse."

"I'm glad to 'ear that. 'Ere, I'll clean up that mess."

She vanished, and returned with a pail and some old rags, and cleaned up with efficiency. When she had finished: "Do you want me for anything more, sir?"

"You want to get away?... Oh... Well, would you mind dropping in a note at Nurse Perkin's on your way?"

I scribbled a request for the nurse to come and spend the night with Miss Maitland. Mrs. Wilson took it and departed. I resumed my watch on the girl in the bed.

Her eyelashes moved slightly. Presently her right hand began to flutter weakly around the coverlet as if seeking something to hold on to. I let it grip my wrist.

Suddenly her eyes were open and she was staring at the ceiling. Slowly she dropped her gaze until it met mine. She seemed a little perplexed. She whispered something I didn't catch. I bent nearer.

"Say it again," I said.

"What's going on?" she said in a soft, husky voice.

"Oh, nothing in particular. You were taken ill. You've been sick. How do you feel now?"

"A bit... headachy. Pains in the tum... Oh, lord, I remember now. So I didn't pull it off? I don't seem able to pull anything off."

"Pull it off?"

"Yes. I meant to shuffle off this mortal coil. But I seem to have missed the exit."

Her voice was stronger now, but not loud. She had a naturally soft voice, and she spoke slowly as if there were no hurry about anything in the world at all.

Her eyes were no longer puzzled. They regarded me with a faintly quizzical quality. I could not make up my mind what colour they were. I suppose I should have put "grey" on a report, but they were not any one colour. The irises gave the impression that they were built up in a sort of crystalline formation, splinters and chips and narrow facets radiating from the pupil, irregular segments that apparently contained no pigmental hue of their own but reflected colour from within. I think Lena's eyes were like the sea, whose colour is not inherent but a reflection of the weather in the sky, blue on sunny days and grey on cloudy ones. Similarly—a fanciful supposition for a physician, I admit—Lena's eyes reflected the weather in her soul.

Just now I was certain that humour was within her as she took in my probably somewhat shocked expression at her straightforward admission.

"I suspected as much, you foolish girl," I said. "Here, finish this tea."

I picked up the cup with my free hand. This movement drew her attention to the fact that she was still holding my wrist.

"What am I doing—taking your pulse?" she queried. "I imagined *you* were the doctor."

I ignored that. Gently she let my wrist go and took the cup in both hands. She drank a little at a time.

"You make better tea than I do," was her murmured comment when she had finished.

"I don't mix arsenic in it," I said, a trifle grimly.

She smiled faintly. "It adds to the flavour, but it's a bit... sickly."

"So I noticed. You were very messy. Why arsenic, for heaven's sake? The veronal would have been less messy and much less painful."

"I'm sorry. It was inconsiderate, wasn't it? I'll try veronal next time."

That stung me. This conversation was fantastic. To all my preconceived notions about such a situation, the subject should be tearful, remorseful, angry, frightened—anything but detachedly facetious.

"There'll be no next time, Miss Maitland. I don't know what put it into your head to do it this time. It's a silly way of trying to solve a problem—and cowardly. What's the good of running away?"

"What's the good of standing still?" she countered.

"I don't understand you. What's the trouble?"

She shook her head, the corners of her lips still curled whimsically.

"Nothing that you could do anything about, Doctor."

"To be frank—have you been jilted or something? Are you jealous?"

She really smiled at that. For some absurd reason her smile reminded me of cherries. Even at that moment I paused to think why. It eluded me.

"Have you—got into trouble?" I pursued, awkwardly.

She laughed aloud, a husky chuckle of a laugh, so warm and genuine and human that one could not help laughing in sympathy.

"No, I'm a good girl."

"You defeat me," I said, with a smile and a shrug. "I'm glad I don't get cases like you every day. You didn't do it for fun?"

"Perhaps," she said.

I stood up and gazed around helplessly and at a loss. Through the open door I saw part of the wall of the large room with the hung paintings. A notion occurred to me.

"All your own work?" I asked, indicating the canvases.

She nodded, rather more soberly. She looked at me, a hidden query in her eyes. I thought I had got it. I hardened my heart.

"Pretty awful, aren't they?" I said.

She looked me straight in the eye.

"Yes," she said, not defiantly, but in the manner of one stating a fact.

"Is that the trouble?"

She made no answer. Her gaze dropped. Her finger traced the pattern on the coverlet.

"It's not really a tragedy," I said. "One must accept these things. There's a lot of compensation in being able to appreciate beauty—it isn't necessary to create it."

Her finger halted at the corner of a square. I saw two big tears gather under those long dark lashes, break away and meander slowly down her cheeks.

In a low, muffled voice she said, "It *is* necessary."

And then the tears came in earnest, and I sat down again with my arm around her shaking shoulders. I felt unreasonably ashamed of my cruelty, but determined to remain hard. It would never do to agree with her. And yet—

"I'm sorry if I hurt your feelings, Miss Maitland," I said quietly.

She made an attempt to control herself, groped for a handkerchief under the pillow, wiped her eyes and blew her nose.

"I'm—I'm sorry if you think you did," she answered through the handkerchief. "You couldn't. No one could. I don't care what other people think. The trouble is what *I* think."

"You think you're a failure?"

"I know I am. I haven't got it in me." (Sniff.) "No divine afflatus. And yet the urge to create, create, create won't let me be. God knows I've tried every way to give it expression. I've tried and tried. And my painting isn't good enough for a pavement. My attempts to compose music are only endless imitation. And writing... I'm not even a sedulous ape. The pen sticks in my hand like something immovable. Squeezing words out of it is like getting blood out of a stone—and what words! Schoolgirl essays! False, all of them!"

"Must you create something in the arts? Surely there are other things as rewarding?"

For the first time since the breakdown she looked at me. She smiled a little ruefully with still wet eyes.

"Would you have me knitting jumpers? Designing brassières? Doing fretwork?"

"I had thought of something like landscape gardening," I said, a trifle uncomfortably. "But the things a girl of your age should be thinking of creating are a home and a family. I believe that's what you're really seeking underneath."

"Are you married, Doctor?"

"Er—no."

"Why not?"

"I—um, things never went that way. I've always been interested in so many things… I've never really thought… A country doctor is kept pretty busy, you know."

"What sort of things are you interested in?"

"Oh, medicine, and philosophy, and—well, the arts."

She made no answer, but regarded me with a return of that quizzical look.

I began to get defensive.

"Don't think because I never married that I don't know what it is to bring up children. I *do* know the amount of creative satisfaction that can be got by moulding a child's character and outlook, and guiding its intelligence along the most fruitful paths."

I hesitated a moment, then plunged into the story of Bill and myself. She listened patiently, but before I had finished I felt that her attention was somewhere quite outside ourselves and surveying the pair of us dispassionately.

"Interesting," she commented, when I had brought this tale to a finish. "I must see this Bill sometime."

"He's back from college now. I'll introduce you," I said, a little too quickly.

She gave me a look between amusement and wariness. In that slow, almost lazy, manner she said: "If, by any chance, you have any ideas about making matches, Doctor, please forget them. Things don't go that way for me, either."

"I don't think there's any danger, Miss Maitland," I replied coldly. "As your sex takes very little interest in science, it scarcely exists for Bill. In fact, unless you evince some warmth towards Mr. Einstein I doubt whether Bill will even notice whether you're male or female."

"Who is Mr. Einstein?" she asked, so innocently that I didn't know how to take it. At that time I was not aware of the mocking sprite in her.

I did not answer. I was surprised at my own unaccountable wish for this meeting. Possibly I did think it would be a good thing for Bill to discover women and become a little more worldly than he was. But why I should consider this unstable girl with suicidal tendencies a suitable specimen for a start I could not imagine. There was something undeniably attractive about her. Only—

"Miss Maitland," I began sternly.

"Lena, please," she put in meekly, throwing me rather off balance.

"Miss Lena—"

"No. Lena."

"Will you let me speak?"

"Do go on."

I'd lost the initiative now, but spoke with as much gravity as I could collect.

"You know, I should report this matter to the police. Because no one besides us knows of it, I won't."

"Is that ethical?"

"Don't interrupt. Now, your reasons for this act, however they appeared to you, are to me fatuously inadequate. Perhaps I cannot persuade you of it. But I do want you to promise me one thing. Please don't attempt it again, at least before my next visit. Will you give me your word of honour?"

"That sounds frightfully St. Gertrude's Fifth Form. No, I'm afraid I can't. It all depends on my moods, you see. Nothing to do with my honour."

"You are the most exasperating child—"

I stopped, for she was holding out to me the phial of veronal tablets.

"Take these instead of my word," she said. "And on a bookshelf in the next room you'll find a tin of weed-killer. Not very good stuff. It wouldn't kill the weediest weed. I promise you I'll buy no more of that—I was robbed!"

"I still don't know why you took it instead of veronal," I said, slipping the tablets into my pocket.

"Oh, taking veronal would be just like going to sleep. I think dying ought to be quite an experience, something you've never done before. If you want to express life through art you've got to experience everything in life—and death."

"I can't see how you can express life when you're dead," I said. "You have the most fantastic reasons... I can't comprehend you at all."

"Perhaps I *am* a genius—yes?"—with that provocative smile.

"No, your sense of values is merely perverted—"

There was a knock at the cottage door.

"Nurse Perkin, probably," I said, and went to answer it. It was. I had a few quiet words with her in the other room, telling her that on no account was Miss Maitland to be allowed to get up, or move out of that bedroom, or have anything to eat.

"I'm leaving you in Nurse Perkin's care now, Miss Maitland," I said, showing the nurse in. "I'll be calling again in the morning. Meantime, just try to sleep. Good-bye."

"Just a moment, Doctor—a private word." Lena beckoned me over. She made me stoop down, and whispered in my ear, "My grandmother committed suicide."

I bit my lip, and glanced up at the nurse, who was unpacking her case. Then I gazed straight into Lena's bright eyes only a few inches from mine. I saw the red imp of mischief dancing there among the glinting lights.

Strangely, that impudent message, possibly true, gave me a feeling of relief. I was beginning to take Lena's measure. There was a child in her who, like the baby in *Alice in Wonderland*, delighted to do things just "to annoy". So long as the child was alive in her, nothing was serious. It is only when we are in an adult, weary mood that the world appears sometimes no longer to be tolerated.

"Be good, you vixen!" I muttered, pressed her hand, and left— nearly forgetting to collect the tin of weed-killer as I passed through the outer room.

As I was driving home a memory drifted into my mind's eye of an oleograph that used to hang in the passage of the house where I was born and spent my childhood. It was of a chestnut-haired little girl in a white poke bonnet. She was smiling and proffering a basket of cherries. And held between her white teeth by the linked stalks, dangling from lips as red as they were themselves, was a pair of gorgeous cherries.

That little boy who was me never passed that picture without a look, often a long look.

Thus the "cherry smile".

I thought that if I could have encountered Lena forty years ago, things might have gone "that way" for me after all.

CHAPTER TWO

IN THE EVENING I PAID MY SECOND VISIT TO THE DUMP.
The door was jammed half open: the top hinge was broken
and had not yet been attended to. I squeezed through the gap.

Under a couple of naked electric globes Bill and Rob, in shirt-
sleeves, were working away in the midst of a disordered clutter of
equipment which looked as if a power-house and a radio station
had been partially dismantled and their fittings thrown on to a
common heap. Coils of wire were springing apart all over the floor,
and from the raftered roof cables of all thicknesses were looped
and dangling like creepers in a tropical forest.

Bill was bent over a sizable piece of apparatus trying to insert
a screw, which was clinging uncertainly to the end of a magnetic
screwdriver, into the narrowest and most inaccessible crevice
among the soldered wires of the thing. He was standing in his own
light, and Rob was nonchalantly directing the beam of a hand-torch
into the dark crevice.

Bill probed gingerly. The screw became detached, and tinkled
away on a private journey into the interior.

"Blast!" emitted Bill with vehemence, and tore his flaming
hair. He gesticulated wildly with the hand holding the screwdriver.

"If it isn't enough to make a saint—"

Cr-rack! Crr-rack!

The point of the screwdriver had struck upon some live ter-
minal, and vivid blue sparks rasped into being. Bill flung the tool
from him with language more electric than the sparks. Rob laughed
uproariously, noticed me, and jerked his head, still laughing,

towards Bill, conveying to me the unsaid remark, "Isn't that just typical of him?"

Bill caught the indication, and turned to view me in some chagrin.

"Hullo, Bill," I said. "Having fun?"

"He's demonstrating different ways of turning the air blue," grinned Rob.

Bill scowled. "A mere technical hitch. The Master Mind will recover. Meanwhile, does anybody want a cigarette?"

He produced a packet and handed it round. When we were lit, Rob strolled over and recovered the screwdriver and began tinkering with the apparatus. Bill sat on a rough bench and puffed at me: "Well, Doc, what's in the wind? Have you come to give us a hand?"

"That depends. I may get called away any minute. Mrs. Lewis's time is ripe—over-ripe, in fact. Besides, give you a hand to do what? What *are* all these contraptions?"

"It's hard to explain, Doc. Most of them have only just been invented and haven't got any names. If I were to explain their functions I should have to go into a lot of technical jargon, and I know that means nothing to you. I'm not sure even that they'll carry out their intended functions. I'd much rather wait until we got them going properly, and a demonstration would speak for itself—pretty loudly, if it comes off."

"They'll function all right, Doc," said Rob, probing patiently with the screwdriver. "The theory is watertight, and a good bit of it has already been tested in practice."

"All right, Bill, if you want to be hush-hush I'll wait and see," I said. "Actually I didn't come here out of mere curiosity. I'm a man with a mission."

Bill raised his light eyebrows.

I continued: "There's a newcomer in Howdean, a young girl named Lena Maitland, and I think you might be able to help her."

Bill's eyebrows dropped into a frown.

"A girl?"

"Yes. Not exactly an ordinary girl. But I'll begin at the beginning."

I told them every detail of my visit to Lena and what had been said and implied.

"I'm sorry for the girl," said Bill at the conclusion. "But, really, what can we do about a frustrated amateur artist? It's entirely up to herself."

"Well," I said, "there are two things wrong with that girl. First, she has lost enthusiasm for everything. Life appears empty and pretty murky to her. Honestly, I do believe that she doesn't care a pin whether she lives or dies. Second, she sees things reflected in the distorting mirror of an artistic temperament. Her values are all to pot. She wants a little common sense injected into her. Now, you, Bill, are just the fellow to get her interested in things again. Any things—that is, any things you are enthusiastic about yourself. I know your enthusiasm is catching: I've had some. Once you even got me interested in carburettors. And you, Rob, are the man to give her the right sort of 'talking to'—not directly, you know, but you talk in such a matter-of-fact way that unconsciously people come around to your outlook, persuaded that it is the sane and obvious one. Soothing, reassuring—that's your suit. You've a better bedside manner than I've achieved in forty years."

Bill and Rob exchanged glances, and laughed.

"And you, Doc, have the nicest line in smooth-tongued flattery that we know," said Bill. "I'm sorry you've wasted it on me. If there are two things wrong with that girl, there are also two things wrong with your proposition. First, I hate being introduced to women. About the only woman I ever wanted to meet was Madame Curie. Second, we are working like mad to get this job done. We'll probably be working most of the night."

"It's tomorrow night I wanted you to visit her."

"Well, and tomorrow night too. This is one of the biggest things ever, Doc—the results may be incalculable for everybody. I'm serious. I'm mad keen to see how it turns out. I really have no time for side issues, especially with the other sex. Perhaps later, when this is over."

"Later may be too late. How about you, Rob?"

Rob stubbed out the cigarette he had hardly drawn upon, and took out his more appreciated pipe. He had in his quiet, efficient way got the awkward screw into its place while we had been talking.

"H'm," he said, stuffing tobacco into his pipe. "I must admit I'm no more keen than Bill to meet the girl. I don't know much about art. I don't understand at all how she can take it so badly. Can art mean so much as that to anyone? Frankly, I loathe the clever girls from Bloomsbury. Girls shouldn't be intellectual—only nice. But that's beside the point. If I can help save her from doing something idiotic, I'll try. But can you make it tomorrow afternoon or the next day, Doc? I've arranged for a pretty important talk with Dad tomorrow night."

"Lord, yes!" exclaimed Bill. "You must see the old man about funds."

"You see," said Rob, "Dad invested a thousand pounds in our project, to set us up. We thought it was enough, but it turns out that it isn't. We need half as much again. I want to try to talk it out of him if I can. We're still quite a lot of vital apparatus short.

Transformers, for instance. Special valves. Oh, heaps of it. By the way, Bill, you won't be able to do much more tomorrow until we get that Heivers transformer."

"Hell, no!" exploded Bill. "Oh, hell, hell! Another hold-up!"

"Thanks for your offer, Rob, anyway," I said. "I don't know about tomorrow afternoon. It's too soon. She may not be well enough. It'll take her a good long day to recover from the dose she took. I'll see her in the morning. But if Bill can't get on with anything here tomorrow night, he might as well go and see her as sit here kicking his heels, and probably the apparatus too, in furious inactivity."

"I think so," smiled Rob, and sucked a match flame into the bowl of his pipe.

"Oh, you artful pair!" said Bill petulantly. "Shyster lawyers ain't in it. All right, Bill the sucker will go. I'll stop that girl killing herself if I have to kill her myself to do it—I probably shall."

"Good man, Bill," I said. "I'm sure someone is dusting off your seat in heaven at this very moment. I'll call tomorrow about seven and take you round… All right, I see I'm not popular here now. I'm off before you change your mind. I'll shut the door behind me."

"I don't think so," Bill fired after me, and of course I couldn't— the thing was hopelessly jammed.

"You might get this repaired," I said, as I squeezed round it.

"There's an idea: that's a job I *could* be doing tomorrow night—" began Bill thoughtfully.

"Good night!" I shouted, and was away.

The dilatory Mrs. Lewis did not get me out of bed that night, and next morning when I saw her the labour pains had died away again. The stork takes these turns of mind sometimes.

My next visiting patient was Lena.

Nurse Perkin opened the door, a small, rather worried-looking woman in the fifties.

"Oh, Doctor, I'm so glad you've come," she said relievedly. "The patient won't go back to bed."

"Won't she?" I said grimly. "Let me get at her."

Lena was reclining in the armchair by the fire, in her scarlet-and-white pyjamas, holding out her bare feet to the blaze and smoking a cigarette. An open book lay on the arm of the chair at her elbow. Her colour was a good bit healthier than yesterday.

"What is the meaning of this, Miss Maitland?" I said.

She breathed smoke towards the fire, not a plume, but the tenuous shapelessness of inhaled smoke. She stared pensively through it at the flaming coals.

"There is no meaning," she said dreamily. "Life has no meaning. It is only an experience, like a beautiful view or the scent of a flower. All you can do is try to transmute the experience through art, change it into a form of expression, so that feelings may be recorded and felt again. But it's awfully hard to do. It's the hardest thing in the world. That's why I like to try to do it."

"The present tense is promising," I said. "But you'd better get back to bed, or it'll be the past tense whether you intended it to be or not."

"That's what I keep telling her, Doctor," said the nurse, not (I think) gathering the intent of all my words. "She *would* get up."

"Why not, Nurse?" asked Lena, looking up. "I've had a good night's sleep, which is more than you've had, poor thing. I do think you ought to go and lie down, you know. Go on, there's a good girl: have a lie down on my bed, and I'll bring you in a cup of tea about eleven."

The nurse looked lost. I repressed a smile. I do not think Lena was being facetious on this occasion, only genuinely well intentioned. She lacked self-pity completely. I learned in time that her physical condition was something she just never wasted thought upon, and she took it as a matter of course that nobody else should bother about it either.

"Before you start giving orders, you'll obey mine, Miss Maitland," I said.

"Lena—be nice."

"All right, let's have a look at you, Lena."

I investigated pulse and temperature and eyes. The irises had flashing red points in them today, reflections from the fire.

"Any more sickness?"

"Only of soul."

"Any spasms or pains in the stomach?"

"Yes, spasms of annoyance and pains of hunger: Nurse has locked the larder door and swallowed the key."

"You can have a couple of poached eggs for lunch. You're more or less back in one piece. All you've got to do now is rest."

"Rust?"

"Rest. Well, thank you, Nurse. You'd better get some rest, too."

Nurse Perkin hesitated, looking from one to the other of us. She opened her mouth, then closed it again. But the doubt spoke from her weary eyes.

"Don't worry, Nurse—off you go," I said. "Miss Maitland is a difficult case, but I'll see she's all right. I'll send for you again if you are needed."

"Very good, Doctor." Still dubious, she went.

"I'll have Mrs. Wilson come around this afternoon to do anything you need," I said. "And I expect to call in again tonight."

"I'm afraid you still don't trust me, Doctor," murmured Lena. "But you'll have to. I don't want you to send Mrs. Wilson here again. Nor the nurse. And I should be pleased if you would look upon this as your last visit."

"Are you dissatisfied with my treatment?"

"Not in the least. You have been very kind."

"Then why this dismissal?"

"I would rather not tell you, Doctor, but believe me there is a very good reason."

"Well, Lena, your reasons don't count with me. Since I've known you I've developed a very poor opinion of your reasons for doing or not doing anything. I think you're wilful. At some time you've been spoilt. Somebody should take you in hand. I am not presuming to do that—I hope some forceful young man may come along and do it soon enough. But I want you to understand that no patient dismisses me: it is I who dismiss patients—when, and only when, I am thoroughly satisfied with their condition."

"Who did you say was wilful?" she bantered.

"That's not wilfulness, that's my job," I replied. "I have a certain sense of responsibility, even about irresponsible people like you."

I felt a bit priggish, taking this tone. But I had the idea that I was preparing the ground for Rob and Bill to knock some common sense into her. Writing this now, with fuller knowledge of Lena, I can only say of myself, "Poor ass!" How utterly ridiculous overbearing righteousness, mounted on a base of complete ignorance, must appear to the recipients of it! Lena "spoilt"! It is laughable—or she would have thought it so, and no doubt did. Other people might take such a wild misstatement about themselves more seriously. And to talk of "taking in hand" a spirit so much stronger and independent and self-assured than my own, than most people's, was more pure babble.

"So long as you realize I'm not responsible, that's all right," said Lena, flashing me a bright, but somehow enigmatic, smile from those white teeth and red lips. And then she turned to reach for another cigarette, and proceeded to light it from the butt of her old one.

"I'm sorry, Doctor—a cigarette?" she puffed, proffering me the box with one hand and shying the butt with unerring aim into the heart of the fire with the other.

"No, thank you, Lena. And I think chain-smoking is not advisable just yet."

"Chain-smoking is never advisable."

"Well, I'm advising you to put that cigarette out."

"Thank you, Doctor."

"For what?"

"The advice."

I had run into a dead end again. When I thought I was putting my foot down with authority she seemed to slip from under it like free air, a natural effortless movement. I was stamping upon nothing. A vision of myself doing so, ridiculously, ineffectively, and her contrasting calm attitude, partly mocking, partly indifferent, appeared before my eyes and abruptly went up in red flame. I lost my temper. I reached out and quite rudely took the cigarette from her and tossed it at the fire. I say "at", because it hit the bar and rebounded on to the hearthstone and lay there smouldering.

With that maddening sweet smile Lena reached elegantly down for it and flicked it straight into the hot coals.

"Is that what you were trying to do, Doctor? I like to help you, but I don't quite see the point of this. You know as well as

I do that you won't be gone two minutes before I am smoking again."

"I've no doubt of that," I said truculently, and I hadn't. "Look here, Lena, if you won't co-operate with me, you can't expect me to co-operate with you."

"You mean you won't come to see me any more? That's nice of you, Doctor, to fall in with my request. Now you *are* co-operating."

"I mean nothing of the sort!" I exclaimed—almost a yelp, like an old dog. "I mean I reserve the right to use any means to get you into good health, mental and physical, again. Any means."

"Meaning mean means?"

"You'll find out," I said darkly, gathering my things. The idea grew and persisted at the back of my mind that I, a supposedly wise man of medicine and sixty summers, was behaving like the spoilt child I had imagined this cool and undisturbed girl to be. I felt I could not go away leaving such an impression.

Rather hesitantly, and looking Lena in the face only with an effort, I said: "Lena, let's not be bad friends. Oh, I know we aren't really, and it's only I that's been snapping. I'm sorry I lost my temper just now. Though you are a damned provocative person—yes, you are. But, as I say, I'm sorry I was rough."

"Personally, I think you were about as rough as a sheet of glass," smiled Lena. "But as you want to be forgiven, I'll forgive you. Now we're friends, eh? Cigarette?"

And she proffered me the box.

I swallowed, and took one, and when she took one too, looking at me with eyes that now appeared as blue as the Pacific and as innocent, I said nothing.

But when she struck a match and held it out to me, I saw the flame beneath my nose flickering and dancing, and the hand that held it shook too. I glanced up at her face and saw that the girl was shaking all over with suppressed amusement, and as soon as she saw that I had noticed it it all burst forth—peals of rather husky but most pleasingly melodious laughter.

There was nothing else to do. I had to laugh, too. There had been such an adroit turning of tables that I had no dignity left to stand upon. I knew in that moment that never, as long as I lived, would I ever have the whip hand of Lena. I could not imagine anyone else having it, either.

In the evening I called at the Dump for Bill. I was rather later than I had meant to be. Rob was already away on his diplomatic loan-raising mission to his father.

Bill made me come in and share the pot of tea he was brewing. Over that he began a long discourse on the Michelson-Morley experiment, exhausted it as far as I was able to understand it, and went on to the Lorentz-Fitzgerald Contraction. He made it interesting, but I knew my Bill.

"Is all this anything to do with the mysterious work you're engaged upon?" I asked.

"Well, in a way, yes, but—"

"But not directly. No. I thought not. You're merely hedging for time. Now, you know very well why I've called."

"Oh… that Maitland girl? Hasn't she changed her mind yet? Straight up, Doc, do you think there's any real need—"

"I do, Bill, so locate your overcoat. It's late enough now."

"All right, all right, she's asked for it."

We went.

As we approached the one-time Martins' cottage the only illumination in its windows was the jumping pattern of red light and black shadows from the sitting-room fire. I knocked at the front door and it swung open a few inches: it was not latched.

"Is that you, Doctor?" came Lena's soft voice from somewhere within.

"Yes."

"Come in."

We went in. The sitting-room was empty. Lena, apparently, was in the little bedroom. On the back of a chair, airing at the side of the fire, were hanging her scarlet-and-white pyjamas. Bill removed his overcoat and went and stood on the hearthrug with his back to the fire, warming his posterior. His stance showed a slightly self-conscious determination to be bluff and masterly with this errant young girl. Knowing just how likely this attitude would succeed with Lena, and how little Bill was expecting the unexpected, I concealed a grin by making another casual inspection of the bookshelves, peering in that uncertain light to make out the titles.

I heard Lena's voice.

"Oh, hullo! Are you Bill? I didn't expect to be introduced so soon."

That's one point I can mark up for myself and against you, my lady, I thought, without turning. You're being proceeded against according to my plan. Already my agents are at work. I decided to let the pair introduce themselves, and pretended to admire the binding of a Spencer's *First Principles*.

But for a determined, masterly man Bill seemed a little slow. I heard a sort of gasp, suddenly throttled, and then silence, and then noises like the beginnings of words that got stuck in his throat.

"Er—yes. Er—no," was all he managed. I thought he had let me down. I turned with a little frown. He stood there most awkwardly on the hearthrug, his hands twitching at his side, his face a darker red than the firelight could have painted it (and I knew he was blushing violently in the manner peculiar to his complexion), and looking with a queer half-averted gaze towards the bedroom door. I looked there, too, and nearly dropped Spencer, for framed in the dark oblong of the doorway was Lena, wearing that lovely cherry smile and not a thing else. Her hair was in disarray, and she had obviously only just got up.

Her gaze switched to me.

"Good evening, Doctor Harvey—how's your circulation by the way?… You're late. I'd given you up and gone to bed. So this is your protégé? I think he looks as intelligent as you said, though he seems to be a man of few words. Never mind, Bill, I expect you'll thaw out. Which reminds me—my pyjamas."

She walked over towards the fire. Bill skipped off the hearthrug like a scared deer.

"Don't move if you're cold," she said, looking at him a little puzzledly, and I am certain that puzzlement was genuine. "I only want to see if they're dry yet. They're the only pair I possess now, and I washed them this afternoon."

She examined them. I can see that picture through my memory's eye now: Lena stooping gracefully over the chair, earnestly and absorbedly investigating her garments, with the firelight bathing her slender, perfect figure, dark red shadows bringing into relief the curves of her breasts and shoulders, her tumbling hair looking almost black in that ruby emanation—as unselfconscious as a nymph in her secret bower. What a beautiful painting that would have made, I thought.

She pursed her lips and cocked her head doubtfully on one side as she passed her pyjama jacket through her long fingers.

"Near enough," she decided, and my tension fell away, for I knew that if they hadn't satisfied her she would have seen no reason to put them on. I felt easier when I saw her dressed, or dressed as far as I had seen her attired so far.

"That's it," she said. "Come on, let's all sit round the fire. You're very quiet too, tonight, Doctor. You're not annoyed with me again for something, are you?"

"No—no, not at all," I said with a start. "I was—er—thinking."

"What about? I hope it's interesting. I feel in the mood for a bit of 'argument about it and about' tonight."

"I'm supposed to be paying you a professional visit, if you remember."

"Oh—must you? I feel fine. I haven't felt so fine for a long time. Arsenic must agree with me."

She couldn't have known that I had told Bill about her suicidal effort, but it was obvious that she didn't care if I had.

After Bill had left the hearthrug so precipitately he had taken refuge, figuratively speaking, in the pile of music on the baby grand. He was still looking through it.

"Are you fond of music, Bill?" asked Lena, looking across at him.

I decided to waive the professional side of the visit. Plainly it was not necessary.

"Yes, I am," said Bill. He approached the fireplace and settled on a chair. I pulled up another, and we made a little arc before the fire.

"Tchaikovsky, in particular," added Bill.

"He let himself go, didn't he?" mused Lena. "He wore his heart on his sleeve. I like people like that."

"Yet he was anything but a simple character," I put in, feeling it about time I came to life. "Full of moods and self-doubt—arising from his sexual perversity, of course. He was probably the most versatile composer of them all. He made a success of everything: symphonies, concertos, chamber music, songs, marches, ballets, concert overtures. Yet he had only to hear the *Coppelia* ballet music of that delightful but limited Frenchman, Delibes, to feel that his own *Swan Lake* was rubbish in comparison, and be so utterly depressed and miserable as to think of—"

(Damn! What thoughtlessness had brought me to this? I thought furiously, but could see no escape. Lena and Bill were watching me and listening.)

"—of ending his life," I finished, scarcely happier than Peter Ilitch himself.

As I might have known, Lena didn't turn one of her brown-and-spun-gold hairs.

"Once he jumped in the Neva, on a winter night, and tried deliberately to catch pneumonia," she said. "And didn't he die in the finish through drinking unboiled water he must have known was thick with cholera germs?"

"I believe so," I said, wishing that the melancholy Russian's name had never come up for discussion. The talk kept driving towards the very subject upon which this evening I had opened my campaign to oust from her thought, to banish by the introduction of brighter things. But, against all my ideas, it was Lena who led the conversation.

"I cannot understand how he could be so continuously unhappy," she said. "He had proved his ability over and over again. He was always working and producing fresh evidences. How could he ever feel inferior? How could he be plagued with self-doubt? It is those who have every faith in themselves, and yet fail consistently to produce anything worth a damn, who should know what unhappiness is. Myself, as a case in point."

"Do you believe that you will ultimately create something that will satisfy you?" asked Bill.

"Oddly, I do. Despite the fact that I've tried every form of expression I can think of, and achieved every degree in them between downright failure and mediocrity—which is really failure, too—but never one example which hinted at promise, never one thing which I felt I could do again better. Yet I believe this desire to create was not made part of me unless at some time it is destined to be consummated. In this life or the next," she added pensively.

"You believe every need is, by some obscure workings of Nature, tied up with its eventual satisfaction?" queried Bill, with an appearance of seriousness at least, although I suspected that he was inwardly amused at such irrationality.

"The law of demand and supply?" I said, intelligently perhaps.

"Well, it's rather more of a spiritual matter than human economics, Doctor," smiled Lena. "Of course, it's not rational. I believe it, probably as most people believe such things, because I want to believe it. But even such a belief may bog down temporarily after years of attempts that bring no results and lead one only into a state where even attempts are no longer possible."

"You mean—" I began.

"I mean I shall be telling a disgusting tale of woe if you drive me into explaining what I mean," she evaded. "Sometimes I wish there was no such thing as belief. Only absolute knowledge. To *know*, one way or the other."

"There is no such thing as absolute knowledge, there is only faith," said Bill.

For once Lena looked surprised.

"That's a strange statement for a scientist to make, surely?" she said. "I thought you people had most things taped and measured, sorted and popped into their pigeon-holes?"

"Einstein rather upset the solid world of pigeon-holes," said Bill. "Nowadays we believe that pigeon-holes have no definite size or position in space and time. Only relative ones. But that wasn't the point I meant. You think we *know* things. We don't. We know nothing. We say we 'know' that when sulphuric acid is poured on zinc it produces hydrogen. That's because of the thousands of times sulphuric acid has been poured on zinc and it *has* produced hydrogen. We say therefore it has been experimentally verified. But because it's always happened every time so far doesn't necessarily mean to say that it always will happen every time. A man may catch the 8.25 train every morning for years and think therefore he always will. But one morning the 8.25 doesn't turn up: there's been a railway strike, or the engineer forgot to put the water in the boiler, or the wheels fell off. The same with the chemical experiment. Some accident that never happened before might happen. One day a man may pour sulphuric acid on a bit of zinc and it will turn pink and give off *Night in Paris*. Every such experiment is only an act of faith. We don't really know what will happen. We merely believe what will happen."

There was to come a time of stress for me when I was to recall every word of Bill's argument on this occasion. When I was to cling to them as my own act of faith.

"That may be true," conceded Lena, slowly and thoughtfully. "But at least you do *know* that you have poured acid on the zinc. Whatever may happen, you can't deny that as a fact."

"Can't I?" smiled Bill. "Last night in bed I chased two spotted antelope around the terraces of the Empire State Building. If my memory serves me accurately. But does it? Maybe I was dreaming.

Supposing I thought I poured sulphuric acid on zinc two minutes ago. How do I know whether or not that was only a dream too? It seems to me that I poured it. Perhaps I really did. I believe I did, but do I *know*?"

Lena and I both burst out laughing.

"But, come," gurgled Lena. "You were asleep when you were chasing antelope. You were wide awake when you poured acid on zinc two minutes ago."

"Lena, if you keep on speaking as if I, Bill Leggett, did pour some acid on zinc two minutes ago, you'll have me falling victim to the power of suggestion—I'll be believing I really did: I'll be thinking I *know* I did!... How do I know I'm wide awake? How do I know I'm not just dreaming I'm wide awake? How do I know I'm not in a hypnotic trance and it has been suggested to me that I'm wide awake?"

"This is getting a bit complicated. Say that again slowly," I put in.

"Say what again?" asked Bill blandly. "I haven't said anything. I haven't spoken for the last ten minutes."

"Oh yes, you have. I heard you," I said.

"That proves nothing. Joan of Arc heard voices. The people around her didn't."

"Just a minute," I protested. "I can produce a witness. Lena, hasn't he just been talking about dreaming and spotted antelope and hypnotists?"

Lena turned a poker face on me.

"Dreaming? Spotted antelope? Hypnotists? Dear me, Doctor, I think you're sitting too near the fire. Do you feel a little giddy? Would you like a drink of water?"

"Perhaps he merely dozed off," said Bill solicitously.

"You pair of scallywags!" I exclaimed. "I *know*—"

And paused irresolute, and broke down into laughter, in which, I noted with a faint, childish feeling of relief, they joined.

"You see," said Bill, "the memory is an unreliable instrument, and not to be trusted overmuch. Especially mine. I often think I'm remembering something correctly which turns out to be wrong in all sorts of details when I come to examine it more exactly. A bad fault for a would-be scientific mind."

The talk after that veered from the qualities of the disciplined scientific mind to the undisciplined artistic mind, which quite naturally went on to Vincent Van Gogh, whom Lena and Bill found they both admired more than averagely.

It was good to see Bill's enthusiasm drawing out and leading on Lena's own enthusiasm, and I was congratulating myself on my own acuity in foreseeing this when there came a knock at the door. In the shape of young Rose Lewis it was a summons for me: her mother was at last on the threshold of adding another Lewis to the world's population.

So I had to go. But not without the satisfaction of something done. As I struggled into my coat I watched them there. Bill now standing up and leaning with one elbow on the mantelshelf while the other arm gesticulated eagerly to add degrees of force to his points, and Lena reclining easily and carelessly in the armchair, like a cosy and lazy cat, one pyjama-clad leg crossed over the other, and the dainty toes of her dangling foot wiggling unconsciously near the inquisitive tongues of the fire-flames, her perfect, petite face uplifted to his, calm, amused—and interested.

It was well past midnight when I got home after assisting the entrance into this life of one who was to be called "Henry Arthur Lewis", who came trailing the usual clouds of glory of which the doctor, and the nurse particularly, take a less appreciative view than the poet.

I was scarcely in, and had not yet tasted the peg of whisky I had poured, when I was disturbed the second time that night by a knock on the door.

Opening it, I was somewhat surprised to see Bill there in the moonlight.

"I was just walking back from Lena's. I saw your light. May I come in?" he said, coming in.

"Do," I said sarcastically. "Have a drink?"

"Just one."

I poured it. He drank half of it.

"Well," he said, sitting down and throwing his gloves on the table, "you certainly introduced me to an interesting person tonight."

I noted that his eyes were quite bright, and he seemed even more than usually full of restless, nervous energy.

"You kept her up late enough."

He threw a glance over his shoulder at the grandfather clock.

"As late as that? H'm. We didn't notice it," he said unaffectedly.

"She's still my patient, you know, and ought to have some rest."

"Rest is rubbish. You want your patients to live, don't you, Doc? Especially her."

"Do you think she will condescend to?"

He gave me a sharp look.

"Don't be cynical about her, Doc. She's a nice kid, really."

"'Kid' is good," I said. "She's probably more mature than you'll ever be."

He actually winced. I was immediately sorry. Late work and consequent tiredness generally put an edge on my tongue. In the resentment of weariness I let things go that normally a moment's thought would have me restrain.

"You may be right about that," he said quietly, the bounce seeming to go out of him.

"Have you learned much about her?"

"A lot. A lot that I don't think you know. She's a strange history, almost hard to credit. But I've heard of stranger lives—Corvo's, for instance. It's true enough. Would you like to hear something of it?"

"I would, very much."

And so Bill listed what he had learnt.

Lena was an orphan. "Not a semi-orphan like myself," said Bill. "She has no idea who her mother and father were. Her parentage and babyhood are a complete mystery. Her earliest memories are of herself at the age of three or four living a nomad and almost savage life, a little girl who slept on the bare ground in woods and wandered all the days of the year in fields and lanes in the less populated parts of the country, living on fruit, berries, potatoes and turnips, stolen eggs from chicken-runs, stolen milk from cows. She even stole clothes from cottage laundry lines. She did not know it was supposed to be wrong. She saw other people take them. She assumed therefore that she had a right to take them. But once she was chased by an ugly, angry housewife, and after that she was careful to take things unseen, often at night. It is amazing that she was never picked up or questioned by the police or anyone. The reason is probably because she was always moving on, always in remote rural districts, and never stayed long enough anywhere to be associated with any missing property. She always avoided people, anyway. She was not like a lost 'civilized' child, instantly detectable as such. She was a self-possessed, if untidy and strangely dressed, little girl, who always seemed to anyone who did see her to know where she was going and what she was about."

"That does explain to some extent the most remarkable thing about her character," I interpolated. "I mean the way she makes her own rules. She never grew up under the threat and correction of society's rules or the rules of family and parent. They counted for nothing, and apparently still count for nothing, with her."

"I envy her that freedom," said Bill. "As you know, I had rather too much parental control, and I still have the marks. Self-doubt. Uncertainty. No wonder I took to science. But even that… Science is a faith, yes, but a hesitant faith, eternally doubting, eternally questioning, constant revaluation. What wouldn't I give for Lena's unqualified, if unsubstantiated, faith in herself! She was standing on her own two feet in this world in the figurative sense before I was in the literal."

He paused in silent introspection for a little while. Then gave himself a sort of shake, and continued:

"But this is Lena's tale. She led this wild life for about six of her most formative years. Then somehow she got into a convent school. I am not quite clear how the school came to get hold of her—all this information did not come out chronologically. It came in disconnected and unrelated chunks that, by apparently casual questions, I pried from her in the general run of our conversation. She did not set out to tell me her life-story. I am only piecing it together from an enormous amount of talk we had, largely about other things.

"At the convent school she learned to read and write, and had a pretty good general education, including music—did you know she is a fine pianist? She is. I asked her to play some pieces on that baby grand. Her technique is perfect, her interpretation personal.

She could make a really great pianist, I believe. But she said she was not basically interested in 'executive' work or interpreting other people's work. It had no lure for her. She must create her own work. And she had failed in music, as in everything else—she showed me her efforts at sculpture: I could not pretend they were good, and she would have seen through it if I had. 'A volcano has done better with stone haphazardly,' she commented herself. But this convent… What she became really interested in there was designing clothes. You see, she had never before had any especially designed for her: only garments of all sizes and shapes stolen from other people's washing, things fitting only approximately, from a limited choice.

"They wanted her to stay on at the convent school as a teacher. But she left when she was eighteen and got work in the designing department of a dressmaker's in Regent Street. She was good, she was quite good, but she was in no way exceptional. She worked like a slave, ever on the hunt for ideas, thinking and sketching far into the night. She kept her eyes open, she went to Paris, but inspiration never came to her in flashes. The best she could do was get a small idea and keep pegging away at it until she had worked it up into something passably original. 'Ninety-nine point nine per cent perspiration,' she said it was. In Paris she saw the masterful ease and speed with which some designers worked, and the incomparably better results they obtained. She knew it wasn't in her. She resigned from her firm. She had worked hard and been paid well, and had saved a respectable sum as capital to live on.

"She turned her attention to the older arts, painting particularly. She knows the Louvre inside out. She lived in the Latin Quarter, got to know the up-and-coming young artists and learned what she could from them. For a long time she acted as a model, to get into the studios of the established and study their methods. Perhaps that's why tonight she showed such unconcern at appearing in the nude," he added inconsequently, with a slight smile. "Or it might have been because she was only expecting a doctor."

"Rubbish!" I said. "You don't have to look for ordinary excuses for her. The only reason Lena does anything is because she feels inclined to do it, and because she is not in the habit of considering any reasons why she shouldn't. If an archbishop had called then she would have behaved no differently."

"You're right," said Bill. "She is not ordinary. Because of those early free years out under the sky she is, in some ways—primitive. For instance, comfort means so much less to her than us. Tonight while we were talking the fire died out, and there was no more coal. I was soon shivering. She, sitting there in thin pyjamas and with bare feet, was still talking away just the same: she hadn't even noticed anything. She laughed when I had to put my overcoat on. She said that when you had to sleep out on winter nights without a bed, you got used to cold. Even at this time of the year she goes swimming in the river every morning at dawn—Brrr-rr!"

"I've noticed this indifference to physical feeling," I said. "I think she does feel it—she must feel it: but she got so much into the habit of thinking it part and parcel of life that she attaches no importance to it. That's the trouble with us well-fed, shielded, comfortable people—pain and discomfort are comparatively so rare that we notice them more than we should."

"Talking about being well fed," went on Bill thoughtfully. "Do you know she's had nothing to eat for four days now, except dry bread? After her studies in Paris she spent a good deal of her capital in the requisites for pursuing the arts actively: paints, canvases, brushes, music, the piano, books... She thought they would be an investment. Surely, she thought, she would be able to sell some paintings, some manuscripts. And from then on she worked without haste and without delay, continuously, and produced not a single thing she thought worthy of even offering for sale. Her money dwindled away. She moved into that six-shillings-a-week cottage. Still she could make no money. Now she hasn't a penny left. She had one slice of bread and apple in the larder, and that was all—I looked. She has no coal, and very few clothes. She said she hoped you still thought she wasn't responsible, because she couldn't be responsible for paying you or Nurse Perkin just yet, anyway—that is why she requested you not to come any more."

I remembered a few things. I remembered calling her "spoilt". The recollection of that alone was enough to make one feel ashamed. I remembered saying she could have two poached eggs for lunch. With no food to speak of in the house, and no prospect of any, she had taken that without a murmur. And the time when she said she was glad I thought her not responsible—now I understood the puzzling humour at the back of her eyes at that moment. And how I had thought it strange that she should have only one pair of pyjamas—though perhaps the mystery of that was why she wore pyjamas at all.

"Confound the girl!" I swore. "She had only to tell me!"

"She's not the sort to ask for, or even expect, help. I only found out these things myself by some practical investigation, elementary detective work and cunning questioning."

"But couldn't she have sold the piano?"

"She had come to realize that point, that she would have to sell the piano in order to go on living. And inevitably follow that up with her books and paints and everything she was trying to work with. That was when she lost interest in going on living. Anyway, she said, so far she had found no justification for living."

"Couldn't she go back to fashion designing?"

"Doc, I'm beginning to believe you don't understand her at all. It's against her whole nature to 'go back'. She couldn't go through all that slavery again, years of 'standing still', as she called it, knowing that she couldn't get anywhere. The one thing she lives by is the impulse to go on exploring, trying new ways, to satisfy that urge in her. It was the frustration of that, and her final impossible position, that decided her to finish with this life."

"I see it clearly enough now," I said. "I thought perhaps she had congenital tendencies. She told me her grandmother—But she must have been joking."

"No, Doc, that was true, about her grandmother. But no doubt she told you just to be provoking—a devil of mischief seems to get into her sometimes. Tonight, for example, when I—"

He paused, and laughed. "No, it's too personal. What a girl that is! She doesn't care a damn."

"Well, someone's got to do some caring, that's obvious," I said. "She can't go on living on air, and probably won't want to try."

"I'm coming to that. You remember the main object of my visit was to try to get her interested in life again? When I saw how serious the need was, I told her something of the work Bob and I are doing now; that is, I told her about one expected development of it."

"You told her that?" I repeated like an incredulous parrot.

"Yes. I think this particular development is just the thing—possibly the only thing—to catch her interest as she feels now."

"You're trusting her with the information before you've even completed the work? I'm pretty curious about it myself, you know."

"Sorry, Doc, but it wouldn't save *your* life if I told you. Don't think I'm worried about patents or anything like that. I don't think that anyone but Rob and I—and I'm not at all sure about Rob—could even understand the principles of this thing without long and exhaustive study. That's why I shy at beginning to try to explain them to you—I know your limitations that way. Just as soon as we have something to show, something working, I promise you you'll see it. I don't think you'd really believe it without the evidence of your eyes."

"All right, Bill, I'm content to leave it at that. But what about Rob? What will he think of your giving things away to a queer girl you've met only once and he hasn't met at all?"

Bill's lips set in that line that denoted he was going to be obstinate, even to the point of mulishness. He spoke quickly, biting off the ends of his short, abrupt sentences.

"He probably won't like it. But he'll have to stand a bigger shock than that. Doc, Lena can't pay the rent of that cottage any more. As I said, she hasn't a penny. She absolutely refuses to accept loans: she sees no chance of repaying them. Charity I did not dare suggest. Anyway, you know we're pressed for cash too. She will not go back to mere drudgery for food. That was clear. Now that situation has only one end to it, if something isn't done. We know what the end will be. I know we could say 'It's unfair exaction: if she will make no effort, she should not expect anyone to make efforts for her: she's playing on our consciences.' But actually she does not expect anyone to make efforts for her. I'm sure she'd rather they did not."

"I agree, but what can one do?"

"I thought of a solution. I told her of this aspect of our research, and she became interested. I said her knowledge of art would be invaluable when we got to the production stage, and would she like to become a partner? It would give her a unique opportunity for creative work in the realm of art—you'll understand that later,

Doc. Meantime, I told her, Rob and I badly needed some immediate partnership at the Dump, in the form of feminine assistance. If she would come daily and shop and cook for us, keep the place reasonably tidy and darn our socks and do all those necessary domestic jobs which diverted far too much of our present attention, our work would be appreciably expedited. And we'd pay her a weekly salary for it."

"Good lord!" I ejaculated. The picture of Lena as a sort of cook-housemaid was indeed hard to get into focus. "And what did she say to that?"

"She laughed, and then agreed. She'd do it, if only to square your bill, she said. But I really do think the prospect of becoming an active partner appealed to her. I was insistent on the engagement being a strictly business affair, and made her take a week's salary in advance. At least she'll be able to get something to eat in the morning."

"Good work, Bill, I think you've done the trick. If Rob raises any objections, I'll give *him* a common-sense talking to. But I don't think he will, somehow. Not after he's met Lena."

"Perhaps not," said Bill, rising. "Well, Doc, sorry to have kept you up late like this after you've been working—how did it go with Mrs. Lewis, by the way?... Good." (At my thumbs up.) "But I thought you'd like to know our trip wasn't in vain tonight. I hope Rob's wasn't, either. I'd better push along and find out. Good night."

"Good night."

When he had gone I pottered around a bit longer. There was something vague on my mind which hindered me from a decision to go to bed. Suddenly it came to me what it was. I hadn't had any supper, I was hungry. And Lena had had almost nothing to eat for four days, and must be a sight hungrier. I wondered whether that had stopped her from going to bed too, or at least to sleep.

I went to the larder and delved for things. I cut a pile of ham sandwiches, wrapped them up, and stuffed some fruit and chocolate in one pocket. Then I went out through the still cold of the moonlit night to Lena's cottage.

There was no response to my knock. As I had expected, the door was not locked. I let myself in.

The sitting-room was dark, chilly, empty. In the light of a match I saw the bedroom door was open. I stumbled over the books on the floor to it, and struck another match there.

Lena was in bed, lying face downwards. Her face was buried so deeply in the pillow that it would be a wonder if she hadn't suffocated. Her features were completely hidden save for her hair, which seemed to be growing out of the pillow like a clump of long, waving, glossy, yellow-and-brown grass. Her arms were bent and asprawl around her head as though she had pillowed her head on them and it had slipped off. For a moment a nasty little doubt gripped me.

I shook her by the shoulder. The match burned my thumb. I dropped it and struck another. Lena's eyes were open and blinking sleepily in the light.

"Hullo," she yawned. "Who's there—a burglar? I'll swap you my jewels for a cigarette."

"It's me, Doctor Harvey," I said, with more relief than grammar.

"Oh, good—whatever it is—morning, is it?"

"Not exactly, not yet. Where's the light?"

I saw it as soon as I spoke—a candle—and lit it.

"What brings you in these wee sma' hours, Doctor—do you want some help with that baby?"

She struggled up on to her elbows to get a better look at me.

"No, it's just a queer idea I've got. I thought I would like some company for supper."

I put my unwieldy newspaper-wrapped package on the bed as I spoke and opened it. I laid the fruit and chocolate on the paper, and as an afterthought tossed down a packet of cigarettes too.

"That's very nice of you indeed, Doctor. I don't think it's at all queer. You're always saving my life, one way or another. I've been dying for a smoke all evening—I ran right out of them this afternoon."

And she picked up the cigarettes, broke the packet, offered me one, which I refused dumbly, and lit one herself from the candle. She took a deep draw, lay back on the pillow, and expelled the smoke straight up into the air with a simultaneous sigh of relief and contentment.

An unpredictable person. Never, I thought, would she cease to surprise me.

"Sandwich?" I indicated.

"Thank you—if you don't mind me eating and smoking at the same time."

"I suppose it would make no difference if I did."

She smiled, and took a bite out of a sandwich.

"Do you usually sleep face downwards?" I asked, chewing also.

"About all you can do on an empty stomach is sleep on it."

"Well, get busy and fill it, and then you can sleep on your side," I said.

We both got busy, in silence, until nothing was left but the cigarettes. I rose.

"Must go along and try some sleep myself now," I said. "Good-bye."

"Good-bye, Doctor," she said. "Perhaps I'd better get some more sleep myself—I've got to get up and go to work in the morning."

An odd little interlude, and one that sticks in my memory very clearly.

CHAPTER THREE

M Y ROUNDS BEING FINISHED UNUSUALLY SOON IN THE
morning, for once in a while I managed lunch at a reasonable hour, and afterwards strolled down the long winding lane that
led out of the village and along the valley to the clay area, where
the Dump stood alone in desolation.

The sizzling of frying came from the lab, and there in one
corner was Lena examining the progress of three eggs, their whites
trembling round the edges and bubbling and spitting in a little pool
of grease in the pan upon the gas-ring.

She looked up as I entered, and smiled. Cherries and eggs!

"Good morning, Doc—as I gather they call you in these parts,"
was her greeting.

"'They' being them, I suppose?" I said, nodding towards Rob
and Bill, who were sitting on packing-cases and talking over some
matter. ("But that would get us *somewhere*," Bill was saying.)

"Yes, them," she said with a little laugh, her eyes sparkling and
alive, not like the sleepy girl I had supped with very early in the
morning (or was that only my dream?).

"Them" paused in their discussion.

"Someone's talking about us," remarked Bill. "Why, hullo,
Doc. How's things?"

"What things?"

"Oh, any things."

"Fair to middling," I replied cautiously. "How are things
with you?"

"Oh, anyhow."

"Which means?"

"Which means that the old man wouldn't part with a penny," said Rob. "In fact, he was the reverse of helpful. He said that if I couldn't make an elementary estimation of opening stock, he had no further faith in my business ability, and I must look upon the thousand pounds he had given us not as an investment, but only a loan. And if we couldn't return it within six months' time he would sue us. Obviously he believes we're wasting our time and means me to return to family affairs. He said he wouldn't dream of advancing any more money unless we showed him something concrete."

"Unfortunately, we're not manufacturing concrete," put in Bill.

"Isn't it possible to show him *something*—I mean, cook up something that looks like a result, and perhaps get his backing and then really start producing?" I asked.

Rob gave a genuine chuckle and Bill a hollow, mock one.

"Dad's first and foremost a business man," said Rob. "I know him. His head's very hard and it's screwed on in the correct clockwise fashion. Besides, it wouldn't be playing the game."

(I noticed that Bill gave him an odd look at this last remark.)

"Is it inquisitive to ask how much you are trying to tap him for?" I asked.

"It is. Five hundred pounds," said Bill, turning on me quickly.

"Well, now, I've saved up a bit to retire on—God speed the day!—and some of it is already invested. But I'd like to make another investment. Would you accept a third partner if he deposited five hundred pounds?"

They hadn't expected that. They looked at each other, Bill whistled, and they looked back at me.

"That's very decent of you, Doc," Rob said quietly. "If I weren't sure you were on a safe thing I would never consider it. The point is, though, would you instead consider taking a fourth partnership for three hundred and fifty pounds?"

This was something I hadn't expected.

"Fourth partnership?" I wondered, and then remembered Bill's offer to Lena. "Oh yes, of course—Lena. But why only three-fifty pounds? Have you found some way of paring it down since yesterday?"

"No," said Rob. "The equipment we need to finish off all this"—he flourished his hand to indicate the conglomeration of apparatus around us—"cannot be got for less than five hundred. We sent our third partner, Lena, out for some eggs this morning. It was three hours before she returned with the eggs—and a hundred and fifty pounds in cash, to deposit for her partnership, she said. She'd gone and sold her piano to Baynes, the dealer. We were discussing how far we could get with that when you came in."

He cast a sidelong glance at Lena as he was finishing, and I saw the amused approval in it. There had obviously been no difficulty about Lena's partnership.

"Are eggs done when they start giving off smoke?" asked that young lady inconsequently. "I've never done this sort of thing before."

"What colour is the smoke?" asked Bill gravely.

"Blue."

"And what colour are your eyes?" continued Bill.

"I wouldn't know."

"Let me see… They're blue, too. Yes, the eggs are done."

"They're field-grey," I said. "The eyes, I mean."

"I'd say turquoise—if I were sure what colour turquoise was," said Rob.

"She's got chameleon eyes," said Bill. "You can't trust those sort of people. Shifty."

"About these eggs…" said the imperturbable Lena. "Including Doc, it works out to half an egg each. One egg is done for: it looks like a bit of brown paper: I'm afraid it—caught. Take it off my salary."

"Don't include me: I've had my lunch," I remarked.

"Oh, then that complicates it. Let me see… Three people. Two eggs. That's two-thirds each. Why, that's nearly a whole egg each!"

"Good work, Lena, but try to make it a hundred per cent next time," said Bill. "Let's get on with it. Pass the bread, slave… No, cut it first, girl, cut it!"

It was hard to believe that Lena was really a comparative stranger here. I had never seen a trio fit so naturally and spontaneously together. I had imagined Rob might be a little stiff and proper towards her at first, but if he had, it had already worn off. Perhaps he had very sensibly decided that the conventional attitude was out of place with this girl of no illusions and no pretensions. He was already taking her as a matter of course, but not entirely casually: there was a hint of respect in his attitude towards her: he could sense there a person of real character.

Bill's initial shyness seemed to have passed altogether. He treated her most of the time as if she were a kid sister, joshing her along. Yet beneath this surface rudeness I divined that there still remained something of the awe he felt at that first encounter.

There was no doubt about it. We all looked up to Lena in some way. It was as though she held some mysterious power, though one could not imagine anyone less ostentatious, anyone less likely to strive after an effect. That was probably the secret of it: we admired, and envied perhaps, her complete independence and self-sufficiency.

She had set up no opposing fortress wall against extraneous opinions. There was no defence mechanism, no counter-attack of "Take it or leave it!" No determined toughness. Spears of hostile opinion lost their mass in her presence: became rods of no weight at all, of nothingness, in the very hands of the would-be thrower. The fastness of her inner self was more unapproachable than the remotest lamasery in Tibet. There in that quiet lonely place Lena made her own decisions by her own standards, made her own pattern of life, and nothing outside could disturb them. Such people are rare in the male, rarer in the female, and we men recognized that and silently gave our tribute.

Over the skimpy lunch, plans were discussed, though it was mostly reiteration: all the equipment had already been decided upon. I wrote out my cheque and passed it over.

"Results, in concrete, in a fortnight, Doc—I promise you that," said Bill, taking it.

"I'm not worried," I said, "only—still curious."

"Come here, to this very room, a fortnight today," said Bill. "Your curiosity shall be satisfied. We'll show you."

"If we're still alive a fortnight today on my cooking," said Lena.

I looked at her. It was in my mind to say something about the gesture she had made in parting with her piano. But there was nothing much I could say. She would merely point out that she had only loaned the piano, and would get it back with interest when the wheels began turning. She would make it appear just a reasonable act and not a chivalrous one.

So all I said was, "I'll be here, anyway."

That was rather an assumptive statement for a G.P. to make, but actually a period of good health seemed to set in around Howdean at the time of the appointment. I was not bothered overmuch, and again walked the fair distance to the Dump on my own flat feet for the exercise and the air.

It was my first visit since I made the promise to be there. I had called once, briefly, upon Lena at her cottage to sign her off, as it were, as a patient, and she told me Rob and Bill were working like a couple of madmen. At least, Bill was mad enough; Rob, in his steadier way, was not letting up either. They had even taught her to solder: there was an immense amount of wire-soldering to be done, and they kept her there all hours at it, and at other odd jobs: I was lucky even to happen upon her at home.

"I'm enjoying it," she told me. "At least I'm helping to create something, even if I don't know properly what it is. But I know it's something worth doing."

So I walked into the lab with my curiosity stretched at its tautest.

The first thing that caught my eye was a pair of shining glass domes, like the dust-covers that used to enclose and preserve Victorian waxed fruit, only each of these was about four feet tall and correspondingly wide. They stood side by side on an assemblage of rough planks, which in turn overlaid a compact assortment of electric motors, accumulators, coils and condensers and switch panels.

One of the domes was entirely empty. The other contained a gold-framed oil-painting, depending slightly askew from four rubber-insulated wires, which ran up from its corners and passed over a hook and then out in a bunch through a small washered and packed hole in the apex of the dome. There was something familiar about the painting. I stepped nearer to make certain.

It was indeed Boucher's "Madame Calonne", which I had seen so often hanging in the library at the Heath house. That faintly surprised-looking lady from the eighteenth century with the brown, wide eyes, the beauty spot on the chin, the powdered wig and the tiny beribboned hat stared back at me, reflecting my perplexity.

Rob emerged from somewhere behind the domes, saw my face and read it and smiled.

"Yes, it is," he said. "Madame herself, loaned for the day by kind permission of my mother, in the absence of my father—in town, on business. But I'll have to return it before the old man comes back late tonight, or he'll go mad. It cost him thirteen hundred."

"Is this pertaining to the concrete you're going to show me?" I asked.

"Yes, indeed. We could have carried out this demonstration with practically any old thing: that box of screws, one of Bill's discarded shoes, a book… But we decided you'd be more impressed if we did it with something of worth and rarity, preferably of colour and detail. So I borrowed this example of the skilful François. We're all set—we've just been waiting for you. I'll get Bill and Lena."

He went and called out of a back window, and soon Bill and Lena came in laughing (Bill breathlessly) and carrying tennis racquets and a battered shuttlecock. Lena had lost her hair-clip in the game, and her gold-streaked hair floated around her head as she moved, like seaweed in a gentle current. But she was as cool and upstanding as a young daffodil, while Bill looked as if he had just run a mile: his face was nearly as red as his damp hair, and he was generally pretty limp.

"Blinkin' girl—had me runnin'—all over place," he gasped. "Phew!" And threw his racquet on the floor and himself in a chair.

"Better get your breath back, Bill," said Rob. "You've got to deliver your little lecture to the Doc before we get started. Else he won't know what the devil's happening when we do."

"Wai' minute," panted Bill, "Phew!"

"Cigarette?" asked Lena maliciously, offering him her open case. He was much too done even to reach for one, so she slipped one behind his ear. Rob and I refused, so she lit one for herself.

"Dunno how you… do it," got out Bill. "You smoke… twice's much me. An' look at me! No breath."

"It's because you rush at everything too much," said Lena calmly. "You will go half-way to meet things that are coming towards you anyway. Discriminate, my boy, and take your time doing it."

"As Bill is temporarily out of action, I'll begin the lecture," said Rob. "But he'll have to take it over when it gets a bit intricate. I'm not too sure of my subject, and anyway he knows more than I do how much you know about these things—"

"I'll tell you now—nothing," I said. "Explain as you would to a child of ten—I mean a normal child, not the insufferable little know-all Bill was at that age."

"Very well. Be seated, Doc. Lena, you know about this, so would you like to get a brew on meantime? The Doc will probably take an aspirin with his. Well, now, Doc, take matter."

"Eh?" I said.

"Matter. The stuff everything is made of. This bench, that chair, the door, the air we breathe, every blessed thing. They're all made up of atoms, as you must know. Moreover, however different these objects may seem, chalk or cheese, they're all composed of formations and arrangements of this one little thing, this unit, the atom. Think of it as a brick. Other bricks added to it in all sorts of fancy ways, and sometimes with most intricate brickwork, make all the buildings we call 'materials'. But however elaborate these erections, these materials, are, they can all be broken down to the common brick—the atom."

"I've got that," I said.

"Good. Now I've got to tell you why you mustn't imagine the atom as anything so solid as a brick at all."

"Oh, I know that too," I said. "Sometimes I read the newspapers you know. At school I used to think of them as gritty little particles, like grains of sand, but I realize now they are little lumps of practically nothing at all."

I was over-rash.

"We'll take that as read, then," said Rob with a smile. "You remember that Millikan found that the charge e increases only in multiple integrals, and Faraday's electrolytic results bear out—"

"Whoa!" I cried. "I'm sorry," I added humbly. "I'm that dullish child of ten again. Forget I said anything. Go back to the beginning."

I bore the pair's laughter with, I thought, admirable indulgence.

Rob continued: "Very well, Doc. The atom consists of a central nucleus, which is a bundle of positive charges of electricity called 'protons', and around this nucleus, circling in different orbits like the planets around the sun, are revolving an exactly equal and balancing number of negative charges of electricity called 'electrons'. Now, Newton thought—"

I can't quite remember what Newton had thought, nor Dalton, who followed him. As for Thomson (J. J.), Rutherford, Dirac and Planck, they came in to confuse utterly a conception that was already clouding. Bohr had something to do with the Theory of Indeterminacy, which either explained or didn't explain why electrons jumped from orbit to orbit without apparent cause and oddly taking no time at all for the journey, and Rutherford shot millions of *alpha*-particles (which might have been the same things as 'photons'… no, on second thoughts, perhaps they were not) from a cathode ray tube at atoms in the early attempts to split them. Gentlemen named Siegbahn and Hahn were somehow involved with "Uranium 235", there was such a thing as "heavy water", and an Italian named Fermi had discovered something pretty important, too.

That was my net result from Rob.

I must pause here, because I feel I am making a fool of myself before the reader, or at least revealing too clearly the hopeless moron I am in these matters. I can sense the stifled impatience of the readers of the admirable popular works of Jeans, Eddington, Sullivan, and the other scientist-journalists. It is strange that such readers should know more of atomic physics than I, who was taken into the confidence of two of the greatest nuclear physicists of our day.

But I am aware that the ordinary run of folk are still in the dark regarding the basic principles of the Leggett-Heath Reproducer, of which there was only one model, and about which no secrets were divulged. Yet I cannot give more than a rough, and possibly inaccurate, account of these principles, for that is all I know, and there are reasons why I cannot extend that knowledge now. Even if I wished to, which I do not. The agony of the four-sided triangle remains too fresh with me.

Somewhere in the middle of Signor Fermi's doings, Bill broke into Rob's exposition with a loud laugh.

"For goodness' sake, Rob, cheese it. Look at his face—you lost him way back among the *alpha*-particles!"

Rob stopped in mid-sentence and looked at me inquiringly.

"I'm afraid so," I said apologetically. "I couldn't quite get the hang of these electrons and protons as 'electrical charges'. I can't visualize an electrical charge on the loose, so to speak. I'm really quite lost without a mental picture."

"You couldn't get far with a mental picture," said Rob. "Atomic physics has passed beyond simple analogies or working models of the Kelvin kind. One is just at a loss trying to think of any material conditions adequate to represent states that can only be conceived mathematically."

"I'll have a go," said Bill. "Look, Doc, I know these 'charges' are of a practically indescribable consistency, especially as nobody quite knows what electricity is. They are not simply matter, nor yet simply waves. Someone christened them 'wavicles'—that is, half wave, half particle. The best way to picture them is as ball lightning—floating globes of force, the things that come down the chimney on rare occasions in thunderstorms and float round the room like toy balloons, but glowing weirdly and spinning about their own axes—you must have read about many such instances.

"Ball lightning is a pure chunk of naked electricity, a segment from the general flow between earth and cloud, caught by chance in a cross-current of an unrelated, intense electrical pulsation, and chopped clean out of the main stream. These chopped-out bits have a habit of contracting upon themselves like the bits of a chopped-up snake. Each twists back on itself like a dog after its own tail, and becomes a sort of knot of pure force. Balls of lightning remain in this condition until they drift into a cross-current similar to the one which had cut them out and sent them spinning in the first place. Then, strangely enough, one flip of this same current that fashioned them is sufficient to shock and unbalance them, so that they fly apart and their electrical energy flows freely away again."

That was not a very exact analogy, but the best he could do, said Bill. He went on to tell of his discoveries at the Cavendish Laboratory.

His imagination had been fired by the work of the General Electric Laboratories, New York, who in 1945 first created matter from raw energy. The G.E. Lab people devised a machine called a "Betatron", which shot high-powered X-rays, produced from smashed tungsten atoms, into hard steel, and thus brought into being brand-new electrons, freshly created particles of matter. The possibilities arising from this synthesis gripped Bill. He threw himself heart and soul into research based on it, in the course of which he stumbled entirely by accident on a new principle.

He found that when a current of electricity of a certain intensity is passed through an object, any object, the strength of the current being in very exact proportion to the object's mass and conductivity (there being no absolute non-conductors of electricity, those widely believed to be such being in actuality only very poor conductors), this sets up an invisible field of force around the object, a network of innumerable fine lines of force, which form a sort of trembling mirror image of the object. Only it is not a reverse image, as in a mirror. It is an exactly similar image, a duplication existing more or less as a possibility. (Here, Bill said, Bohr really came into his own—to define this possibility state, you had to go into the geometry of hyper-space, fourth-dimensional mathematics, the laws of Probability, and heaven knows what—even Rob could not follow him here.)

However, by some radio set-up, whose principles I didn't even attempt to grasp, impressions of these lines of force could be collected and retransmitted along a radio beam directed at a neighbouring receiver, where they were reformed in exactly the same ghostly shape.

That was the arrangement I saw before me. In the glass dome "container" of the receiver was the sympathetic possibility image to be formed. Then a projector of some kind was to fling a barrage of short waves across the duplicate lines of force, somehow cutting across exactly at right angles. The plan was that this would chop them into small segments, which should instantly twist back on themselves like springs released from tension (similar to the birth of ball lightning) and become tiny knots of energy—electrons and protons, in fact, in precisely correct relative positions to the electrons and protons composing the object being duplicated.

For that was the purpose of the invention: to duplicate to the last atom any material object under the sun.

I gathered that this projector was not particularly powerful. The whole startling result was obtained by the nature and angle of the impact of the short-wave barrage. The bulk of the power was latent in the duplicate lines of force themselves: they were like strings of stretched elastic, and as easily cut. Free energy, it seemed, was only too eager to be transformed into material if someone could turn the right key.

"And this is the right key, eh?" I said, getting up to examine the two glass domes and their attendant appendages and adjuncts.

"Yes, that's it, Doc—thanks to your help," answered Bill. "It's pretty rough and ready, but it works. It's already been tested. Look at these."

He handed me two bottles of aspirins, exactly identical.

"Yes, I could have bought them both in the same shop myself," I said drily.

Bill and Rob exchanged grins.

"Told you he wouldn't believe it till he saw it happen," said Bill. "O.K., Doc, get ready to take that back."

He came over to the Reproducer (as it came to be called) and played with switches.

Lights jumped into existence on panels. A big dynamo began to snore in the far corner. A dozen electric motors started humming in a dozen different keys. A spark-gap lit the place with a vivid, leaping blue light which chased the shadows out of the gloomier corners, constantly retreating and springing again. Then Bill switched on powerful downward-directed lamps over the two glass domes, and I turned my constant attention to these latter.

Now both Rob and Bill were at my elbow, watching meters, adjusting resistances, and yet keeping an eye on the receiving container too.

Nothing in particular seemed to be happening at first. The receiver dome remained as empty as ever it was.

Then a fine horizontal line of gold, a mere stretched thread, appeared inside, something over two feet from the floor of the dome, and apparently resting upon nothing. Very slowly it thickened, lengthened away to the right, then suddenly ran swiftly, stopped, and dropped a perpendicular from its end!

The gilt picture frame was embarking upon its dual existence.

Why that should appear first I cannot guess, unless it was because of the higher light-reflecting quality of its surface particles.

Very soon the whole general rectangle of the frame had linked up, a golden oblong, its top line thickest—indeed now it was a wide tape and the vestiges of moulded beads were springing along it.

The noise was tumultuous now. The dynamo was not bolted down as securely as it might have been, and it seemed to be roaring in an attempt to free its fettered feet. The vibrations were setting the floor a-tremble, and they came through the soles of my shoes as though the leather were but paper. The electric symphony of the small motors was almost unendurable: I remember making the mental comment: "Thank God Mossolov never got into here!"

The air itself seemed to be oscillating with electricity. My mouth was prickling with it, as though my tongue were on the prongs of one of those flat batteries for flashlamps. A pulse began to beat in my head. The golden frame appeared to advance and recede and bend before my too fixedly staring eyes.

I was forced to look away.

Lena was at my side, red lips curling back from those so-white teeth in her smile of mischief, her eyes oddly reflecting the intermittent violet fire of the spark-gap, as if someone were turning a pair of sapphires in their setting under a bright light. She was offering me a cup of tea with two aspirins prominently placed in the saucer.

I accepted the collection.

"Are these the original aspirins or the fakes?" I bawled.

She couldn't make me out for the din.

I drank the tea in two gulps and disposed of the aspirins in one. I felt that I needed them.

Bill and Rob were still warily watching their instruments.

The duplicate had materialized to a recognizable extent. A phantom sketch of Madame Calonne hung there as if daubed on glass. She was yet tenuous. The eyes were two empty holes. Through her I could see the sheen of the curving interior of the far side of the dome, and even objects behind that sheen. But steadily she solidified. The network filled in, became a fabric. Colours brightened as if a dull coating were being dissolved away, sepia grew in the eyeholes, the beauty spot stood out suddenly with almost startling definity, the hairs of the white powdered wig could be picked out almost individually, the rose in her dress glowed as vividly as the original... And again Madame mirrored my surprise.

A red lamp screwed on the coarse planks lit up like a traffic light. Automatically everything seemed to cut out. The spark-gap died in a last flash, all the motors stopped with choked growls like a pack of frustrated hounds, and the big dynamo began to run down with a note oddly sweet now, a falling cadence like the violins in the Largo of the "New World" Symphony, deepened into the realm of 'cellos, became a throb, a whirring, a fluttering, the breath of a sigh... and was silent. All was silent.

And I looked from Madame Calonne to Madame Calonne and I could not see a spark of difference. Boucher's painting was no longer unique. There were two of Madame Calonne, and each was made of the same common material, wrought into shape to the ultimate atom, the last electron.

"Unique" was a word that had suddenly lost its essential meaning during the last five minutes.

I pondered upon this miracle and all that it would mean, and voiced in awe the suggestion that another Sistine Chapel could come into existence this way. And they made light of it in their fashion...

Rob lifted the two domes by some hoisting mechanism, and reaching into them detached both paintings from their wires. (The duplicate painting had sprouted wires of its own, mere dummy wires that terminated where they passed into the tight hole in the apex.)

"The primary idea of these domes," he said, "was to have the original and the duplicate both suspended in a vacuum. You see, the volume filled by the object in the container is actually filled by air in the receiver dome. We thought the displacement of this air might affect the accuracy of the building-up process. But tests have shown us that it doesn't make the slightest difference. However, we're retaining the domes as a feature of the apparatus to prevent anything being accidentally jarred or interfered with—it wouldn't do, for instance, for a wasp to try to fly through a half-formed duplicate: Madame Calonne might have had a wasp jammed on her chin as well as a beauty spot!"

I fingered both paintings, weighed them in my hands. It was impossible to tell them apart. I would have defied any connoisseur to do so. The colours matched perfectly, and every speck, every hair-line was co-existent and accurately in place to the nth degree.

I looked round at them all, Rob, Lena and Bill, and I was still full of "wild surmise".

"All this wants talking over—a good talking over," I said.

"Sure," said Bill. "Just give me half a chance!"

I did, and we chattered away like magpies for a long time and by no means exhausted the subject. During the course of the talk Rob produced a sheet of foolscap covered with his own fine writing.

"I got this out yesterday," he said. "Our deed of partnership. I'm sure it's unnecessary, really, but we might as well do things in the proper style. Sign, please."

He passed it to me. I glanced at it. It began: "*We the under-signed…*" and that was as much of it as I bothered to read. I signed it. Immediately Bill scrawled his signature beneath mine. Lena wrote hers quickly but neatly, without reading the document. Rob took it back, looked it through once more, and carefully inscribed his signature at the bottom.

"I'll make out fair copies of this and let you have them later," he said.

"No need to write 'em out," said Bill. "Just run 'em through the old duplicating machine." He jerked his thumb at the Reproducer.

"Why, of course," smiled Rob.

I have my copy beside me as I write. Or perhaps it is the one that I signed myself. I don't know, for the copies and the original got mixed up. I have just read it for the first time. It is very formal and straightforward. There was never any query brought up about it.

I made a provisional appointment to meet them in the saloon of the "Pheasant" in a couple of hours' time. I had to get back for my evening surgery, which turned out to consist of three colds, a whitlow and one earache. My slack period still held, so I was able to make the saloon not more than five minutes late, having told my housekeeper where I could be found if needed.

They had just arrived. Rob had a large flat brown-paper parcel with him. "What's that?" I asked absently.

"Madame C., of course," he said. "I must get it back in the library before Dad gets home. Still, there's no hurry for a couple of hours."

"I told him to give the old man the copy, for a lark—he'd never know," remarked Bill.

"And are you?" I asked Rob.

"No, I couldn't do that," he said. "We must play fair."

And again I caught Bill regarding him strangely.

The waiter brought the tray of drinks to our corner by the potted palm.

"There's still so much to discuss, it's hard to know where to begin," said Rob.

Bill pushed a foaming pint tankard under his nose.

"Begin there," he advised.

We men all got our noses into our tankards. Lena sat back in her low armchair, the inevitable cigarette between the fingers of one hand, a glass of dry sherry in the other, her shapely knees carelessly crossed and her short wine-coloured skirt not concealing the fact. Her now pale eyes seemed to indicate that she was far away in thought. The ensemble was a picture of utter sophistication—it was a libellous illusion.

I noticed the locals—mainly lower middle-class tradesmen in this bar—sliding sly looks at her from time to time, and was unreasonably irritated. I suppose she had acquired some undeserved reputation already (among people eager to create gossip to give some interest to their own dull lives) as "that strange artist girl from London" who lived alone. Smoking and drinking and hobnobbing with men—even such well-known and respectable men as ourselves—would no doubt add to it, especially as she looked like one of "they film stars". Still, who could blame any man for stealing glances at Lena? You could not but be interested, whichever way your interest lay.

And then we went into hectic discussion of the commercial and cultural possibilities of the Leggett-Heath Reproducer. Over our constantly replenished glasses in the palm corner that night we planned much of what came later to amaze and, I trust, improve the lot of the world.

When we had thrashed things out sufficiently to satisfy ourselves that we had at least laid the rough foundations for our future work, Rob looked at his wrist-watch and exclaimed: "Good lord! It's gone nine. I'll have to hurry to beat Dad home. Would anyone like to come along and have a spot of supper at the house?"

I said: "No, thanks, Rob. My conscience is already nagging me for being away for as long as I have. I'd better be getting back to my post and advising my patients to lay off the drink."

Said Rob: "When the dividends come rolling in, Doc, and it won't be so long now, you'll not have to remain chained to that post any longer. In fact, I see no reason why you should not retire right away, now."

"H'm. I'll think that over," I said.

"Leave me out of the supper, too, old boy," remarked Bill. "Not that I shouldn't be glad of something properly cooked, after what Lena did to the steak today, but—well, you know your Dad and I don't hit it off too happily. He's still got it in for me for leading you away from that nice job he had all planned for you at the factory."

"Rubbish," smiled Rob. "But he always comes back from these business trips with a headache, so perhaps you'd better not make it worse for him: you *will* argue with the man. How about you, Lena? Would you like to meet Mother and the Menace from the City?"

"Yes, I would," she answered. "Perhaps Mother can let me into the secret of this cooking business."

"Good," said Rob, rising and tucking Madame Calonne under his arm. Lena stubbed out her cigarette, rose and stood beside him. I could not help noticing what a pleasing pair they made.

Rob, with his black, neatly brushed hair and strong, handsome face—a young face, but carrying in its line and set all the suggestion of the man of maturity and decision. His suit cut and worn to perfection. His movements deliberate, confident.

And Lena, so pretty that it almost hurt, her gold-veined hair combing back in waves as smooth and free as those far out on the undisturbed ocean, back from a clear brow that had never yet creased to a line of worry nor seemed that it ever possibly could. Easily erect, her shoulders back, her bosom firm and bold, her serene spirit looking straight and direct at the world which she neither feared nor loved.

They struck me as an anachronistic couple from a future when mankind has shed the pettiness and foggy ignorance of this stage of civilization like an old, clinging dead skin, and stands, as upon a rock, on its own integrity and sure, unclouded knowledge.

I am sure the effect of this alignment struck Bill too, for he sat looking at them as I did.

"So long—be seeing you," said Rob, and Lena flashed a parting smile. They went out, Lena on Rob's arm.

A moment's silence.

"Come on, drink up, Doc," said Bill suddenly. "The night isn't young, you know."

I drank up. "Hullo," I said, noticing something. "How long have you been on whisky?"

"Oh, several rounds back. I'm not a cask that one can keep pouring beer into all night. I don't know how you do it."

I said: "I don't know how you can mix spirits and beer. I think it's a sickening habit—literally. You'd better ease up. I've never seen you drunk before."

"I have been completely drunk three times in my life before, Doc. I do believe this is going to be the fourth time."

He beckoned the waiter over, and ordered again.

The impulse to remonstrate crossed my mind and passed. Bill was out of my leading-strings now. Besides, he had worked hard enough lately, and achieved enough. Let his mind have a break and a rest, if only in the befuddled cradle of alcohol. I had had enough myself now to feel benevolent and tolerant towards everybody. I had forgotten already about any possible patients.

We drank. We talked, but of nothing important. We had spoken enough of the Reproducer that night. Our talk showed reaction in light nonsense.

Came closing-time. When Bill stood up he had to put his hand on my shoulder to steady himself. His face was flushed and perspiring. He was breathing through his mouth as though it were too great an effort to keep it closed. His eyes were rather starey, and his tie was awry.

When we stepped out of the brightness into the abrupt darkness of the night he was as helpless as if he had stepped off the end of a diving-board. I guided him down the High Street with his arm in the crook of mine. We managed not too badly like this, but it was obvious that I should have to see him all the way home.

When we were clear of the village he began to talk, at first slowly and deliberately. But presently his speech became a steady, fast stream of words, sailing easily out of his now uncalculating mind into the night as if that mind were a bobbin on a free spindle and someone was hauling, hand over hand and unceasingly, the thread of discourse from it. It lasted most of the way down that long winding lane to the Dump.

In that discourse Bill revealed something of what went on behind the self-conscious, facetious, self-opinionated and yet unsure façade he presented to the outer world.

It was the first development in the unprecedented multiple tragedy that, for want of a better description for a series of situations almost beyond description, I have called the four-sided triangle.

"Yes, Doc, I'm plenty drunk and I like being this way. Sometimes I seem to be able to see things so much more clearly. No effort at all. Lucid. Like Lena's mind. Not confused with hopes and fears, like I am most of the time. Don't care a damn what anybody thinks. Wonderful thing, alcohol...

"I get the world in perspective this way. This is what I should be all the time. But I'm not. I'm rags blowing in the wind. I'm not—integrated. There's not a thing about me I can trust. Self-doubt, self-doubt all the time. What do I look like, what do I sound like? I keep wondering all the time. Am I being impressive or just a bore? Do I look to others like the overgrown school-kid that stares back at me from mirrors? Do I *mean* anything in this life? Is there a God, and if there is does Bill Leggett mean anything to Him?…

"I've no foundation of faith, I'm not constant, not even about science. Science is only tinkering with machinery; it doesn't know anything about the purpose of the machinery. Or isn't there a purpose? Lena doesn't think there is, but that doesn't make any difference to her outlook. She's sufficient unto herself. I'm not. I want something to lean on. Like your arm now. Lord, for a consistent faith, even if it were misplaced—so long that I believed!

"Like Rob. He's had it all set for him. To play the game, to be a worthy servant of the British Empire, and to keep to the British moral standard. Stiff upper lip, understatement, no complaining, no giving in as long as the job's to do. I always want to chuck it when I get sick of anything. I was never at home at Trinity, except in the lab. Hated rugger. Seemed a lot of running about and mess and unpleasantness for damn all. Proved nothing. I can see I was wrong to dodge that. I might have proved myself to myself. I still have the opportunities, but it's too late: something paralyses me into inaction every time. Chronic doubt.

"I envy Rob, meanly and miserably. I admire him, as though he were the school hero and I was a fresh, green kid. It got that way at Cambridge and it seems to have stuck that way. I feel the inferiority sometimes so badly that I almost hate him, as I somehow hate the standard, the priggish standard, he upholds so steadfastly. Steadfastness is always an admirable quality, even if a man is steadfastly wrong. Everybody respects a man who is consistent. You know where you are with him. He is a unit. He is all of a piece. I am all pieces and they are all over the place.

"And yet, you know, I get glimpses. Glimpses of a reality more fundamental than anything Rob even suspects..."

He went on about these glimpses. I was too fuddled myself to follow. I doubt whether I should if I had been wholly sober. Disconnected fragments about Dr. Rhine and Extra-Sensory Perception, Dunne's Time Theory, Ouspensky, Schrödinger, Wells, and the nature of a racial mind are all that survive in my memory.

I picked up the thread again somewhere in the midst of more morbid analysis of "the emotion-ravaged, fear-torn, doubting creature called 'Bill Leggett'."

"But it is Bill Leggett who doubts, not I. The real I only emerges as the sweet power of the grape melts away Bill's chains, or when sheer wonder has set him free. Free from the pain of the never-healing wounds of his early life."

It was here that he went into intimate detail about his sufferings at the hands of his father and his father's women, and of the dreaded visits of the unmentionable Uncle Joe. For reasons of decency I am not prepared to make that matter public. It comes under the adjective applied to Uncle Joe.

Bill went on: "Bill Leggett's knowledge grew, you see, but his emotions were bottled up, denied outlet, and they never grew. His emotional outlook is still that of a thwarted child.

"Supposing you visualize the emotions trying to develop as, say, the human skull develops. Now, Bill's skull got nowhere. Every tendency it had to expand in any direction whatever was jealously watched by a semi-mad parent and promptly and furiously hammered back 'into place', lest the son be greater than the father, which was absurd—in Leggett Senior's bleary view. Bill has the cramped skull of a mere infant, containing his emotions under pressure, like a steam boiler.

"It was different with Rob. Have you read the *Cannibal Island* book of the Martin Johnsons, describing how a certain savage tribe, the 'Long-heads', make a practice of binding their children's skulls almost from birth? Their belief is that 'superior' cannibals have long, narrow, back-projecting heads. And so each baby's head is tightly bound with unyielding cloth while the skull is still soft, leaving only one direction for it to grow freely: backwards. Thus it is encouraged to grow up in a frame, so that it will finish in the 'superior' shape. That is Rob, in the frame of his family, the code of his class and of his public school. But at least his emotional beliefs were encouraged, even if they were directed and set.

"Lena's is the only head among us that has grown and developed naturally and unhindered. By the time the convent school got hold of her it was too late to malform her fundamentally. She had already worked things out for herself. All the convent did to her was to suggest to her that sex and domestic life were unnecessary to living, and, indeed, not even to be desired. And it steered her creative urges instead into the arts, where they have got hopelessly lost, seeking a fulfilment that does not lie there.

"Your diagnosis was correct, Doc. What Lena lacked in her early growth was a home, and the intimate, personal family life in that home. She never had experience of it, and even now she has still not had experience of it. And she doesn't know what she has missed. But, instinctively, she feels the loss, the gap, in her life. So she wants something to fill that gap. Of course, what she really wants to create (without realizing it) is a family and a home of her own. A created existence with herself as the nucleus of it, watching and guiding the clinging children, receiving the homage of the husband and yet guiding him, too, in her way, and fashioning a living place full of beautiful, loved and lovely things. I can see now why she was so attracted by my project of filling the home of the ordinary person with *objets d'art*. It fitted in with all her subconscious wishes.

"Alas, that interest is dying before we really start. She half realizes that she is not going to create, with the Reproducer, anything that would completely satisfy herself. I can sense that...

"You know, a couple of mornings ago I actually went swimming with her at her usual place. At least, I went: in point of fact, I dodged going in at the end. It was too damn' cold. There was frost on the grass. Her usual place is at that bend in the river where the bluff is. That must be thirty feet high, and there's an outcropping of rock below it. Two sharp tongues of jagged rock reach out into the river, and little more than a metre separates them. Her way of going in is off that bluff into the space between the tongues. A thirty-foot drop into a safe area little more than a yard wide. However good a diver you are, that's a chancey business.

"And I could see by the not exactly careless, but uncaring, way she took off that it didn't matter a tinker's curse to her if she did happen to hit anything. Despite all our hopes, she's back in that state of not particularly wishing to live, and quite indifferent about dying. And I know she takes that unnecessary risk every morning, and I don't like to think what the edges of those rocks may do to her if—"

At this juncture a bright white light shot suddenly between us from behind and sent fantastically lanky shadows of us, absurdly high-stepping, reaching far before us over the tarmac surface of the lane. There was the bray of an automobile horn.

I pushed Bill away to the side of the road, and he stumbled and half disappeared, nearly dragging me after him. The car brushed past us, much too fast, and became a weaving, diminishing red tail-light in a fading white glow.

And Bill lay half in and half out of the ditch muttering to himself. Lately, in a manner I have not tried to represent, his sibilants had thickened, terminations of certain words were more frequently dropped, and something like a stutter had cropped up. More noticeably, since he had been talking about Lena, something of the maudlin note of a certain type of drunk had crept in.

Obviously this "setting free" action which Bill had claimed for alcohol was good only for the first stages of a bout. After that, a delayed action started catching up, steadily befuddling, wresting away control of the body, letting emotion seep in again loose and uninhibited, until at last body and mind together had about as much volition as a marionette with broken strings.

I had to stoop to try to heave him up.

He was mumbling, half under his breath and over and over again, what sounded like a line of poetry, though I did not, and do not, recognize it:

> *"Said the Rose: 'To punish, I die...'*
> *Said the Rose: 'To punish, I die...'"*

I had to carry him partly now as we lurched along. Thank goodness there was not much farther to go: I could already see the black roof of the Dump in silhouette against the stars, over the hedges.

"I see with the eyes of the seer. I speak with the tongues of the prophets," he burbled, as we made slow progress. "O, hear ye—"

He stopped suddenly. He stood swaying. I sensed, rather than saw, that he held up an admonitory finger.

"Doc," he said, "I must be serious. Oh, it *is* serious. That girl, that silly girl... doesn't know what she wants. But I do... know what she wants. Ah, I know... what I want, too. I want her. I love her."

The maudlin note was more evident.

"Love her... since that night... by the fire. 'Tisn't just that. Companionship... want her companionship. You know, I never had mother... not really. 'Swhat's wrong with me. Need motherin'... sometimes. Silly. There you are. Lena... need Lena."

"Then why don't you tell her?" I said.

He made a queer sound between a gulp and a noise of ridicule.

"You know how it is... She doesn't realize... doesn't know what she needs... She might... She might..."

"She might turn you down? Well, that can't be helped. It doesn't stop you from trying."

"But it *does* stop me..." (Foolish laugh.) "The thought—*does* stop me. Know what it is—pride. Just pride. Can't help it. There it is. Sensitive. Too sensitive. Can't help it."

"Perhaps you can't," I said, a little wearily. "But can I?"

"Yes... you can. There's a race on... between Lena happenin' to find out... what she wants... and... and... it being too late... for her ever to..."

"I see what you mean," I said.

"It's a close race... Either may happen... any time... now. I see with the eyes of the s—"

"Yes," I interrupted. (He was intolerably heavy to hold up.) "But what can I do?"

"Obliged if you would... probe her, Doc. See the lie... of the land... for me. She is on the point... believe me... on the point of reali... zation. If you think there is... a chance... I'll try... cold sober... I could never try... like this. Not drunk...

she'd never believe I meant it. Must try sober... if chance... pride or no pride."

"O.K., Bill," I said, after this painfully protracted effort. "I promise you I'll probe, and let you know."

"Thank you... kindly," he got out, and collapsed on me as limply as a rag doll but not as lightly.

However, it was easier to carry him in that condition, by the "fireman's hoist", than in the fashion of the previous hundred yards. I got him to the Dump pretty near in a state of collapse myself, and put him to bed.

He came partly conscious once to be very sick, but it was a very small part, and he only frothed instead of speaking. I left him in snoring, drunken slumber.

Half-way back along the lane I stopped once and gazed up at the eternal glittering stars to assure myself that this day had been real. As I contemplated the black gulfs between the stars, falling away through unfathomable distances to the places where man's feeble light could never reach in all his history to be, I felt awe and a queer inward trembling about this strange new force we had uncaged upon this planet.

What would it lead to? What change in the destiny of man might it make? Or was it perhaps a thing destined already?

I never dreamed, in the smaller personal sense, just what a grip it was to fasten on me and those near me. It was as well I did not. I had disturbing dreams enough that night.

CHAPTER FOUR

NEXT MORNING I WAS DRIVING THROUGH THE VILLAGE WHEN I saw Lena stepping from the doorway of a grocer's carrying a bulging shopping bag. I pulled up at the kerb beside her.

"Taxi, lady?" I inquired.

"I'll have to pay you in potatoes," she smiled. "The shopping purse is empty."

"That means you've got it all, anyway, so hop in—I'm going by the Dump."

She got into the seat beside me, putting the bag in the back. I let a bus get in front of us before starting off, and followed its slow course along the High Street. I did not want this journey to end too soon, before I had done my probing for Bill.

It was difficult to think of a plan of approach. Even though I knew that if the situation were reversed Lena would ask straight out what she wished to know, with no sly hesitations, I could not bring myself to do that. For myself to do so (but not for Lena, who had no such habits) would appear to me to be a violation of the behaviour long known as "good manners", and I should not escape awkwardness.

But, as it happened, my opening gambit led almost straight to the point.

"You'll soon be getting your piano back now?" I half stated, half asked.

"Maybe," said Lena.

"Maybe? Why, if our plans work out cash should be coming in in two or three weeks."

"Yes," said Lena. "But I'm not frightfully anxious to get the piano back."

I frowned my displeasure.

"I don't like to see that attitude coming back, Lena," I said. "I thought you were going to make an effort. I thought you were interested—"

"Doc," she interrupted, with a quizzical look, "you've barked up the wrong tree altogether. I *am* interested in the Reproducer, up to a point. But now I'm more interested in—something else. The piano would be no help."

"Is this 'something else' a secret?"

The quizzical expression became a smile.

"I don't believe in secrets, Doc," she said. "In any case, you already know of it. You knew of it before I did."

"Meaning?"

"Meaning you were right when you said that what I was really seeking was a home and a family. Perhaps it was started by your suggestion, but it came to me as plainly as anything last night. When I saw Rob's home and family. I met his mother and father, and young brother and sister. In that lovely house."

She paused, looking into her memory, and seemed to muse.

Presently: "Would you believe, Doc, that that was my first real experience of a home, a natural, happy home? It was. For once I envied a person for her position, and not for her artistic ability. I could have changed lives with Lady Heath, if I could have done what she had done: made that fine house into a wonderful home, created that cosy family circle. I felt quite outside of things and alone. I wanted to start *my* home and *my* family. And then, suddenly, I knew that would satisfy me completely, and that art was just a side-street that I had thought my main road."

She stared reflectively at the back of the bus.

I saw my cue.

"I'm not surprised," I said. "There's a man who knows you so well that last night he told me that you were just on the point of realizing this."

She looked at me now, eyebrows a little raised, and some unidentifiable expression behind those unfathomable eyes.

"Bill," I told her.

The expression changed, but did not come to the surface.

"He's a nice lad, as well as a clever one," she said in her slow way. "I've become quite fond of him."

We were getting ahead so well now that I took a chance and pulled out round the bus and left it behind.

As we approached the long winding lane along which I had steered Bill on the previous night, I ventured: "He's become rather fond of you too. He hesitates to express it, because he's extraordinarily sensitive about personal relationships, but I know he feels that way. In fact, I know he's head over heels in love with you."

Her expression was clearly surprise this time.

"Dear Bill!" she exclaimed. "How can he imagine that I could be of any help to him? I know next to nothing of science. I could do little but hinder and distract. I cannot see what use he imagines I could be."

"My dear girl, he wants a wife, not a laboratory assistant. If I'm any judge, he wants a wife with a pronounced sympathetic side—in fact, with a mothering quality. For he still has a childish longing for the mother he lost. I know what he can see in you, if you cannot. He can see someone without a thought for herself, but plenty to spare for others. Also a spirit which supplies his needs for steadiness, patience, understanding, reassurance and comfort."

A silence followed this song of praise. Again she was gazing thoughtfully before her through the windscreen.

Presently she said: "Bill did all he could to help me. I would like to do all I can to help him. I should not hesitate to marry him if, as you say, he really needs me. I believe I could come to love him, to love children from him, to share a home with him. Only there's one thing which prevents that."

"Eh?"

"I have found that I'm in love with Rob—very much."

I nearly ran the car sidelong into a hay-waggon on a bend.

"Good lord!" was all I could say.

"It's only just happened to me. Last night, in fact, when I found out what I really wanted. He was part of it, in that setting. He goes with it. It might be an accident of circumstances. I don't know. Perhaps it could as well have been Bill. But I carried home with me a mental picture of Rob sitting opposite me at the supper-table and laughing across at me at some remark I made to his father. That picture stayed in my mind all night. It would not let me sleep. All I have known since is an ache and a longing to be back with him. Even now something is reaching out ahead of me to the Dump, impatient to be there quickly, and I am straining after it. I have never known anything like this. I never knew anything could hurt so much."

Lena was still surprising me: always doing something I had not in the least expected, and leaving me groping for comments.

"I don't know whether to sympathize or be glad," I said. "I still haven't been 'that way'. But if there's anything I can do...?"

"Nobody can do much," she said with a little smile. "It's just a matter of how some people feel. Rob particularly, of course. The one thing I can do is tell him of my feeling, and probably he'll tell me if it means anything to him or not. Then we shall know where we are."

"You're going to tell him?" I repeated, slowly and stupidly.

"Yes, of course—directly I get back now. Can it do harm?"

I could not see that it could, and said so. After all, how could I expect Lena to go about hugging this feeling to her breast, nursing it, gazing moon-eyed at Rob every time he came near and coyly and cunningly trying to prise his view of her from him? That was not Lena's way. She would think such a performance unnecessary and, in its way, absurd.

"I wish you all luck, my dear," I went on, and an inexcusable curiosity got uppermost for a moment. "What if he doesn't return those feelings?"

"I'm sorry, Doc, I can't enlighten you. I don't seem to be able to make plans ahead based on different 'maybes'. I only seem able to do anything about the future when it becomes the present."

At which moment in time we arrived at the Dump. I carried her bag in for her.

Only Bill was in the lab, working at the bolts in the feet of the dynamo. He had an oil-can in one hand and a spanner in the other. Black, glistening streaks of the oil smeared his forehead where he had been running his soiled fingers through his hair.

He glanced up. He was perspiring, and the trace of a frown lay upon his smudged brow. I guessed the bolts were recalcitrant, and moreover had been the recent recipients of some blistering language.

But he smiled when he saw us. "Hullo, Doc. Hullo, Lena—you haven't been gone long. Did you get the apples?"

"Yes," she answered, feeling around in the bag. She selected a huge pippin and threw it to him. "If you *can't* wait for lunch," she said.

He took a large bite and grinned through it—a shocking sight.

"Time is purely relative," he said. "It's my lunchtime now."

"So we see," said Lena. "Where's Rob?"

"Oh, he's out in the yard bricking up the foundry."

"I thank you."

As she passed me on her way to the back exit, for all her casual walk and absent-seeming appearance I perceived that her mind was taut and set on having this thing out. She glanced at me, and I strove to convey by facial expression an encouragement I knew she didn't need. She acknowledged it with a faint, wry smile.

Bill didn't notice. He was testing the head of one bolt for play with his fingers, still munching away at the apple.

I walked slowly over to him.

"Bill," I said, "remember last night?"

"Gosh, not half!" he said. "My head still feels as if I've just come off a roundabout."

"I mean what you asked me to do?"

He merely looked puzzled.

"Regarding Lena," I supplied.

"I'm afraid I don't," he said.

"Then it doesn't matter," I said, turning away.

"Come on, Doc, what was it? You can't leave me up in the air like this."

I hesitated. I had rather let well alone. Only there was a likely chance that he would get the information in a more unexpected and shocking form very soon, and perhaps I could ease its path. In any case, he would know eventually: Lena would be as honest to him as to me.

"You told me you were in love with Lena. You asked me to find out how she felt about you. I did. She said—"

"Stop, Doc!" he broke in hoarsely. He had flushed deeply, and his eyes held sudden agony. "I don't want to know. I was too drunk to know what I was saying. God—to think…! Do me a favour and forget it, Doc. Please, I…"

His voice trailed away, he blinked and suddenly bent over his work again, wrenching hard with the spanner.

His distress was like a knife in my own heart. A sudden welling-up of tenderness and compassion for this foster-son of mine filled me. And rage that humanity had to be tormented through its feelings in this way. Why did nature take such a clumsy, tortuous path to gain her ends? Why must birth and growth always be a friction and a suffering?

Nature staggered blindly through the human crowd like a senseless, flailing idiot, sending reeling and bruised all she came by chance to contact. All her spreading ramifications since the beginning of time were a confused tangle of blind alleys, merciless squeezings out, brutal tramplings and oppressions, square pegs bludgeoned stupidly into round holes, preventable maladjustments and enforced compromises, manifestly unsatisfactory. Like a small child trying to fit together a jigsaw puzzle it has lost patience with and jamming the pieces together anyhow in a temper. "Get *there*!"

So it seemed to me then, and so it has always seemed to me.

All I have concluded from a lifetime of studying man and his sickness of body and mind is that if the liver and intestines are in good condition and the sexual urges satisfied, then God's in His Heaven and all's right with the world. But if all or any of these are out of order or frustrated, then during that time there is no God and no Heaven, and the world is a sorry, grey, dismal mess. We are in invisible cages in Nature's mad zoo, cages too big or too small for us; but the bars are very real.

Sometimes an unclassified being like Lena comes along and causes us to wonder. But then even her self-sufficiency proves to be so only up to a point. She wanders far in her isolation, but she is not entirely free of that jungle: it grows and reaches after her.

I, at least, I told myself grimly, have no illusions. I would never acquiesce, with resignation, with these Fates of the Greeks, this Universal Irony of Hardy's, this Blind Process of Wells's, this Nature of my own observation. I would fight back, and stand by anyone who fought back.

These were my thoughts in that space of furious sympathy.

I don't know quite how long I stood there in reflection, but I was aroused by the entrance of Rob and Lena, hand in hand.

One look at Rob's beaming face and the quiet serenity of Lena's was enough to tell me the outcome of that deliberate interview.

I caught Lena's eye, and shook my head with the slightest of indications towards the oblivious Bill. She comprehended at once, and sought to restrain Rob. But it was too late. His cheerful voice rang out across the lab: "Bill! Doc! Congratulate us! We're going to be married!"

Because I knew what reaction to expect, the sudden stillness of Bill's back as he bent over the feet of the dynamo was like a printed page to me. He was numbed, momentarily paralysed, in utter blankness. As his thoughts began to move again, a tremor shook him, and I knew pain coursed within him as raw as sulphuric acid. Then his shoulders came ever so slightly back, he stiffened, rose slowly and turned, his face still a little blank. And then he forced a grin, a mockery of his old free grin, but brave enough to arouse no doubts in the happy Rob. A marvellous effort, and I respected him for it, respected him more than I had ever done before.

Bill was not so immature as he believed himself to be; be the occasion great enough, and he could summon the control to meet and deal with it.

Nevertheless, to help, I spoke first, if banally.

"Heavens, that's a quick one! This is so sudden!… Yes, of course I congratulate you, Rob, Lena. I wish you all the happiness in the world. Now, where did I leave my breath?"

Rob laughed and Lena smiled faintly; and then Bill came across to them, still grinning, and shook each of them deliberately by the hand. He could not yet trust himself to speak. With her hand in his, Lena still smiled at him; but her eyes were not the blue they were when she was happy—they were cloudy grey, and something quite apart from the smile lay back in their depths. And because I was in a state of super-sensitiveness just then I could see quite clearly what that something was. It was a compassion as deep as my own.

The drinks were got out.

Afterwards, Lena came out to me alone just as I was starting up the car.

"Doc," she said, leaning over the door.

"Hullo," I said.

"I'm terribly sorry about the way Bill was hurt a little while back. I meant to break it gently to him in my own way. But I was in such a happy daze myself at the unexpectedness of things that I just didn't think to warn Rob in time."

"Does Rob know now?"

"No."

"Then don't tell him. It's something that will have to be forgotten now. Bill, most of all, must forget. There is only one way. You must get married as quickly as possible and go on a fairly long honeymoon. The two of you in the Dump with him every day just now will only be a constant torture to him. You must give him a chance to forget. I'll do my best to get him deep into work and make him lose himself in it. He'll probably feel he must do that, anyway. It's the natural consequence with energetic people like him. But I'll see that he does. I've got a young doctor coming in a couple of days to take over my practice: I've sold it—I've retired. So now I'll be able to plunge into getting the Reproducer Company under way and take Bill with me."

"Doc, you're an old wise man. Wiser than I'll ever be."

"Nonsense, Lena. You make me feel almost like a kid sometimes. There's another thing—get a house, arrange about a house, before you go. Not too far from the Dump, but far enough not to display your domestic life before Bill and me: for I shall be living with him at the Dump when you've moved out."

She said nothing, but kissed me lightly on the forehead.

"What did Rob have to say when you marched up to him and said you loved him?" I said, no longer matter-of-fact.

She gave a soft, husky little laugh.

"He dropped the brick he had in his hands, looked down at it, tried to pick it up casually, dropped it again, and then suddenly abandoned it and threw his arms around me and hugged and kissed me quite madly. How wonderful that was! I knew how right I was: the satisfaction, the gladness, was—overwhelming. Art, forsooth!"

"So I imagine he had been feeling 'that way' some time?"

"Yes, the silly, lovable man! Said it began when I went shopping and brought back pound notes. Said he couldn't get out of his head the sight of me standing there with a handful of pound notes. Why do men—dissemble? Why couldn't he have told me right away? We could have had days of happiness behind us that have been wasted."

"Supposing he had done? You would have told him primly that you were sorry, but your desires didn't go 'that way'. Remember?—they didn't. Not until last night."

"Yes, but—"

She stopped, nonplussed for once.

"Lena, I can already see changes in you. You're becoming human. You've already become aware of the fear of losing things. 'Wasted days', indeed, from you! Once, time meant nothing at all to you. And life not much more."

"As usual, you're right, Doc. I've changed," she whispered. "Those old blank days are past. Every minute of life means something to me now."

"And you won't go diving off that bluff in the mornings any more?" I asked sternly.

"Has Bill been telling you things?" she said with mock shame. "No, all right, I won't—too often. But that wasn't much of a risk, you know. I've been diving since I was a little girl. It's fun."

"Do it where there aren't any rocks," I said. "I've retired. I shan't sew you up. Well, good-bye, Lena. Have your fun from life now: you've earned it."

"Good-bye, Doc. Thank you for the advice. This time I'll take it."

Lena and Rob were married within the week.

I don't know what Sir Walter thought of this (as it must have appeared to him) almost indecent haste, but he obviously thought it a more worthy cause than his son's "tinkering about with atoms", for he gave the pair the fine old red-brick house "Hawthorns", which stood on a rise overlooking the village and the whole valley. One might have churlishly said that he was glad to get rid of a piece of property which he had not been able to let for years, only he gave a *carte blanche* for the furniture, too, and that silenced one.

When we had seen them off on their honeymoon—they were to spend three weeks on the Cornish Riviera—I took Bill aside.

"Bill," I said, "we've got to do a bit of re-orientation. For one thing, the fellow who is taking my practice is planning to get married himself and would like the whole of the house. Of course, I didn't sell the house with the practice, but he may as well have it, fittings and all. I'm finished with medicine. I'm eager to get to work on our Reproducer Company. I know it's a private company, and there won't be anything like the book-keeping of a limited company. But all the same there'll be plenty once we get going, secretarial work, too, and we've got to get an office and system fixed up and worked out. But I like to live near my work. Now that Rob's gone, how about me moving in on you?"

"I should be glad if you would, Doc," he said, and looked as if he meant it.

So I moved into the Dump, and the two of us became very busy fixing up a room as an office, getting in desks and filing cabinets, a typewriter, ledgers, and all such paraphernalia, and working out a system of accounts. We planned out, too, the details of a press campaign to launch our venture and to inform the world of the new treasure box that had been opened to it.

While we were so engaged Bill seemed, if not exactly happy, then at least not too miserable. It was a good thing that he had the habit of throwing himself wholeheartedly into any work on hand, so long as visible progress was made in that work.

In fact, it was too much of a good thing: in less than a fortnight of hard work everything that could be done had been done. The whole set-up could only wait now on the return of Rob and Lena for the button to be pressed and the Reproducer Company to start into motion.

And Bill, with time on his hands, began to mope about the place, bestrewing the floor with half a dozen empty cigarette packets a day.

It was the one condition of things I had wanted to avoid. For the life of me I could think of no new activities to keep him occupied.

He refused to be tempted out to any amusements. He even cold-shouldered my sudden inspiration and suggestion that we spend a few days in London and attend a series of symphony concerts which were due to open.

But on the evening of the third idle day he was so sick of himself that he agreed to have a walk up to the "Pheasant" and a few drinks with me.

"A *few* drinks, mind, Doc!" he emphasized. "I don't want to make such an idiot of myself as I did last time."

Nevertheless, the few drinks mellowed him appreciably. For the first time in many days he began to make cracks in the old fashion and even laugh. As he loosened up, he became quite voluble. Opinions on everything under the sun came tumbling out just like old times.

The domination of the Roman Catholic Church over the artistic energy of the Renaissance in Italy. A condemnation of "The Last Judgment" as "a glorified snakes-and-ladders board" and Michelangelo's egotism in putting himself in a good position on it while depicting the one man who criticized his work adversely as serpent-wrapped in Hell. The more genuine insight of Cézanne. Debussy and Mallarmé. How the beauty of mathematical equations might be represented by pattern painting or pattern music. Discoveries of effects in supersonics, and development of rocket propulsion. All those things and a dozen others came under review.

On that walk back he was the same old Bill, opening up fresh worlds of perhaps to my imagination.

And then, without warning, he switched on to something which I think had been fermenting below the surface of his mind for a long time.

"Doc, if I weren't slightly oiled I shouldn't have the nerve to ask you this. As it is… Well, anyway, how *did* Lena feel about me?"

"She is very fond of you. She was surprised at your interest, and couldn't fathom how you could get in any way bothered about her. But she said that if it hadn't been for Rob she would probably have married you. She believed she would have come to love you, and liked the idea of sharing a home with you. So you see, my dear Bill, you needn't have been half so nervous and touchy about it as you were."

He was silent for a little while.

Then he said: "I'm sorry I was so touchy about it, Doc. Only I was very het up over things, torturing myself about her. It came as a shock to learn that I had been acting suitor by proxy, so to speak. I must have been very drunk. The trouble was, you see, that I really knew, though I wouldn't admit it to myself, that Rob was much more the type she needed. They seemed so *right* as a pair. God knows exactly why I feel so inferior to Rob, but I do. The idea of me trying to sell her second-class goods… It makes me feel bad, even now. But what Lena said helps a lot. It's wonderful, really, that she should care at all."

"Not particularly wonderful: you certainly have points," I said, trying in my small way to help break down this ridiculous inferiority complex.

"It makes it easier to be a loser. I'd rather get second place than be nowhere."

"Of course."

He fell silent again after that, and meditated through the short remainder of the journey.

He said only one more thing before he turned in.

"My greatest asset is my mind, Doc. If I can use it right, who knows?—I may not be a loser at all, even now."

To which statement he would add nothing. I went to bed puzzling over it.

Next morning he was up before I was, which was a rare thing. Moreover, he was in a good humour.

"There's your breakfast, Doc," he said, pointing to two boiled eggs and a pile of cut bread. "Maybe not perfect, but at least I didn't crack 'em, as Lena always does."

"Don't say nasty things about people behind their backs."

"It's not a nasty thing: it's a statement of fact," said Bill, ruling a couple of parallel lines on the drawing-board he was working on. "Furthermore, I've said it to her face before now."

"One thing, Rob will be able to hire a cook now and get some good food," I said shamelessly, in my turn.

"Oh, Lena used to get good food," said Bill. "It was the things she used to do to it afterwards."

"Lord, if she could hear us!" I speculated.

"Those eggs would be bouncing off our heads," chuckled Bill. "You're fond of Lena, too, aren't you, Doc?"

"In my own particular way, yes," I said reservedly. "She's such a—genuine person."

He made no answer, only busied himself with the board. He was whistling between his teeth, and obviously in high spirits.

"What are you designing now?" I asked, with a mouth full of bread.

"Oh, this?… It's a larger, improved Reproducer. The one we've got is all right for a start, but small and terribly makeshift. When we get a bit more capital we'll enlarge and rebuild it into this one. More compact design, yet three times the capacity. And it'll look more finished, and won't make half the row the present one does."

"You are, I take it, sticking to our original plan never to have more than one?"

"Too true," replied Bill. "And no one but ourselves must ever operate it. We can trust no one else. I don't think that even now, Doc, you comprehend all the unsettling things that might happen if this got into the hands of people without foresight or scruples."

"I comprehend a good many."

"Believe me, there are possibilities you haven't imagined yet. Take the case—"

He paused.

"Perhaps we had better not take the case, on second thoughts," he went on. "Rob had rather you didn't, anyway. And as things are, there may not even be a case."

"You're being very cryptic lately," I complained.

He grinned.

"Ha, ha," he emitted sinisterly, like a stage villain.

"Is that as far as we go?" I pursued.

"*Quien sabe?*"

"Confound you and your secrets! I'll ask Lena."

"Lena wasn't told any more than you. She can't keep secrets. Besides, who said there was a secret?"

"Oh, go and play with your toys," I said impatiently. "You kids—!"

He worked all morning on his designs, and I was relieved he had of himself found something to turn his attention outward. I believed that my frank report of what Lena had said had settled his inward doubts and reproaches, and he had accepted and decided to make the best of things.

I thought that his remark about his greatest asset being his mind, and in the using of it not being a "loser" after all, meant possibly that had he married Lena he would have to devote much of his thought and time to her, thought and time lost to his career in science. And that therefore in a way he was glad the matter was no longer uncertain: it was settled and done with, he knew where he stood, and he was unattached and free once more to attack the forts in the unconquered lands of science.

In the afternoon he went out on a lone expedition to the village.

When he returned he came in the rear way, and I did not know he was back until he startled me by emerging suddenly from his bedroom. By his somewhat guilty expression I judged he had hidden something there he did not wish me to see. As it happened, I was right. But I asked no questions. If it was not my business, it was not my business.

Then he got going again at the drawing-board, and was still producing sheets of mechanical drawings when I went to bed.

I had dozed off, and was awakened by the harsh whine of the dynamo, joined by all the other hellish noises the Reproducer made when in action. That electric taste in the air even got past the shut door of my room, and the vibrations of the still not properly chained dynamo shook my bed like the tremor of an earthquake.

I half made to get up and investigate. Then I thought this might be connected with Bill's "secrets", and he would resent my prying. If it were not, then he would tell me in the morning why he was working the machine at this time of night. So I lay back and endured it like a stoic.

At last it ceased.

There was a silence, and then tinklings as of glass jars being moved and impinging one upon the other. Again a silence.

"Damn the thing!" came Bill's voice faintly.

After a little while came a queer sustained buzzing. The key of it changed a few times. Abruptly it stopped.

I lay listening with ears cocked with curiosity now.

More muffled exasperation from Bill.

More buzzing. It went on a long time.

A long silence after that.

Then, "Curse the blasted thing!" came Bill's voice with unusual vehemence. "Oh, hell, hell, hell!"

The last repetitive expletives, a common series of his, were on a rising note, half a wail, almost on the road to tears. More than a touch of hysteria. The unstable Bill had been disappointed near to grief by some experiment he had set his heart upon: somehow it had not come off.

There was the crash of breaking glass. No accident, I judged, from experience of him from a child. He had flown right off the handle, lost his temper and thrown or kicked something. I had seen him, when he was a schoolboy, make himself physically sick with the rage of frustration.

As then, I did not interfere. To pay attention to it would only magnify its importance in his eyes.

The last sounds I heard that night, when I was too near the indefinite border between consciousness and sleep to be more than faintly and drowsily surprised, were the cloppings of a shovel hitting hard earth: Bill was digging in the rear yard.

In the morning I had forgotten about it until I noticed the splinters of large test tubes on the lab floor.

Bill was not up, so I made a stealthy investigation of the yard... Whatever he had buried was a small thing: the patch of newly turned and trodden-down earth was hardly more than a foot square. I gazed at it, wondered, and shrugged my shoulders. I noticed other small patches of less freshly dug earth.

When he appeared, quiet and rather sullen, he made no mention of the previous night's alarums and excursions, and so neither did I. He read *Nature* at breakfast, tore to ribbons (with words) quite vindictively an article by a renowned physicist, glanced over his plans and elevations once more, and abandoned them to tinker at the work-bench on some new gadget he was fitting together.

In the afternoon, now in the dreadful state of having nothing to do myself, I went for a long solitary walk over meadow grass-tracks and through empty woods.

I was not accustomed to this condition of being at a loose end. I half regretted that I had given up my practice so suddenly. The only saving thing to reflect upon was that Lena and Rob were due back next day, and we could all get to work.

I looked forward to seeing Lena again. Bill's glowering and unsettling tantrums wouldn't last long in her presence: her cool ridicule and laughter would sap them of all their angry life. She would bring out the old Bill of crazy jokes, burning enthusiasms, and a head half in wonderland.

Her absence had certainly left a gap in my existence. I missed her as I had missed Bill when he went away to college. Life seemed to mean something and be altogether warmer and brighter when she was around. Even in those times when life meant nothing much to her. There was no great mystery about this. She was beauty, she was unfailing good humour, she was reassurance in her refusal to be upset by the little worries that vexed us lesser mortals, she was realism and honesty, sympathy and grace, and I missed all of these things.

When I returned to the Dump the tang of electricity was yet in the atmosphere of the lab, and I knew that Bill had been using the Reproducer again. Obviously not successfully, for he was sitting humped up in a chair, his chin cupped in his hands, staring in front of him in silent misery.

"What's wrong with you lately, Bill?" I asked. "Is there anything I can do?"

He did not answer immediately, but continued to gaze dolefully at nothing.

Presently, and almost grudgingly, he said: "There's nothing wrong with me, Doc. It's my theories that are wrong. I don't know whether you could help. I don't think so. But it's more a question of 'would' than 'could'. I don't know if anyone *would* help. I know Rob would not. No, Doc, I'm on my own in this: I have to be. I haven't given up hope yet. I'll appeal to you before I do."

"Why not appeal now?" I suggested.

"I'd rather do it alone, if I can. I don't mean 'No trespassing'—don't take it that way, Doc. Only—the outcome is something I'm still not sure about. I can't make up my mind. If I actually get a result, it may decide things for me."

"All right, Bill," I said. "Only for goodness' sake don't worry so much. You'll be grey before you're thirty. Try to be a bit larger towards things, if you see what I mean."

"I feel what you mean," he said. "But all I see is that this is the most important thing that I have ever tried to do. It means everything to me. I can't help believing it is serious, and the uncertainty of it is hell. I haven't Lena's divine detachment. It matters an awful lot. If it doesn't come off, my life will be emptier than Lena's ever was."

He said this so straightly and sincerely that my slight irritation at his evasiveness melted away. I felt paternal and solicitous again. He was so much that red-headed youngster of years past when at odds with life in the perplexities and doubts of adolescence, seriously trying to square them for himself in his own way.

"I'm sorry," I said. "I hope it works out all right. But it's up to you. Don't give in too easily."

His lips tightened.

"I won't," he said, his voice firmer.

He got up and went over to the work-bench, and resumed work on his new gadget. There was a small electric motor in it, and a glass tube and piston—a sort of pump—and appendages of rubber tubes with silver-plated fittings.

"Do you mind my asking what it is?" I said, sauntering over and regarding it curiously. "It looks rather more in my line than yours, but I don't recognize it. But then I'm not very up to date with clinical gadgets."

"It's not quite an orthodox one," he said. "It's my adaptation of a product of the Institute of Experimental Physiology and Therapy in Moscow. It's based on Dr. Bryukhonenko's 'Autojector'—you may have read about that?"

"I'm afraid not," I said, but he made no attempt to explain further.

He worked on it the rest of the evening.

I had been in bed scarce half an hour that night when the rising scream of the dynamo tore across my nerves, and in a moment the full racket of the Reproducer in action once more shook the house. I had something of a headache to begin with. After another quarter of an hour of taut endurance, without relief, I could stand it no longer.

I got up, and was wrenching on my dressing-gown when the machine was switched off and the clamour fell away to a silence that seemed to be pulsing with wild, pressing power.

But I would not risk the chance of a renewal of the experience. In a sort of determined ill temper, I shoved open my bedroom door and marched out into the bright-lit lab. At least, it was brightly lit when I walked out. I had not gone two paces, my dazzled eyes had not adjusted themselves, I had not even seen Bill, ere all the lights went out with a click.

Complete darkness. I came to a sudden halt. I became aware that I had not put my slippers on: the floor smote cold on my bare soles, and my toes retracted sensitively lest they encounter unseen and unpleasant edges.

"What the devil!" I fumed. "Are you there, Bill?"

"Yes"—coldly.

"Did you put the lights out?"

"Yes."

"Why, for heaven's sake? What *is* going on?"

"Some private business," came Bill's voice, hard, deliberate, incisive.

"That's all very well. If only you would keep it private. I don't want to see any of it. Far less do I want to hear any of it. I've got a headache, and I can't stand any more of that racket. If you want to carry out secret experiments in my absence, then I'll get right out of it—I'll take a room at the 'Pheasant', any time you wish. But, please—let me have some sleep tonight."

"I have finished with the machine for tonight."

He was still speaking in abrupt, clipped words, the way in which, on rare occasions, I had heard him speak before. It meant that the hot rage of frustration and bafflement had reached and passed a certain switch-point of intensity that turned it into a solid, cold fury. A volcano iced over, under terrific pressure, a mood of temper with no susceptibility, a mood in which deliberate murder is done or incredible deeds in war. The ultimate ferocity of a cornered fighting animal at bay.

"In fact, I am finishing with the whole damned affair tonight," he went on. "If nothing comes of it this time, the whole shoot can go to merry hell. I'm sick of being driven like this. I'm sick of this hole-and-corner business. I'm getting beyond caring what people might think. If you want to see—see!"

And with the word, he switched on the lights.

When I could see, I perceived him standing with his back to the domes of the Reproducer, facing me, feet apart, as if he had planked himself there as an obstacle. His mouth was set, his eyes hard and bitter. He thrust his hands into his trouser pockets.

"Look," he commanded, with an indicatory sideways nod and jerk of the chin towards the twin domes at his rear.

I gazed past him. In each of the domes was a small brown shapeless object. I padded over for a closer view. When I made out what they were, I exclaimed softly.

I suppose my imagination must be pretty limited. Or perhaps it has weakened with the years. I seem almost certifiably dull at perceiving obvious developments. I sometimes wonder if I ever get any genuine ideas of my own. Those that I ever had seem to have been borrowed from brighter people, like Bill or the writers of books.

The object in the container, and its obviously just formed duplicate in the receiver dome, was a rabbit, lying still and apparently dead.

Why had I never considered the possibility of duplicating living things? Simply because no one else had suggested it. Because Bill and Rob and Lena had talked only of paintings, sculpture, medical appliances, jewels, and I had accepted all unconsciously the suggestion that only inanimate objects were within the scope of the machine.

But this was different again. The memory of Bill telling me there were possibilities I hadn't imagined flashed into my mind. And how he had pulled himself up at that.

Perhaps it wouldn't work after all. Those rabbits, or more correctly that rabbit, did not look alive to me.

"Are they both dead?" I asked quietly.

"Neither is dead. But only one is alive," Bill answered shortly.

He took pity on my bewilderment. He thawed out somewhat.

"The one in the container is alive, though drugged. The duplicate is not dead: it has never died because it has never lived. That's what's beaten me all along the line: the duplicates *won't* live."

"Perhaps they weren't meant to."

"Don't be sententious, Doc. It sounds too much like Rob. That was his opinion."

"How does he know of these experiments?"

"We included similar ones in our last tests before we showed you the Reproducer. We always chose times when Lena was out.

It was much too important an idea to get loose. If it worked with animals, there was no reason why it should not work with human beings. Think what might arise from that, if the power got into irresponsible hands!"

But he gave me no chance to think. He went on:

"Countries with declining birthrates could increase their population at will, bringing out great masses of people with identical outlook, appearance, tastes: all individually lost. Think how a ruthless business magnate could produce endless cheap labour from one foolish, willing serf! How any new upstart of a dictator could produce a million fanatical fighting men from just one selected follower—and never fear man-power shortage for his armies: all losses automatically replaced! My God, the chaos that could come upon the world!"

His coldness had vanished now. He felt the horror of these things as he revealed them. It goes without saying that I felt them no less. I fell back on the comforting assurance that so far nothing had proved that such events were even potentially possible.

"It's a dangerous line of thought and should not be pursued," I said. "I can understand why Rob wasn't happy about such experiments. In fact, I wonder why he ever agreed to the original experiments."

"My dear Doc, let us get ourselves straight about this. Knowledge as such, little or great, is not a dangerous thing. It is the unscientific education of the public and politicians who may mishandle it that is dangerous."

"The point is," I said, "that it's not wise to bring razors into a house containing too many imbeciles."

"Is it wrong to invent razors, then? Are all men to be cursed with filthy beards because some fools will not learn to use an instrument for its proper purpose?"

"No, it is not wrong to invent them. Only you must retain a sense of responsibility for them after you have invented them. Keep them in the right hands, and away from children and fools."

"Then as far as this particular case is concerned, you have no crib," said Bill. "I am trying to fashion a razor purely for myself. I do not want it to get into any other hands than mine. It need never go beyond us two. Not even to Rob—indeed, I know he would refuse to accept it."

"You have had a difference of opinion with him over this?"

"Yes. When we first got the Reproducer going and proved it on several inanimate objects, I, naturally, as a matter of curiosity, wanted to see whether it would duplicate living things. Rob did not seem very keen. He pointed out that as we had to pass a continuous current of electricity through the subject until the replica was complete, it was not going to be very pleasant for the guinea-pig, cat, rabbit or whatever it was. Which was, of course, mere niggling. Chloroform or morphia would largely settle that. It was an objection out of all proportion to the knowledge to be gained. He had to admit that. So we started—with a guinea-pig… Well, the result was just like this."

He waved a hand towards the rabbits in their domes.

"Two motionless guinea-pigs at the finish. The original one was still doped, of course, but came round after a little treatment. But the duplicate remained just a stiff little body, its muscles contorted and hardened, as the original's had been, by the action of the current. We massaged it, we injected adrenalin into it, we tried every resuscitatory dodge known—including smelling-salts. I spent a night throwing together a miniature iron lung for it, to get its lungs working. The iron lung worked: the guinea-pig's lungs wouldn't."

"I might have tried my hand at surgery for you," I said. "Made an opening over the heart—"

"And massaged the heart itself?" said Bill. "I even went as far as that. No go. We were flummoxed. Even Rob could think of nothing. But then, he wasn't particularly anxious to."

"What did he say?"

"He said he thought we had gone far enough. He said he was a physicist, not a biologist. He had never approved of biology in the line of ectogenesis, and he said this research could be compared to that. It was God's business to create life, not man's. His religious beliefs, my dear Doc, are incredibly crude—all at odds with his common sense in other matters. The trouble is, of course, that they are just inculcated beliefs, part of the bandages tied round his head to shape it in infancy—I've a dim memory of making that analogy before."

"Yes, when you were very drunk," I said.

"Nevertheless, it's a true one. It's hard to credit that such a clear mind should be so hypnotized, so inhibited, by the word 'religion'. But there it is: he is so conditioned. As far as I can see, his religion is a vague anthropomorphism, framed by a code of Christian behaviour and manners, and a solid line of prejudices. He pointed out all the evils I have mentioned which might result from duplicating human beings in the mass, but repeated that his main objection was to the creation of life. We had not the right to bring a single soul into the world. I replied that people are doing it every day—he had only to look at the 'Births' column!"

Despite the nature of the matter under discussion, I could not help a laugh at that.

"He never did go in for ready-made tailoring." Becoming serious again, I added: "But that raises a point. Could these imitation human beings be said to have souls of their own? The problem of Frankenstein's monster or Rossum's Universal Robots in fact."

"You know my views on that, Doc. I don't believe in individual immortal souls. If anything survives, it is the larger soul of mankind. We are drops in an ocean, mingling and intermingling—our individuality is as transitory as spray. If you or Rob say that the soul is a small part of God in every man, then I remind you that God is infinite, you can place no boundaries to Him or shut Him out of any living thing. Infinity means infinity. And please don't say 'imitation' human beings, Doc—you comprehend the function of the Reproducer well enough to know they would be as real in every way as the original models."

"That appears true enough," I admitted. "My heavens!—this contraption of yours has certainly brought some moral problems in its train."

"Not to mention physical ones," answered Bill. "This damned rabbit, for instance. And the cats and the rats and guinea-pigs which preceded it."

"Are those the bodies you've been burying in the yard at dead of night?"

"You heard me? Yes, they are. Only the duplicates, you understand. The originals are running around as healthy as ever. I had been trying different degrees of electrical stimulus to nerve-ends. Absolutely no effect whatever. I got wild and threw things about. This autojector is my last card. It not only acts as a heart-pump, setting up a circulation artificially, but it also oxygenates the blood at the same time. If it fails, I'm done."

"Well, let's try it," I said, peering through the curving glass at the rabbits again.

"Good old Doc," he said quietly. "I should have known I could have confided in you."

He hauled on the mechanism which lifted the domes. He investigated the body of the copy while I examined the original rabbit. It was a brown one with an odd white patch or so, I remember, and was already showing signs of stirring again. Its whiskers were visibly trembling, with some movement of the muscles around the mouth, and the left fore-paw every now and then bent and twitched with a nervous tic.

I felt it. It was warm enough. Most of the muscles were contracted and hard, gripped in a cramp. I started to massage it gently.

Bill looked across at me and smiled approvingly.

"That's it, Doc. Poor little beastie! I hated to get it in that condition, but it couldn't be avoided. However, it'll come round all right and be none the worse."

It did come round pretty quickly, and was soon kicking convulsively in my hands, trying to get away from me, its eyes open and scared.

"It's a wild rabbit," said Bill. "Let it go."

I opened the back door and set the creature down. It lolloped away, none too surely, and I saw the white bobbing tail of it cross the border of the light which streamed out from the door, and vanish into the darkness.

When I returned, Bill handed me the duplicate rabbit.

"What do you think of that?"

It was as rigid and hard as the other had been at first, but not nearly so warm. No apparent signs of life about it at all. The whiskers were like stiff wires, the eyes were tightly shut. The ears, pressed back close to the little round head, were no more pliable than thick palm leaves.

"It's no good your massaging him," said Bill. "You'll not achieve anything, as I can tell you. His blood will just go on cooling until he's as cold as any corpse."

"I'll take your word for it," I said, handing it back. "Put the autojector on to him."

"There are one or two necessary preliminaries," said Bill.

He carried them out. One was to prevent blood coagulation. There were two other operations, the import of one I got only vaguely. That is as much as I think it necessary to say. I do not wish to reveal, even obliquely, knowledge which man is still far from fit to receive.

Finally the autojector was fixed and the little pump worked steadily.

Eighty seconds later the copy-rabbit's hind legs thrust back simultaneously in an unconscious bound that got it nowhere, for it was lying on its side.

Bill sucked in his breath sharply.

Ninety-five seconds: the rabbit's ears stirred, its side heaved.

One hundred seconds: life-like, characteristic twitching of the nose.

One hundred and twelve seconds: its eyes opened.

It was panting now, twitching and bristling and alive in every way, and obviously in a highly nervous state. But it had no proper control over its body, despite its straining efforts. Cramp still largely crippled it.

Bill shut off the autojector, removed the rubber tubes, and doctored the rabbit. Then, eagerly and clumsily, he began to massage the stiffness out of it. Clumsily because he was the prey of intense agitation. His eyes were burning like those of a man with fever. The point of his tongue roved over his dry lips. Every now and then he emitted a strange little sigh of pure excitement.

And suddenly the rabbit wriggled and turned and escaped from his unsteady fingers, and took off from the bench in one terrific bound. It sailed through the air like a leaping gazelle and landed yards away. Its limbs were still a little too weak to meet the shock. Over on its back it went, and over again.

Then found its feet and hopped madly around the lab floor, looking peculiar with its white scarf of neck bandage, seeking escape. But I had shut the door.

Suddenly Bill, who was watching it with popping eyes, burst into hysterical laughter, and sat down limply on a box, shaking uncontrollably and laughing yet. The mounting tension of many days had passed the peak and fallen abruptly down a precipice.

I went for the whisky, and when I returned he was sitting on that box gazing at the ridiculous cavortings of the rabbit, and the tears were streaming down his cheeks and sobs choked in his throat.

I moved him to a chair where he could relax, and dosed him. He quietened down, and lay back holding his forehead with one hand and wiping his face with a handkerchief in the other.

"Phew!" he emitted.

I captured the rabbit, and stood with it in my arms, soothing it and covertly watching Bill.

Presently he looked up at me of his own accord.

"Well, Doc, I've done it," he said. "Life *can* be duplicated. Isn't the secret of it simple? Just pump the blood through the veins until the creature's own heart-pump begins to work in sympathy! Why, we've by-passed all Schrödinger's work!"

I nodded silently.

"The hardest part still remains," he said unexpectedly.

"What's that?"

"To summon the nerve to ask Rob if he will consent to a duplicate of Lena being made—for me!"

The rabbit escaped from my suddenly loosened arms.

CHAPTER FIVE

I HAVE ALREADY ADMITTED THAT I AM DENSE WHEN IT COMES to foreseeing the obvious.

There is some excuse in this case. With a long experience of Bill's highly strung nature and over-leaping impatience, I had not taken the intense importance he had set upon the success or failure of this experiment as unduly unusual, considering the very real significance of the research to mankind.

But this time Bill had not pursued his end in the sheer intellectual curiosity of the scientist. His driving force had been—Lena.

Now, belatedly, I saw what he meant by using his mind so that he should not lose her.

It was impossible! That brilliant mind, set awry by the emotional storms of love, had toppled over the frontier of sanity. He was crazed with a hopeless infatuation.

But—*was* it impossible? After what I had witnessed just previously? That had been no impossible scheme: the living proof of it gazed at me now with wary brown rabbit eyes from under the chair where it had sought sanctuary. A lesser life than a human being's, but the human body was made of the same basic stuff.

One had to admit that it was not impossible for a human body to have been in place of that rabbit. But every ounce of me protested against the suggestion that it could have been—that it ever could be—Lena's body. The mind shut its doors against such an idea and the heart turned it away.

One could accept the general view that there could be two unspecified "labourers" or "clerks" with the same characteristics, outlook, turns of expression, and appearance. But the imagination did not know which way to go when it came up against the idea of someone you knew personally and particularly suddenly turning into unnatural twins. Especially if that someone was so essentially individual as Lena.

Two Lenas!

"You really mean that?" I said slowly.

"Certainly I do."

I made an effort to face up to the fantastic situation.

"Let us set aside the personal issues of this for a moment," I said, a little unsteadily. "First of all, is it really practicable? Will the personality be mirrored as completely as the body? Are you sure you won't produce some grotesque parrot image with no mind of its own—an awful sort of human gramophone record? Is it possible that the second Lena may somehow be fixed as in the moment of her creation, a set and finished being, incapable of further development or reaction? Will the co-ordination of mind and body be all that it should be, or must the new creature be taught to use its body? Is there no danger of the shock of realizing you're not a real person deranging the mind, causing madness?"

"If I hadn't considered all those things, Doc, I wouldn't insist on going on," said Bill, looking at the floor. "Believe me, there is no danger of harm to Lena. I am sure of that. That is the last thing I would risk."

He pointed suddenly to the rabbit, now so far recovered from its fright as to be snuffling around the floor in the direction of the door.

"Has that had to learn to use its body again? No, it is exactly the same rabbit as that which you let out of the door a little while back. Nor has it been driven mad. I can conceive of an unprepared, weak-minded person going off the rails, perhaps, after such a process carried out against his will. But never anyone so strong-minded as Lena, knowing just what she was doing. The 'parrot-gramophone' danger you visualize is non-existent. Every brain cell with its recorded impressions, every nerve with its ability to convey fresh impressions, is reproduced intact and unimpaired. In working order. And as long as there is a flow of blood to nourish them, they will remain so. You have seen how the last difficulty has been overcome."

"I take it," I said, "that though they will be exactly similar personalities at the first moment, they will diverge gradually from that moment? I mean, as soon as they are separated, live in different environments, speak to and are spoken to by different people, have different experiences—in short, are subjected to a multitude of different stimuli—they will grow into two distinctive people? Fundamentally the same, of course, but dissimilar in many details—no more than twin sisters, in fact."

"That is what I do believe," said Bill soberly.

"It becomes a little more easier to accept, looked at that way."

"I know you must be in revolt against the whole thing, Doc. I can understand it—I had a terrible fight with myself until I made up my mind to go through with it to the end. But I have made up my mind. I had to. Once that idea got into my head, it would not let up. I must have Lena—I can't live without her. And here, providentially to hand in a miraculous way, is the means. So providentially that it seems like a thing destined, intended. I can't let the chance go. What would my life be worth if I let it go? One long, aching, intolerable regret!

"I *can't* let it go," he repeated, obstinacy returning.

"I see, and I sympathize," I said. "But doesn't this chance rather rest with Lena and Rob?"

"With Lena, ultimately."

"Just as much with Rob, surely? Can any man be expected to like the idea of a copy being made of his cherished wife and given to someone else? It—it cheapens things, somehow."

"You're being offensive, Doc," he retorted, his colour rising.

"I didn't mean to be."

"It is not as though Lena were to be shared by everybody. I resent your suggestion of common property. I've told you the second Lena will become different—not much different, I know, but she will not be the Lena that Rob will know. She will be my wife. That is solely up to Lena to decide. Even if Lena is married, her body and soul are still hers—Rob doesn't *own* them."

"Don't be silly," I said, getting testy in my turn. "No one said he did. But a husband has certain rights over his wife."

"If you keep making this sound like adultery, I advise you to go back to bed, Doc, before I lose my temper. All I know is that if Rob's position and mine were reversed, such scruples would not deter me for a moment from doing all I could to help my best friend."

"I don't doubt that," I said. "The point you ignore, although you know it very well, is that Rob has a much more orthodox outlook on such things than yourself. Marriage must seem something very sacred to him. You have told me yourself how much the religious aspect means to him. Those scruples would count."

"The distinction between being religious and being a Christian is loving thy neighbour as thyself," said Bill, with a touch of bitterness. "I should have thought the Christian solution was obvious."

"Well, you'll have to sound Rob on that. That's particularly his problem. And you cannot but respect his decision, whichever way it is."

"I still maintain the decision rests with Lena. She said she'd do anything to help me, to the point of marrying me. She did not seem averse to the idea, either. All that prevented her was the fact that she was only one person. Well, now she can be two. Without losing Rob, or impairing their relationship in any way, she can satisfy both of us. What is wrong in that?"

"Nothing," I said, "except that it seems to me that you are presuming on Lena's good nature. You know she will not refuse you, because she never counts the cost. She never thinks to insure herself against any future disasters by weighing and considering and dodging, as we more anxious people do. She just cuts a straight path through life and takes the pitfalls in her stride. She's big enough to take them, where we are not."

"There aren't any pitfalls. I honestly believe that. You don't think I would mislead her?"

"Of course not. But—Oh, well, it isn't my business."

"No. It's Lena's alone."

"Nevertheless," I said, "for decency's sake, approach Rob first. After all—"

"Don't get worried, Doc. I intended to see Rob first. I told you so in the beginning."

"Very well," I said, and found myself at a loose end. My feet became apparent to me as two solid blocks of ice. "Very well, Bill, I leave it to you. Good night."

"Good night, Doc."

I went back to the welcome warmth of bed, but I did not get to sleep for a long time.

*

The next day I learned that Rob and Lena had returned overnight, and after a solitary lunch I was making my way up the rocky and winding path to their new home on the hill, "Hawthorns".

Bill had gone out for a walk in the morning and had not returned for lunch. I judged he had "taken his thoughts for an airing", as he used to put it when he had plans to sort out mentally.

I found the pair rearranging the furniture more to their taste, and planning what "copy-originals" of art they would have where.

Despite the time of year, they had evidently found sunshine in Cornwall, for each was lightly tanned, and this suited Lena's frame of golden-brown hair and made her eyes as blue as the cornflower. She was even more beautiful than the image of her I had held in my memory, and for a moment I could not raise my eyes from her curving, welcoming smile.

"Hullo, Doc," she greeted, with an outstretched hand that did not wait for mine but reached for it and grasped it. "How's the world been treating you? How's Bill been treating you? Has *anybody* been treating you? Here, have a drink!"

In almost the same smooth, deceptively lazy action she had passed on to pour one.

Rob smiled after her, shook his head at me to indicate that Lena was still unpredictable in her little ways, and greeted me more formally.

"Did you have a nice time?" I inquired—one of those idiotically unnecessary questions which nevertheless you can't very well skip asking.

Naturally they had, and told me about it, recounting the favourite incidents with such verve and laughter that it was obvious they were very much in love indeed, and these little happenings were important in their eyes and long to be treasured, remembered and recalled.

I gave them an account of Bill's and my setting in order of the Reproducer Company.

"It's all ready to go, as soon as you're ready," I said.

"Tomorrow?" suggested Rob, glancing at Lena.

"Yes, darling," she nodded over her glass.

"All right, I'll let Bill know," I said.

"Where is he?" asked Lena.

"Oh, he's out walking. I shouldn't be surprised to see him turn up any minute now."

But I was surprised all the same, for the door-bell rang in the middle of that sentence, and it was Bill.

He came in with his quick nervous stride, and from the indescribably dishevelled state of his hair I saw that he had indeed been busy with his thoughts. Traces of strain still showed in his eyes, but I saw that line of obstinacy in his mouth and I knew he had shut his mind to all but his intention, and that this was to be the time to bring it to the point of action.

But he managed a smile and the small-talk that was expected, and although Lena showed no signs of noticing his preoccupation, I felt that her quiet eye had observed it.

Apparently he was revolving in his mind some way of introducing the subject. But either his imagination or his patience failed him, for suddenly he blurted out, in an odd jerky manner: "Rob, I've got to talk to you about something important—alone. Doc, will you see that Lena is—informed?" And catching the astonished Rob's arm, he hustled him out into the garden! Again leaving me to nurse the baby, or one of them.

Lena watched them disappear from view, and then looked at me in gentle inquiry.

"Something's wrong with Bill—I could see it a mile off. Now what's worrying the poor mite?"

"You are," I said.

"So he's not over it? I'm really sorry. It's very difficult, isn't it?"

"You've no idea," I said. "Gosh, you've no idea at all! I don't know how to go about giving you one."

She lit a cigarette.

"Have a dash," she said.

I did, and after a fumbling beginning, got into a free lucid strain, and progressed so rapidly in my account of Bill's experiments and feelings that the climax, his proposal of duplicating her, came too swiftly for my management and slithered out more like a cake of soap escaping from wet hands than a bombshell being fired from a bombard.

"Pretty staggering, isn't it?" said Lena in her soft and slightly husky drawl, and not looking at all staggered.

"I think so," I said.

She started another cigarette from the butt.

"Well, you've prepared me, Doc—thanks. I hope Bill led Rob up to it as slickly. But I'm afraid Rob is having the shock of his life."

I was afraid so, too.

"I don't have to ask you if you would do this thing for Bill, Lena, if Rob agreed to it. The question is—will Rob agree to it?"

"After the shock, yes, I think. But he will be quite unable to adapt himself to the idea at first. And so he will ask for time. He will hate the idea with everything he's got. But his conscience would never let Bill, of all people, go on suffering."

It seemed to me that in the comparatively short time of their honeymoon Lena had got to understand more of the essential Rob than I had in years of acquaintance.

"Here they come," I said. "And now we'll see."

They came in rather stiffly, avoiding looking at either of us, with almost absurdly identical wooden expressions. It drew a bubble of laughter from Lena.

"Goodness gracious, don't be so serious about it! You look like a jury coming in with a verdict of 'Guilty'."

They both smiled perfunctorily, but looked just as anxious afterwards.

Rob took up a stance by the fire. He coughed in a preparatory manner. He was obviously to be the spokesman.

"Er—um—" he began.

"Yes?" said Lena brightly.

"You know about Bill's proposition?" he asked awkwardly.

"Yes," said Lena.

"With my consent, would you be willing—"

"Yes," cut in Lena.

Bill was staring at the floor, but I saw the sudden, all-pervading flush rise up his neck.

Rob looked for a moment out of the window, away from the others, but I caught him in profile. For that moment the mask slipped, and all his confused, but acute, feeling was bare. He must have clung to a secret hope that Lena would refuse, for I saw that hope die. I saw pain take its place. And then the mask was back.

He said in a voice as calm as his expression: "Very well. Now my suggestion is—and Bill has agreed to it—that we wait three months before we attempt this thing. We must give ourselves time to realize exactly what we're doing. A clear deliberate outlook is essential to the case. I know you look lightly upon things, Lena, but I cannot for the life of me persuade myself that this is anything but damned serious. What do you think, Doc?"

"I agree that it's not a step to be taken in a hurry," I said. "I'm sure that Bill is burning with impatience to get it done. But if he has enough sense to wait and make sure his feelings are lasting, and not a passing desire, I cannot show less sense. Three months should be sufficient time, I think."

Lena was looking at Bill.

"Is that all right, Bill?" she asked gently. Her voice was almost a caress.

I find it difficult to write about Lena and avoid sentimentality. Perhaps I have not managed to avoid it. The trouble is that though there was not an ounce of sentimentality in Lena, the weakness is in me and evident. But it must be borne in mind that it is my weakness, and not Lena's.

She was too strong-minded to allow herself to be hurt by the general run of things, but her sensibilities were ever in sympathy with more susceptible people, and she went out of her way to prevent those others being caused pain. It was a sympathy so wide and completely selfless that it achieved that rarest quality, loving-kindness. Her heart was big beyond my comprehension.

But here I am being slab-handed with matters too delicate for my limited expressive powers, and moreover, I am writing with memories of events yet to come in this narrative and with a sense of loss yet gnawing at my heart. It is so easy to be sentimental when one is sad. It is so easy to be sad when one broods upon the past beyond regain.

Perhaps Bill did not wholly deserve that sympathy.

He muttered: "Yes, Lena. Thank you. Anyway, the Reproducer will have to be rebuilt first, and that will take up at least half the time."

I had not thought of that. So a good part of the delay was necessary, and much of the time of grace had to be accepted by Bill quite involuntarily. Nevertheless, it was a breathing space to be thankful for. I wondered how matters would stand in three months' time.

The months passed quickly—perhaps too quickly.

The Reproducer Company, whose activities we had planned that evening among the palms in the saloon bar of the "Pheasant", was launched.

And now radium was no more the rare and precious substance it had been. No longer need the grains of it be hoarded like crumbs from the table of heaven—far, far too few of them for the need of man's pain. From one borrowed needle from my friend, Hake, I manufactured enough to keep every existing cancer hospital in bountiful supply.

The boon the machine brought to the medical world alone was incalculable. Rare drugs, rare preparations, clinical apparatus of infinite delicacy and exactness, which normally took months of labour to fashion individually, were mass-produced. In the container of the larger Reproducer into which we expanded the original we placed ten bottles of a certain scarce drug, which we had scraped together. We duplicated them, and put the new ten in the container with the old. So now we could, and did, duplicate twenty bottles, then forty, then eighty, doubling up in this fashion until the container was packed with something like a thousand bottles and in a few minutes could give birth to another thousand bottles.

In this way, too, the last bottle of vintage wine from an ancient château was never emptied. It became the inexhaustible bottle of the stage illusionist. Wines provided one of our more profitable sidelines.

Apart from certain museum pieces, we refused to handle precious stones. The reason is obvious. The market, based on rarity, would have been broken, and no particular benefit for mankind would have resulted from such a move in any case. We must still have some rarities in our lives to maintain spice.

We were to have much of this museum work, and it was certainly a most interesting activity. Museums in New York, San Francisco, Rome, and other world cities wanted "copy-originals" of the rarest treasures of the British Museum, and there evolved a system of exchanges.

I shall long remember the day when the Rosetta Stone, the *Codex Sinaiticus*, the *Codex Alexandrinus*, the Magna Carta, and the Saxon Chronicles all came down from London under guard, to the humble little village of Howdean.

The art treasures of our world that I have handled personally in the Dump! I used often to stop and reflect, near unbelief, that I, so long a worshipper from afar of these things, should have the originals brought to me and placed in my hands in this quiet backwater where I had dreamed about them for nearly forty years.

But the most rewarding work was that aspect which Bill had revealed to Lena on the night of our first visit to her cottage. It really became Lena's department, and we were her underlings.

It was the mass production of reasonably priced "copy-originals" of some of the world's masterpieces of art for the man in the street and his wife. Despite the fair quality of the modern oleograph, it was a poor, off-coloured smudge beside a copy-original of a painting, in its real paint on real canvas, in its perfect colours, every bit of it exactly as the master's hand had chosen and shaped and left it.

"Matisse for the masses," commented Bill as we worked.

"Murillo for the multitude," contributed Rob.

"Millet for the millions," I managed.

"Monet for the many," capped Lena.

And so it was. As Bill had prophesied to Lena that night, knowing that it would probably catch her imagination, the whole world of art and its complementary world of appreciation broadened enormously and had to be re-oriented. New possibilities opened up everywhere.

It was not merely a case of Rodin statuettes in the hall; Constables, Turners, or Whistlers over the fireplace; Greuze miniatures upon dressing-tables; "genuine" Wedgwood shepherdesses in the nursery, or Chippendale chairs in the dining-room. The current artist of repute had something to work for. No longer was the appreciation limited to the number of people who could visit one gallery in one town, or the casual visitors to the library of a single private house.

In one bound the painter, the sculptor and the metalworker attained the advantages of their fellow creators in music and literature: the advantages of recording and publishing.

The writer scribbles a sentence with his fountain-pen, and the press reproduces it thousands of times in much fairer and clearer form, and distributes it in a thousand places where a multitude of people might read it with appreciation at the same time, or at any time for years to come.

And so with music, which in addition is recorded on wax or film. The film, too, has enlarged enormously the public appreciation for the difficult art of acting, and actors are rewarded by the preservation of performances which formerly perished in a night.

And now, through the medium of the sympathetic Reproducer, each chip of the eminent sculptor's chisel, each stroke of a worthy painter's brush, could move a hundred thousand unseen chisels or brushes with it. And when people had these fine works in their homes, at first hand, knowledge of beauty grew, and so, naturally, did appreciation of it and desire for it. In our way, we started a new Renaissance.

And it was Lena who chose the artists, the subjects, and gauged and guided public taste and demand, and for a person who was not good at putting herself in another's place, so to speak, she did astonishingly well.

The press besieged the place.

Flashlight photos, endless posing, endless explaining, endless demonstration. Being cornered by this and that correspondent: "And what is *your* opinion, Doctor?"

The nosing television camera moving from general views to close-ups, and the sinking feeling and dry mouth when it was directed at myself.

Lena's smiling ease and effortless answers—somehow her direct and non-evasive remarks saw more print than any of ours. Rob's courtesy and tendency to stress that it was not really so very startling once you got used to the idea. And Bill taking on half a dozen reporters at once, talking in his febrile manner with a speed which left them floundering hopelessly far behind but yet with the shaping belief that this was the biggest news story that had broken in years.

After the stunt period, the serious acceptance, the approach of the influential art bodies, and the halcyon days I have described, when the treasures of the world came on their shielded journeys to Howdean.

And all the time the products for the ordinary man were being turned out under Lena's discriminating direction, and steadily, without affecting the production, the larger Reproducer was being fitted together into completion.

There was the day when I gave my friend Hake a quantity of radium needles for the Cottage Hospital which, in their lead sheathing, were rather more than he could carry. It was the first time I had held converse with that hard-bitten man and received no vitriolic remarks.

Christmas came, and was gone, and its passage scarcely noted. Never, not even during Howdean's worst epidemics, had I so little sleep.

But after three months we were on top of the work. The larger Reproducer was finished, tested, and producing four times as much as the original could handle. It was not by any means an entirely new machine: it was basically the old one, built upon, changed and improved piece by piece without being out of commission for more than a few hours at a time. There was still only one Reproducer.

The system of running the Company, which Bill and I had worked out in such detail, fulfilled its objects with a gratifying success. The routine became almost effortless after a time. We came even to a plan of having days off in rotation, but such was our interest in our work that we let our opportunities go as often as not. But it was a relief to have spells of leisure when one chose.

The inevitable day came.

Strangely, it was Rob who brought the subject up, on the eve of that unforgettable day.

The work had been particularly light, and we had cleared up most of the outstanding business by lunch-time.

I was smoking alone outside, when Rob stepped out, puffing casually at his pipe and taking in the bright crispness of the day with an appreciative eye. His presence seemed natural enough. I was on the point of remarking on the weather when he spoke in a low but direct tone, and I realized that the casualness was but an appearance and he had followed me with intent.

"Doc," he said, "I've been speaking to Bill. He is still of the same mind. We have got to go through with this thing. Tomorrow."

"Oh." There seemed little else to say.

"It's like this. I've got to talk the matter over with him. He hints at certain arrangements. There'll be some work on the Reproducer, too—only a matter of wiring. But I want to make tests. I can't afford—accidents. Now, I don't quite know why, but I should feel easier about things if Lena weren't here during these preparations."

"So would Bill too, I'll wager," I murmured.

He smiled rather perfunctorily.

"Yes. It would be like discussing a serious operation with the patient just before the operation. Not that Lena would be nervous. But I am—horribly. So take her out for a car ride, would you, Doc? It's a fine afternoon, the day's business is done—"

"All right," I said. "I'll try to make it sound a good idea."

"Thanks, Doc."

Lena accepted my invitation readily enough.

"I've been reading Wordsworth," I said in explanation. "It's a sign. After being cooped up in here all these weeks, I need the country air, the bird songs, the smell of—"

"Pig-sties," said Lena.

"Pig-sties, and wood smoke, the sound of babbling brooks, the sight of little stone cottages—"

"Nestling," nodded Lena.

"I'm not particular. I can take them unnestled. But the wayside flowers, daffodils—"

"No dancing daffodils. In fact, no daffodils. It's too early yet."

"Never mind, there's stitchworts and things. I think. Will you come?"

"Yes."

When we were five miles away—I was driving—she said: "Well, here I am—dutifully out of the way. Shall we go to a cinema or do you really fancy the air?"

"Lena, I knew I had about as much hope of fooling you as of understanding what makes this car go. But so long as Rob's more comfortable, my failure as a mummer doesn't depress me."

"It was obliging of you, Doc… So Bill still wants to bring another bothersome Lena into the world?"

"I'm afraid so."

"If you meant that rudely, you'd better beware, Doc. You'll have two of us to deal with soon, and if I can't think of a nasty retort, *she* might."

"*She!*" That as yet unborn, unformed creature. I could not get the prospect of it out of my mind. What *were* we up to? How were we going to take—"she"? Even more problematical, how was she going to take us?

I was full of inner qualms for the morrow. There was something awesome in the project. Fear of the unknown, the unencountered—and fear of some terrible, unexpected consequence. Frankenstein and his daemon would keep trying to thrust themselves into my mind for horrible comparisons.

Lena broke into my silent forebodings with a little cry.

"Look, Doc! That cottage, nestling. Isn't it just the thing? Right out of Hardy... Do you think *anyone* can learn to thatch?"

She was as inconsequential as a child. Careless as Omar, nor needing the influence of the grape.

> "Tomorrow? *Why, Tomorrow I may be*
> *"Myself with Yesterday's Sev'n Thousand Years."*

CHAPTER SIX

I T WAS FINISHED.

The thunder of creation had passed away like a summer storm, and though the tang of electricity yet lingered in the air there was the peace and silence of eventless time in the laboratory.

Then a bird sang outside the window, and as if that had awakened my perceptive hearing again I noticed the quick breathing of Bill. When Rob took a pace forward to bend and peer into the glass container, wherein lay Lena, motionless, the silent stillness dissolved quite away.

"Let me see her," I said, stepping up behind him.

He cleared his throat.

"She's all right, I think," he said, still a bit huskily.

I peered in my turn.

"Breathing strongly enough, but too spasmodically. Muscular contraction," I said, noting detachedly from the corner of my eye Bill gazing eagerly into the twin container alongside the Receiver at a pale Lena who did not breathe. "Here, get the case off."

Rob pulled on the chain which raised the glass casing, and removed the wires attached to Lena's head and feet.

"I'll attend to her. You see that the hot bath is ready," I adjured.

He nodded, and went quickly, though casting a backward look at his wife as she lay in her drugged sleep.

Bill abandoned the body he had brought into material existence from a sea of invisible energy, and came around to me.

"Can I do anything, Doc?" he asked. He was trembling and jumpy with excitement.

"Not much, while your hands are shaking like that," I said. "Though you could get some tea made."

"Yes, of course." And he was off.

I regarded Lena's naked body. She had one knee drawn up. Her hands were clenched into little fists. Her eyes were tight shut, her brows drawn into a faint frown. The perfection of her curvilinear limbs was visibly spoiled by the cramp which gripped them.

I began to massage strongly, using all my skill to untie those little hard knots of muscle and smooth them into ease, and particularly to free the diaphragm. I worked without delay or pause, for I wanted to get the worst of it over before the effect of the drug had worn off.

She hadn't wanted to be drugged. She was curious, and wished to remain conscious and observant throughout this unique experiment. The pain she would have had to endure to do so went for nothing with her. But it weighed a good deal with us, and our insistence was unanimous.

"No drug, no experiment," we said.

She protested further, saw we meant it, shook her golden-brown locks with half-real and half-assumed exasperation, and gave in—her first defeat, and a sign of the times: she was feeling for Rob, and putting that feeling foremost. It was like her not to turn her head away but to watch the needle go deep into her arm and discharge its contents, showing no other expression but that of a passing interest.

She was quite unconscious before the actual building of her counterpart began.

Now she began to stir under my hands. I had got her pretty well relaxed, and her breathing was steadier. Presently she sighed and opened her eyes. They appeared a pale transparent blue at first, like that of stained glassware, and were as empty of expression. Then it was as though they darkened with puzzlement. They focused on me and some other flicker of expression passed in them and was hidden, and before I could put a name to it Rob strode swiftly up from behind and was kneeling beside her.

"Lena!" he exclaimed softly. "Are you... Are you all right?"

For answer she smiled slowly and as slowly reached up a bare arm and put a hand behind his head and drew his mouth down to hers.

I became suddenly interested in the still image in the adjacent case. Now that I looked at it properly, I was amazed all over again. I could have sworn it was Lena lying there, knee drawn up, muscles rigid, faint frown and eyes tight shut. But so pale! It was Lena dead, and I could not help a shiver, and there was a queer little tug of pain with the horror.

Still the wires encircled her brow and cut into her small curled toes. I felt a certain compassion for her—already it was becoming "her", this shape of clay fashioned through forces I did not comprehend, and which but half an hour ago was mere dust in the wind—ignored, helpless result of a wild experiment, ignorantly destined for strange birth here. I raised the case myself and released the wires. The flesh was not cold, as I had imagined it would be from the corpse-like aspect, but cooling, and the resisting cramp drew an unpleasing comparison with an early *rigor mortis*.

Bill came in bearing a tray with a large steaming teapot and cups and saucers. His anxious-quick eye sought Lena first, whom Rob was helping into a sitting position and placing a dressing-gown around her shoulders at the same time. Then he shot a glance across at the prone and silent image, as though in a brief irrational hope that by some miracle she had come alive of herself in his absence. And then he made a great show of being concerned with the business in hand.

"Hullo, Lena, how are you feeling? Like a cup of tea?"

"No, like a ball of string the cat's played with."

"Oh, *you're* all right, all right," said Bill. "I've still got to watch what I say."

"I hope the spectacle won't bore you," murmured Lena.

"Dammit, no sugar for that!" exclaimed Bill. "Anyway, sweetness is wasted on you. Here—stir it yourself."

He had been pouring the tea, and now he thrust a cup at her. But it was Rob who took it, quietly smiling as he usually did at these verbal passes, and stirred it and held it to Lena's lips. Unobtrusively she took control of it from him, her natural self-sufficiency still showing unconsciously. As well I knew, she made the world's worst invalid, in respect of acting the part.

"Tell me, Lena, what is the last thing you remember?" I said.

She sipped her tea reflectively.

"Lying on my back staring up at the glass case hanging over me, and wondering whether, when it descended over me, I should look like a railway buffet ham sandwich," she said.

We all laughed.

"I felt someone fixing the wires to my toes, and then the case started coming down, and I was watching it when I must have passed out—I know it never quite reached me."

"You're a pretty good anaesthetist, Doc," Rob remarked.

"Yes, I didn't feel a thing," said Bill.

I may have imagined it, but I thought there was a trace of ruefulness in Lena's laugh. Anyway, I knew that every muscle in her body must yet be aching, and became the officious medico again.

I bade her finish her tea, soak for a while in the hot bath, and go home and to bed, and stay in bed for the remainder of the day.

When she was dressed she came to have a look at her motionless twin. She took in the tenseness and distortion of that frozen attitude, but her face remained impassive.

"Quite a good likeness," was all she commented.

She glanced up at Bill, who was looking at the image rapt and yet with the perceptible evidences of doubt and anxiety. I still could not guess what passed in her mind, but I was sure that it was more than she said, which was simply: "I hope she makes a good wife, Bill."

Bill started.

"Er—yes. Oh, thanks, Lena, thanks for doing this. No other girl—"

He broke off, swallowed, ran his tongue along his lips, and went on with jerky effusion: "And you too, Rob—I—you know what it means—"

Words failed again, so he seized hold of Rob's hand and used his friend's forearm as though it were the lever of a pump, and then inflicted the same enthusiastic form of energy on Lena. He was too violent.

"You're mishandling my patient," I told him. "The prescription is rest, not wrestling."

He dropped her hand as though she had pricked him.

"Yes, of course. I—sorry and all that."

He ran his fingers through the red tangle of his hair. Lena smiled at him and took a step towards the door. It was an unsteady step. Rob noticed it, and without a word picked her up. I expected her to protest her ability to walk on her own feet.

But she lay quietly in his arms. Not with meek acceptance—I can't say that Lena was ever at any time exactly meek—but yielding with a sort of composed satisfaction, as though she had a right to be carried by her man.

Possibly that little episode made it clearer to me than ever before the perfection of their partnership.

Rob carried her to the car outside and made her comfortable.

"Mind now—straight to bed," I admonished her.

"Of course, Doctor. May I smoke in bed?"

I grinned at a memory, and said: "No. I absolutely forbid it." And promptly took out my case and proffered her a cigarette.

"Thanks, I am a bit short," she said, and calmly took a handful.

My grin lost mirth and became an empty grimace. But I got even. I snapped the case shut and dropped it in her lap.

"Take that too, as a present," I said.

"Gosh, that reminds me!" she exclaimed, and obviously it reminded Rob too, for he delved under the seat and pulled out a heavy flat parcel (as I discovered later, a canteen of marvellously designed silver cutlery).

He handed it over to Bill, who received it awkwardly.

"From Lena and myself, and we hope that everything goes off tip-top," he said.

And my grin faded indeed, for I had forgotten even to get a wedding present for Bill and his bride without a name.

I was still cursing myself when the Heaths were gone.

The arrangements Bill had insisted upon were definite enough. Directly the experiment was finished, the Dump was to close down as a workshop for two days. For those two days none of us was to go near it. I could understand how sensitive Bill felt about it. He had not only the task of bringing the second Lena to life, but also of establishing his relationship with her, of probing to find out whether the new Lena was inclined to keep the old one's promise, or whether, indeed, she knew anything about it—and if she did not, awkward explanations would have to be made.

It was no wonder that he was a bundle of nerves just now.

Slowly I followed him back into the lab. Still with the canteen tucked under his arm, he stood looking pensively down at her whom he hoped to make breathe, and speak, and love him.

My part in the affair was finished. Naturally, the Dump could no longer be my home. It was to be theirs. Perhaps later they would build a house of their own near by—for Bill could not be happy too far away from the lab. So I was moving out, and had, indeed, removed the greater part of my kit early that morning to a couple of rooms at the "Pheasant", from which base I intended to conduct a leisurely exploration for some fairly local and suitable bungalow or apartments for a bachelor who did part-time work. Rob and Lena offered me the hospitality of "Hawthorns", which I politely refused, not wishing to intrude upon one couple any more than the other.

Said Bill, in a strange, hushed tone: "Imagine it—Lena, to the last chromosome of the last cell of her body. Even to the genes. Did you know that a gene is only one single molecule in itself, Doc? A little bundle of atoms that yet carries our prints of heredity. In that small crystalline formation of atoms lies the whole key of personality. And to capture all of Lena's individuality we have to get that infinitely small structure exactly right to every electron of every atom."

Then something of his agony of soul burst through.

"Oh, God!" he cried. "I hope I've made no mistake. Just one fault in a brain cell may cause insanity. Just one—"

He broke off and put his hand to his forehead. He had tied himself into a knot of worry.

"That's merely *folie du doute*," I said sharply. "Pull yourself together, man. You know as well as I do that the Reproducer makes no mistakes. Here, I'm staying to see this business through!"

"No, Doc, no," he said. "I want you all to go. As we agreed. This is a rather—personal affair."

"Very well. But before you start I think you had better have a few points on massage. I had a difficult job on Lena, and you've got a similar one here."

I explained, and showed him by demonstration the best methods to break down that cramp before the synthetic Lena recovered from the drug which had been recreated within her inert body. Apparently he grasped them, but I got the impression that he was preoccupied with ends rather than means.

"Do you think you'll be all right now?" I said at last.

He said he did.

And so I left him, his eagerness for me to go tempered with a quality of reluctance to be left without support, to which he gave no voice and probably never consciously realized.

When I had set in order my rooms at the "Pheasant" and had a lonely lunch, a restlessness possessed me which impelled me to thrust aside with sudden impatience everything which I tried to occupy my mind. I took *The Lives of the Poets* into the public park with me, and for the first time realized why so many people found Dr. Johnson a colossal bore.

I closed the volume without bothering to mark my place, and fell into a brown study. It became an impossible mood of self-pity.

I had lost Rob as a companion, and now I was losing the boy who meant more to me than anyone in this life. The focus of their attention had been drawn away by the young, alive personality of

Lena. Yet I could feel no jealousy towards Lena. She liked me, I felt sure, and I flattered myself that in me she found a more mature understanding of life, and the situations in which it put us, than existed in the two younger men. Despite our disparity in ages, we met sometimes in places of wordless wisdom and knew that we had met.

That was something. So long as I knew her I should feel that I was not entirely alone and cut off, an old man for whom there was no further need.

That was at the heart of it: to feel needed. When I had passed on my profession and responsibilities, that essential quality of life had largely gone with it. Continually people in their trouble had come seeking my attention, my knowledge and action, and in their helplessness investing me with significance. I was the omnipotent Father-Ruler of my little tribe.

After my abdication, the Reproducer had supplied me with something of that sense of power, the ability "to scatter plenty o'er a smiling land", as one of the elect few. But the Reproducer was not my child. It was wholly Bill's and Rob's, and I was not so much even a junior partner as a sort of fortuitous and not particularly necessary middle-man.

My egocentricity was unpardonable, but none the less it existed—a conditioned existence, maybe. But I believe that all men have a subconscious wish to play God to greater or lesser degrees, and for the average man a dependent wife and family assuages that desire.

I began to perceive that my bachelorhood had been a mistake, and an irretrievable one now. Divested of the work that had blinkered me, I saw now the cold and empty spaces that stretched about me, bridgeless, linkless, the gulfs between our private lives, the loneliness of each little fearful or vain and self-absorbed ego. What time had people for those who could serve no personal use for them—not heal nor instruct them, give them material or monetary gain, nor yet love them or flatter them in more blatant ways?

It was a day of hard, sharp sunlight, casting deep shadows, and in those shadows there hid hard, sharp breezes, which now and then leapt out upon one with mischievous vindictiveness, slashing with a thin cane, and were back in hiding in an instant. From under the trees behind, a sudden sally caught me now, and I shivered. Perhaps it wasn't only the breeze.

There were groups of children playing in the green park, careless of the wind, the future, or the meaning of life, happy in the all-important present, with probably nothing larger than the table at tea-time shaping in their anticipation. I watched them, brooding like Gray over the unheeding young Etonians.

There was one small girl, of perhaps eight years, playing alone not so far from me. She was banging an old tennis ball about with a somewhat gutless racquet and notable strength, considering the disproportionate size and weight of the said racquet. The ball was liable to fly off at all angles from the untrustworthy thing, and presently it shot in my direction, bounced flatly and rolled right up to my feet. She came running after it. I picked it up.

She stopped a few paces from me, gave me a shy, uncertain look, then dropped her gaze and seemed interested in the ground at her feet. But not before I had noticed an odd similarity to Lena—something in the eyes, the shape of the nose, firm little chin, and gold-flecked hair. Lena may have looked just like that in her strange childhood.

I held on to the ball.

"Didn't go where you expected it to that time, did it?" I smiled.

She was, apparently, still abashed, and stubbed her toe gently at a thick tuft of grass to divert my attention from her to it, and did not answer.

"What's your name?" I persisted.

She shot a brief glance at me from under her lashes, immediately lowering her head again.

"Madge," she whispered, almost under her breath.

I took a coin from my pocket, unseen by her, and slipped it underneath the ball in my hand.

"Here you are, then, Madge, take your ball," I said. "Hold out your hand."

I laid both ball and half-crown on the little palm, and she was so surprised that she nearly dropped them. She gave me another quick look, almost guilty, as if she thought she had done wrong, and then turned and ran in obvious excitement. She went only a few yards before she came to a sudden halt, seemed to think, and then trailed slowly back to me, still looking shyly downwards.

Then she looked up and smiled straight into my eyes, and said, "Thank you." And ran way again like a capricious kitten.

A ridiculous pleasure with myself came to me. Even if in a negligibly minor way, I had played the All Powerful for a moment. That little girl would remember, perhaps all her life, the old gentleman who quite unexpectedly bestowed riches on her for no reason at all. The episode—and I—would be dominant in her thoughts for the rest of that day. I might even become a favourite anecdote in her later life, and thus, nameless, achieve one legend which would survive me. A cheap glory, for half a crown!

There was another quite irrational but satisfying feeling, too. Somehow I identified the little girl with Lena, and to get her indebted to me and in some awe seemed to my incomprehensible mind a riposte at Lena herself, a cunning stab at her provoking self-sufficiency.

The evening I spent in a cinema, watching a young couple suffer their way through a whole chain of coincidental misunderstandings, until at last a friend of the family exclaimed, "But didn't you know—?" and so sent them, after a babble of explanation, headlong into each other's arms, forgetting and forgiving, and at the threshold of eternal bliss. The ending didn't make me any happier, though. I still felt outside of things, and when I climbed the stairs at the "Pheasant" and opened the door upon my silent and empty sitting-room, loneliness swept through me like a winter wind through bare trees.

"Forlorn! The very word is like a bell..."

I wished with all my heart that someone, by some unlikely circumstance, would summon me from my comfortable, quilted bed to come out into the middle-night and take up the burden of guidance into this world of some fresh-arriving, bewildered little soul.

In the morning that awful depression, with all its maudlin musings, had departed quite away. Sunlight flooded my breakfast table with a brilliance that washed the pale tea-stains out of the cloth, and made the cruet sparkle as if it were part of the Regalia, silvered the spoons, and made *The Times* hard on the eyes to read—and the paper seemed full of interesting things this day. The bacon was crisp, the eggs in the condition of semi-solidity I approved, and even the toast was warm.

I congratulated the publican's wife, and considered how to spend the day—a brand-new day, as the life-loving Arnold Bennett would have regarded it.

A call at "Hawthorns" was the first and most promising item on the agenda, and the labour of my climb up that hill was paid for with Lena's welcoming smile.

"'Morning. How's the cramp?" I said.

"Quite gone, thank you. Sneaked away while I wasn't looking."

"Pity," I said heartlessly. "It was about time someone cramped your style."

"Really amazing," she murmured in an aside to no one at all, "how he takes after his son. Gets more and more like him every day. Such courtesy, such chivalry. He'd never hit a lady in the mouth if he could kick her in the stomach."

I winced.

"Must you mention your stomach?"

"You mean—it's unmentionable?" she breathed. She gazed down at it wide-eyed, and patted it in a gently exploratory fashion. "Doctor, tell me the worst!"

"The worst is yet to be," I assured her. "May I see your husband?"

"He's on the terrace. Will you come?"

She led the way through the open french windows on to the wide terrace. Rob was sitting with his back towards us, in a wicker chair by a wicker table. She stole up behind him, and hissed: "Rob! There's a man come to see you about my stomach!"

He rose hastily, turning, justifiably startled. His gaze passed from his wife's face of pure innocence to me. I caught a glimpse again of genuine anxiety behind his eyes, hidden in a moment as he saw who I was. He assumed a casual air with a masterful ease, and tried to accommodate himself to Lena's mood of gentle madness.

"Oh yes," he said. "Doctor, will you arrange for an operation for my wife, to remove and dispose of the offending growth?"

"That means disposing of your wife *in toto*," I said. "Or would you wish to keep the stomach?"

"If you do, you'll have to feed it," Lena warned Rob.

He ignored her, and said: "No, throw away all of the wife, and *my* stomach. The one has ruined the other. Home cooking, you know."

"It's a conspiracy!" declared Lena. "I'm retiring to the pantry for a while to draw up my defence."

"Yes, it *is* showing," I nodded.

She gave me a look of utter disdain and withdrew with dignity, pausing only to hand me a glass of lemonade from the wicker table as she passed me.

"Do try this sulphuric acid, Doc—it's delicious."

Rob and I, left alone, looked straight at each other. Then his mouth quirked humorously as he realized that both our inner attentions were occupied with the same thing. He relaxed again into his chair, motioning me to one beside him.

"No word from Bill?" I asked.

"No. I was scarcely expecting any this morning. He said two days. But something is happening down there."

He pointed over the brick balustrade.

The terrace offered us an uninterrupted view of the whole valley and the village therein. Away on the right, on another shoulder of the rise on which "Hawthorns" stood, the level white balconies of the hospital showed, blotted with the black and irregular stains of firs. Almost directly below was the main street and the red roof of the "Pheasant"—I could see the window at which I had breakfasted. Someone—no doubt the chambermaid—opened it as I looked, and it flashed in the sun.

One could follow the hedged lane across the fields between the great oaks as it wound, almost back upon itself, past the Dump, which lay below the hospital shoulder rather than this one. In the clear air of that morning details stood out like print under a reading-glass.

I could see a yellow saloon car, beetle-size from this distance, standing in the lane outside the Dump, and a thin black stroke leaning at an angle against its bonnet.

"Surely," I said, "that's Pike and his taxi?"

"Correct," nodded Rob. "All I'm waiting—"

The telephone burred in the sitting-room behind us.

"That might be it," said Rob, rising and making for it.

I heard the muffled sound of his voice as he answered it, but did not gather the sense. Anyway, he said little: the other subscriber seemed to be doing all the talking.

He returned.

"Bill?" I queried.

He nodded briefly.

"They're off. Look," he said.

The thin black stroke that was Pike, owner of the village's sole taxi, had disappeared behind its property, and now reappeared, bent like a bracket, obviously lugging something very heavy. A quick little figure—even at that distance, Bill's spasmodic, undisciplined walk labelled him plainly—came behind Pike, and together they heaved and pushed to get the portmanteau, as it was, on to the roof of the cab.

And then a third person came into view around the car, feminine, hatless, with a slow, easy walk. All you could make out of her was her shoulder-length hair and her white, neat dress. And then she leaned lightly against the bonnet of the car, one hand on her hip, watching the efforts of the two men, in such a characteristic, lazily elegant pose that I could see plain in my imagination the faint, amused smile that went with it. And a queer little thrill shot through me, for I was looking at Lena, distant but unmistakable, and yet I knew that Lena was still in the house behind me.

"It's like something out of Le Fanu!" I exclaimed softly.

I could not take my eyes off that impossible little figure in white to observe Rob's reaction.

But there was a pause before he answered as quietly: "I'm afraid, Doc, neither of us will ever become entirely used to the idea."

We saw them get into the taxi, and we watched that minute car crawling along the lane as if it were pushing itself by reaction against the thick white clouds of road dust which rolled out behind it. Until nothing was seen but a faint corona sinking and settling behind the hedge at the farthest visible point of the road. Even then we still remained staring with our eyes focused to long distance and our thoughts as far away.

I started when Lena's voice broke into the reverie.

"Ha'penny for your thoughts—I won't rise to a penny."

"We've just been watching your double, Lena," I said.

"Up and doing?" asked Lena with interest. And at my nod: "Why didn't you call me?—I'd have loved to have seen her. Where is she now?"

"Gone away to marry Bill by special licence, and on a honeymoon to Eastbourne," said Rob. "Bill just spoke to me over the 'phone. He said everything's gone off fine, and Dorothy—he's named her Dorothy—is in good health and quite understands the situation. They've decided to leave for Eastbourne right away. Bill wanted to, and Dorothy seemed quite eager to as well, he said. By the way, Dorothy sends you her love, Bill says."

"Bill says? Didn't she speak herself?" asked Lena.

"No."

"Funny," puzzled Lena. "If I were her I should like to say hullo to me—sisters under the skin, and all that."

"You must tell yourself off some time," I said, with a rather uncomfortable attempt at humour.

"Only *I* am myself—no connection with any other firm of the same face," said Lena with emphasis. "Nor shall I hold myself responsible for any debts contracted by Dorothy. No, Dorothy will have to answer for Dorothy, and I'm sure she would prefer to. I don't want any other women—even myself—telling me what I should do. I have enough on my hands as it is with this bully."

She was sitting gracefully on the arm of Rob's chair, and now she snuggled herself against him and began to stroke his dark hair with amused affection. Absently he took her other hand and touched his lips to the back of it. But his eyes were looking into the blue distances where his friend still journeyed with a strange mate.

The all-seeing Lena noticed where his attention lay. Still regarding him fondly, she deliberately tweaked out a hair from his temple by the root.

He jumped. "Gosh!" he exclaimed. "You—you little cat, what's that for?"

She held it before his eyes.

"Look, darling, it's a grey one. You didn't really want to keep it, did you? You're not old enough yet. You're worrying too much, my clever lad, much too much for your years. Come on, let's have a game of squash."

She bounced up, pulling at him. He came reluctantly to his feet, glancing sideways at me.

"Doc, about that operation," he said. "If you will kindly amputate my wife's stomach at the neck—"

Lena's irrepressible spirits broke our pale cast of thought, and the rest of the morning we capered around like children. Where that girl was there was *life*. I do not, even now, regret that her gaiety blinded us to the shadow of the four-sided triangle, which on that day fell across our paths with a growing heaviness. For us to have stood and regarded it with foreboding would have accomplished nothing but our own unhappiness and the realization of worse to come. Because it was as inescapable and certain as the predicted darkness of a solar eclipse. The causal conditions existed. The effect could not of itself help coming.

CHAPTER SEVEN

I T WAS A MORNING OVER A FORTNIGHT LATER.

I was alone in the Dump, packing heads of Queen Nefertiti. The lovely Egyptian had had the oddity of Hydra thrust upon her by one of the impersonal miracles of the Reproducer. As I disposed of each offshoot in its straw nest I had doubts about the taste of our including her in our Art Replicas list. It was not the lady's unique Semitic beauty that was in question, but our prodigal scattering of it about the globe.

We were not exactly spreading appreciation of an artist's work, unless people were really interested in those marvellous, almost imperishable enamels. We were more perhaps of the nature of vandals robbing a tomb, disturbing the intimate and personal, and brazenly displaying our loot to the largest possible audience. Possibly Queen Nefertiti had meant her face to be preserved for the sole and private appreciation of one man. Perhaps Akhnaton, and perhaps not. Yet again, if some clairvoyant vision had been granted her in her life of the manner in which her appearance would be widely admired thousands of years hence, I do not think she would have been displeased. Women of all eras have been vain, to different extents, but always unconquerably so.

Except Lena. Or was I misled there? Was Lena so vain that she concealed her vanity?

That, I thought, was about the most ridiculous suspicion that had ever crossed my mind. Lena was always Lena, and she never adapted her personality to impress or please anyone else, be he king or commoner. She would not do anything deliberately to hurt anyone's feelings, but she did not have to put on any act to avoid doing so. No one but a neurotic could fail to see that there was no spite in her, and her brand of mock malice was reserved mainly for Bill and me, because she knew we liked cracking at her and getting something back.

But—vain? Did she ever designedly show off her unusual beauty? Did she ever display any of her wide knowledge of art that wasn't immediately relevant to the point under discussion? Did she ever break out into that false modesty that conceals the strongest vanity of all? She never did any of these things.

Perhaps, I thought, paradoxically, the very fact that she didn't care a rap what people thought of her meant that hers was a really colossal vanity, an impervious self-esteem?

I wandered off into a mental debate about the distinction between self-esteem and self-respect, and wondered whether a complete egotist could be as unselfish as Lena or love a man like Rob better than herself—oh, damn it, I was thinking contradictory nonsense! It was useless trying to analyse Lena: there were too many elements of which I had no knowledge at all.

This morning she was away driving Rob to the station and seeing him off. He was spending the day in London with the officials of the Tate Gallery, conferring upon the selection of further specimens for reproduction in a national education scheme. But she was due at the Dump any time now, to give me a hand with the packing.

I was thinking upon quite other matters than her when I heard a car arrive and stop outside. There were low voices, and then Lena stepped in through the doorway. She was dressed in a blue frock with white trimmings, which I hadn't seen before, and it suited her very well. The sunlight streamed in behind her and transmuted her alloyed hair into pure gold. Against the light, her eyes appeared darker than usual, almost as deep a blue as her frock. They were the first thing I noticed about her. There was mischief in them, that unmistakable glint that betrayed her expression of quiet repose.

"*Hul*-lo," I said. "You're up to something. I know the signs. All right, come on, catch me out, and then we'll both split our sides laughing. You might let the Queen here in on it too."

She smiled, and my cherry reflex impression darted as usual through my head, and then she regarded the royal head in my hands.

"Queen Nefertiti?" she said.

"Well, it isn't Jane Austen," I said crudely. "Don't tell me your memory for faces is that poor. Why, you chose her. Remember?"

"No," she said.

"Only the other day," said I in a near-shriek.

"Indeed?"

There was a world of mockery in that one drawled word.

I put the head down carefully.

"I think I get your little game, Lena. It's that trick you and Bill played on me that first night we had a pow-wow at your cottage, when you tried to suggest I was dreaming and didn't really know anything for sure. Now say you don't remember that!"

"I remember it perfectly," smiled Lena. "You were chasing spotted antelope around the roof of the Empire State Building."

"Bill was," I corrected. "That is, Bill dreamed he was—had, I mean—"

"You're getting in an awful muddle," pointed out Lena calmly.

"I'm not very good at talking this nonsense stuff," I retorted. "I'm not Alice in Wonderland."

"Are you quite sure now?" asked Lena archly.

"Let's change the subject," I said abruptly. "Did Rob catch the train all right?"

Her face went solemn, the mockery retreating into the unseen fastnesses behind her eyes.

"Has he gone away, then?" she asked. "For how long?"

I threw up my hands, and coincident with that gesture came the sound of a car outside starting up and moving off.

"Hey! Who's going off in the car?" I exclaimed, and stepped past Lena. Immediately, in the doorway, I bumped into Bill, who was coming in carrying a suit-case. Over his shoulder I saw the back of Pike's yellow taxi retreating with a following column of dust down the lane.

"Going somewhere, Doc?" grinned Bill. "Want a taxi? Shall I whistle him back?"

"No—no," I muttered, confused. "So you were who she was talking to out here? I thought I had heard voices. H'm. Well, how are you, Bill? Enjoyed the holiday? Where's…?"

And was momentarily paralysed on that word by an incredible suspicion, and then, thinking rapidly, was certain. I spun round to gaze round-eyed upon the girl behind me, who returned my rude stare with open amusement.

"So you are really Dorothy—not Lena?" I breathed.

"True enough, Doc. Shall we split our sides laughing now?"

Still I surveyed her, certain, and yet wondering at her. It was Lena to the life all right—the same carelessly free and yet pleasing hair style, firm little chin, relaxed and easy carriage, perfect figure—rather wide shoulders, narrow waist, and legs in the film-star class. And the smile of sheer impudence.

Again I had to pull myself together. I glanced in inquiry at Bill, wondering whether an introduction was really called for. His quizzical grin told me that he had read my glance and thought my habit of social correctness humorous in this instance. So I held out my hand to Dorothy.

"Pleased to meet you, Dorothy."

"Haven't we met before?" she said, taking my hand firmly none the less.

"I really couldn't say."

"I seem to recall that once we shared a friendly stomach-pump."

"I do wish you'd leave your stomach out of convers—" I began too quickly. "Oh, I'm sorry. For the moment I was thinking of Lena. She can't keep off her stomach."

"Poor girl. What an uncomfortable position to have to maintain! Does she imagine she's in Napoleon's army?"

I was nonplussed, and Bill laughed his convulsive laugh until his eyes watered.

"Oh, dear!" he gasped. "The Doc doesn't know how to take you, Dot. If you were Lena he'd be throwing things at you now. But now he's shy, 'cos he can't decide whether you're a stranger or not. And actually it's the same old Lena getting at him all the time."

"It's not. I've reformed—literally," said Dorothy. "I'm nothing to do with that rude girl. You do believe me, don't you, Doc?"

She looked at me beseechingly, but laughing behind her face, as it were.

"No, I don't," I said gruffly. "The pair of you have got the same imp in you. I'm making no distinctions between you and Lena after this. Be warned. And if I box one's ears for another's remarks, I shan't apologize, for it will be all the same to me. You're not escaping my wrath, Lena, just by calling yourself Dot..." I heard the distant but growing hum of a car. "If I'm not mistaken, my dear Watson, our original rude girl is approaching now."

Bill sobered down and cocked his ears.

"I think you're right, Doc. That's Lena's car."

His face was a study in reflection. Now he was due in his way to feel rather out of his depth, as I had just been, hovering between the two Lenas, one of whom he had fallen madly in love with and the other he had married.

Dorothy lit a cigarette and leaned comfortably against the work-bench.

"This should be interesting," she said quietly. "I do hope I don't disappoint me."

We all waited in a rather taut (so far as I was concerned, at least) silence, while the car drew near and pulled up with a thin squeak of brakes. A door slammed out there.

And in sauntered Lena.

She looked straight at Dorothy, and no sign of surprise disturbed the composure of her face. Only friendliness and some curiosity showed. Then I noticed that Dorothy was wearing exactly the same expression. It was like watching someone else looking into a mirror.

"Hullo," they began simultaneously. "So you—"

And both realized they were going to make the same remark, and broke off at the same place. Then laughed aloud, with glances at Bill and I to see if we were amused at this little hitch. I suppose I was. Anyway, I laughed a trifle uncertainly, and so did Bill.

"Well, what do you think of each other?" asked Bill. "Er—you speak first, Lena."

"I've been wondering what I should think ever since I passed Pike's taxi going back and guessed Dorothy was here," answered Lena. "And now it comes to it—I'm left without a word. Almost. Although my first impression is that I didn't think I looked quite like that. I thought I—"

"Was a bit taller? Had fuller breasts?" broke in Dorothy. And at Lena's smiling nod, "Yes, I thought so too. One can't really get a complete and proportionate view of oneself in mirrors, even triple ones. I've never properly seen the back of my head, for instance."

Lena turned round and presented her back to Dorothy, who surveyed it critically.

"H'm. Could be worse," was her verdict. "Our legs aren't bad, are they?"

"Let me see," requested Lena, and made an investigation of Dorothy's rear view.

"Don't mind us," commented Bill drily. "How women love to study each other, Doc! I think men are only a secondary consideration with them."

"I was thinking about feminine vanity only a little while ago," I said. "I thought of someone who might be an exception. But now I don't think she is."

Without looking at us, or revealing any sign of having heard us, Lena asked of Dorothy, "And do you, too, detest the awful superior air of the male?"

"Yes," said Dorothy, turning about again. "And it's as baseless as the fabric of Prospero's vision. By the way, would you recite a little Shakespeare? I'm curious to hear how my voice sounds."

So Lena, quite unselfconsciously and with beautiful rhythm, delivered the *"Tomorrow, and tomorrow, and tomorrow…"* extract, while Bill and I exchanged further amusedly patronizing glances, like indulgent parents watching their two children playing for the first time with a newly bought toy, and Dorothy listened to the Macbeth cadences with an attentive ear.

"Doesn't sound like my own voice sounds to me when I speak," stated Dorothy, after *"… signifying nothing"*.

"I know what you mean," said Lena. "It's the first time we've heard our voice speaking outside our own head, as it were. I gather that most film actors don't recognize their own voices when they see their first shots of themselves in talking-films. Come to that, their own appearance looks unfamiliar to them, too, at the initial view. They notice all sorts of little mannerisms they didn't know they had. Do I seem rather like a stranger to you? I mean, like someone you knew well long ago, and then have met again, and she has got some new traits from somewhere and made little changes in her appearance?"

"Thanks for saving me asking it," answered Dorothy, stubbing out her cigarette. "That's it exactly. I know you're me all right, as I would recognize and know a photograph of myself. But it isn't a good photograph. That is, we don't think it's a good photograph because it doesn't quite fit our mental conception of ourself."

"We are not amused at us," croaked Bill, but I was too interested in trying to see through their eyes to heed his pawky humour.

"It's a relief, I think," said Lena. "I mean, this apparent difference. It won't be quite like talking to oneself. And, of course, living different lives in different places, having different experiences—and experiences *do* change one, you know—we should manage to become definitely separate personalities."

"Oh, my ideas have changed in some things in this last fortnight," said Dorothy. "For instance, do you like fish and chips in bed?"

"*Comment?*"

"I mean, eating fish-and-chip suppers out of newspaper in bed?"

"Really, Dot..." began Bill, half laughing in protest.

"I've never tried. Sounds a bit tricky," said Lena.

"Oh, it's easy with practice. And quite fun. You mustn't wipe your greasy fingers on the sheets, though. You suck them, and then dry 'em on the newspaper," said Dorothy calmly.

"*Mama mio!*" groaned Bill, sitting down and holding his head.

"It's one of Bill's ideas, and he's converted me to it," went on Dorothy inexorably. "A ridiculous habit—"

"It isn't!" objected Bill, avoiding my not so covert smile.

"But I like it, and shall probably do it quite often. It's a bit of *my* life, you see. I don't suppose it will ever be a bit of yours, Lena."

"No, I can't imagine Rob taking to it," reflected Lena. "Oh, well, we have our little ways too. It doesn't matter how you enjoy yourself so long as you do."

"Excuse my interrupting this discussion of niceties, ladies," I said. "But I suggest that you go out for a little stroll together and get used to one another. The conversation is veering towards the personal, and I think you had better retire into privacy for a while. I would retire myself, only I must get this consignment of Nefertiti away today, and I don't think you two are going to be of much help to me."

"I'll help you, Doc," exclaimed Bill, jumping up. "Now run along, you girls. Make friends."

"Pleasant fellow, the Doc," murmured Dorothy, as the pair went slowly towards the door. "But sort of old-fashioned."

"Just what I've always thought," nodded Lena, as they linked arms and passed from view.

Bill looked at me. "Well, Doc?"

"I think it's going to be a great success. Congratulations, Bill."

"Thanks. It's turned out even better than I expected. Those differences… There *are* differences, don't you think, Doc?" (This a little anxiously.)

"Undoubtedly," I said, with the private reservation that in my view they were very small.

"Yes. I was a bit apprehensive of meeting Lena again. But it was all right. She did seem like another person to me—not my Dot. Gosh, Doc!"

He heaved a sigh of relief-cum-satisfaction, and beamed.

"I *am* happy! I really am—at last."

"I'm glad. You've deserved it, Bill. You've had a pretty rotten deal up to now, and it's about time the luck turned. Not that it's just luck, of course. You've fought for it, you've thought and worked for it. I really respect that. I don't think Dot will ever let you down."

"Of course she won't, Doc." He looked off into space for a moment, pulled himself back with a snap, gave a little burst of cheerful whistling and broke off suddenly to exclaim, "Come on, let's pitch into these heads and get 'em away!"

He peeled off his jacket and rolled up his sleeves, and plunged into the packing with zest.

"Was the weather good at Eastbourne?" I asked, starting again also, but more easefully. And for the next half an hour, as we worked, I heard of the things they had done and seen, the people they had met, the fun they had had. He was just like a schoolboy returning from his first summer holiday.

> *"I was a child and she was a child*
> *In that kingdom by the sea..."*

I had accepted now that what I had missed in life was gone for ever. Yet there remained the ghost-memory of a pang...

*

That evening the same group of us—Lena and Dorothy, Bill and I—were gathered in the sitting-room at "Hawthorns" awaiting the return of Rob, and dinner. The chauffeur-gardener was also awaiting Rob, with the car at the station. The train he was expected to catch was due in at 7.32. It was striking a quarter to eight when Lena said: "It looks as though he's taking the next train. And I'm getting hungry."

"Dash it, Lena, you've only allowed him thirteen minutes!" I said. "It's a good fifteen minutes' drive between here and the station."

"I do it in ten," countered Lena.

"Everyone doesn't drive like a maniac," I said.

"I could do it in ten," smiled Dot.

"And I," chimed in Bill.

"Trapped in a room with three maniacs!" I exclaimed. "Will Rob get here in time to save me? See next week's instalment!"

At which appropriate moment the door opened and Rob walked in.

"Foiled again," said Bill.

Rob had stopped in surprise, as well he might, when he beheld Lena and Dot sitting demurely together on the settee. For a moment his eyes wavered uncertainly from one to the other of the girls. Then his training came out. The mask of polite imperturbability was slipped on, for the rules say that when you are most surprised you must endeavour to appear not in the least surprised.

"Introduction, please, Bill," he said, and Bill looked at him doubtfully. As I did, I suppose, because I didn't know whether he was insisting on being rigorously formal or whether the request was an adroit way of covering up the embarrassing fact that he could not distinguish Dot from his own wife. Obviously Lena thought the latter, for she gave a little cry, "Rob, don't tell me that you can't remember any of my dresses!"

"I remember that one perfectly," he said, smiling at her.

"That's odd," she frowned. "I've never worn it before."

Treacherous Lena, who always walked right through your defences by an unexpected way!

Here Bill saved Rob's face by giving the introduction.

"Rob, meet Dot. Dot, meet Rob. And now one of you says, 'Haven't I met you somewhere before?'"

"Haven't I met you somewhere before?" smiled Rob, over their clasped hands.

"The answer to that in the Book of Etiquette is, 'No—go away at once, or I shall call a policeman,'" answered Dot.

There was something in the tone of that remark which made me look at her curiously. No, I could read nothing from her calm face, only—her eyes were that sort of grey I had come to associate with Lena's less-happy moods.

"If you want to know the time—" began Rob.

"It's *dinner*-time," put in Lena pointedly.

I remember that dinner mainly as a discussion between Lena and Dot about their food likes and dislikes. They were exactly similar. Both detested cabbage, both went for pickles in a big way, and both had second helpings of sherry-soaked trifle.

"There's one advantage to this sort of thing, Dot," remarked Lena. "I'll never have to baffle my brains to think what to buy you for Christmas. I'll know it's something I want myself."

"Yes," said Dot. "I don't suppose we shall ever be able to surprise each other."

We all joined in this exploration of the possibilities arising from identical tastes, and Bill was in good form and managed to think of some really humorous potential situations.

Throughout it all Rob maintained his studied, correct manner towards Dot, as if indeed she were a new acquaintance and familiarity was not yet of enough standing for him to kid her along as freely and easily as he treated Lena. I was a bit irritated by this attitude, for I myself found it quite simple, and in a way natural, to accept Dot as Lena II, so to speak: she certainly knew all my little idiosyncrasies and the private jokes Lena and I had long had between us. I blamed it on Rob's hereditary conservatism.

He will thaw out slowly, I thought. Meanwhile, every now and again, when the others' attention was occupied by some debatable point, I caught him covertly glancing at both Dot and Lena, and obviously comparing them. And behind that unobtrusive observation I sensed that he was still as amazed as ever. But I detected something besides amazement, and I could have sworn it was a persistent doubt—doubt and apprehension.

We were talking of how we were to stick to the story that Dot was Lena's twin sister, who had been living and working in Eastbourne. Bill was unblushing in his averment that he had met her down there some time ago, and had been carrying on a courtship by correspondence.

"It'll be all right until someone questions me about my work," smiled Dot. "I can't invent lies very quickly—I'm not at all good at that sort of thing. Tell me, what shall I say?"

"Oh, say you sold sea-shells sitting on the sea-shore," advised Bill. "Or jumped off Beachy Head with a parachute twice a day; if wet, in the pavilion."

"It's your father, Sir Walter, whom I'm wondering about," said Dot, turning to Rob.

"That's who I'm wondering about," said Bill gloomily. "He'll think it's just like me to marry a parachute jumper by mail. I can never convince him I'm sane and normal."

"Don't listen to him, Dot," smiled Rob. "You'll be all right. I'll introduce you to him and Mother tomorrow, if you like."

"We've already been introduced," said Dot, looking at him quizzically.

He looked blank for the moment.

"In my previous incarnation," she explained.

"Of course," said Rob quickly. "Of course. Forgive my stupidity. This—situation certainly needs some getting used to. But no doubt it will seem quite normal in time."

"I found it very strange myself at first," said Dot. "However, I'm finding my feet now, especially after that walk and talk with Lena this afternoon."

"What did you talk about?" asked Bill curiously.

"Oh, shoes and ships—we both find that shoes always pinch our toes, because we used to gallop around barefoot at one time, you know. And ships make us sea-sick. We like purple sealing-wax, we hate cabbages, and we're easy about kings."

"It's queer," said Bill, fixing Dot with a stern eye, "but sometimes you drivel just like another girl I know."

"It's turned out nice again," remarked Lena airily. "I thought it looked like rain at one time."

The talk slipped into lunacy for a period, until Bill suddenly proclaimed: "Enough of this nonsense! I want to make a serious announcement."

"Oh, go on!" we said.

He produced a sheaf of scrawled notes from an inner pocket.

"I have here, all worked out, a method of releasing atomic power easily, cheaply, safely, and in far greater volume than hitherto. No elaborate apparatus needed. A child of six, with a normal I.Q., could understand it."

"He's off again. Children's toys this time," I groaned.

Rob looked interested, and Bill moved his chair up alongside him and, quite forgetting us, spread the sheets under Rob's nose and began explaining eagerly.

"You see, giving p a value of eight-point-seven-five, and assuming—"

"He worked all that out on our honeymoon," remarked Dot drily.

"You gave me inspiration, love," said Bill in a rapid aside, darting her a glance in which he achieved the remarkable combination of sarcastic affection—perhaps affectionate sarcasm sounds better. And continued his pouring exposition to Rob.

Lena, Dot, and I looked at one another.

"If we had a fourth, we could play bridge," said Lena.

"Have you heard that one about the mad scientist?" I ventured.

"Probably," said Lena and Dot together.

"If you wait half a moment, I'll explain it to you simply. Don't be impatient," shot out Bill, which latter exhortation I thought was humorous, coming from him.

"He thinks we're children of six," murmured Lena.

In a minute or so Bill treated us to his explanation. It seemed that this was a wholly different business from the principle of the Reproducer. That did not release atomic energy at all. That was merely the application of electrical power in the form of a lever, inserted at a crucial point, which diverted the flow of atomic power back on itself in a closed circuit. (I hope I have got this right.) It did not tap any of that power for extraneous purposes.

Whereas this new effect was a chain action of toppling balance, as it were. You pushed a boulder which set other boulders rolling, and each in their turn made others overbalance until you had a regular avalanche of tremendous weight rushing along. Then, using something analogous to a water-turbine (I am aware I am mixing metaphors, but that's the incongruous picture I got in my untechnical mind), you tapped the thrusting power of this torrent or hurtling mass, and ran it into accumulators which stored it, in easily portable form, for any purpose you may need it in any place.

"As you know, there are already machines in existence accomplishing some part of this effect," said Bill. "But they are crude, clumsy, and tortuous beyond all belief. Compared with this, they are like the early cumbrous printing machines put beside a modern portable typewriter. With this a man could carry in his attaché-case enough power—and, mark you, be able to apply that power safely and easily—to pump all the water out of the North Sea."

"Now, what would he want to do that for?" queried Dot.

Rob coughed.

"Bill's running on a bit ahead, in his usual fashion," he said. "This is only a hypothesis. I think he's got something here, but there's an awful lot of experimental verification to be done before we start predicting."

"Unnecessary," jerked Bill. "Obviously the theory stands by itself. You could build the machine right away, and it would justify every claim I make."

"Well, that's finished that," said Lena brightly. "What shall we invent next? Any suggestions? I've always thought there was a great need for corkscrews for left-handed people. Why should they all have to be turned right-handed? It's a dictatorship of the right, nothing less. We want a *democratic* corkscrew. I think—"

"You don't. You never did," interrupted Bill rudely. "I'm telling you this is the greatest thing since—since..."

He groped.

"Since the Reproducer?" I asked.

"Well—yes."

"It's plain that you want to plunge into this new thing," I said. "In that case, what's going to happen to all the work we're doing with the Reproducer?"

"I should like to know that too, Bill," said Rob.

"I was coming to that," said Bill. He took a breath. "Well, look, folks. I don't know how you feel, but speaking for myself, I can't come back to that sort of work. It's not my sort of life. It's become scarcely more than piece-work. Repetition, repetition, repetition! I'd go nuts. I'm a research physicist, not a factory hand. It's not your sort of work either, Rob."

Rob looked non-committal. "You're not suggesting we stop our reproduction work altogether? We can't trust anyone else with the machine, you know," he said.

"Oh no." Bill turned to me. "You really like the work, don't you, Doc?"

"Yes, I don't mind being a common labourer at all," I said. "Honest sweat, and all that. Seriously, if you take that occupation from me, I don't know what I shall do. I'll go nuts myself, probably. I really think it worth while, and I enjoy doing it. It gives me great satisfaction to be able to spend my declining years usefully. I don't mind taking the whole show on myself, if it can continue."

"Oh, I want to go on with it too!" exclaimed Lena and Dot in their now familiar chorus fashion.

"I mean, I should like to step in and help," amended Dot.

"Good," said Bill. "The three of you should be able to manage all right, especially as work isn't too heavy these days. If it does get more than a handful for you, you can always start packing and accounting departments with outside labour—not here, of course, but in the village. That will leave Rob and me free for this new venture."

"I seem to be conscripted," smiled Rob. "But if it's all right with everybody, I *would* rather like a change."

It was all right with everybody.

CHAPTER EIGHT

Time went by, and things ordered themselves—to outward view at least—in the new circumstances.

Dot was taken locally as Lena's twin sister, and with no great surprise (although some souls remarked that never before had they seen twins so completely alike), for more people than ourselves had accepted the paradox of always expecting the unexpected from Lena. It was just like her to turn out suddenly to be a twin.

Sir Walter and Lady Heath took to her straight away and without reservations, for they had got over their doubts about Lena, and, indeed, grown fond of their son's wife. So they looked upon Dot as another Lena, and never knew just how apposite this attitude was.

In the Dump life was crowded, literally. On one side of the lab Bill and Rob worked away on their new experiments, bringing more and more apparatus into the place and threatening to encroach upon our side. In fact, preliminary cables were already tentatively wriggling along the floor in our direction, and presumptuous wires slung themselves slanting through the air dangerously near the frontier. As the two girls and I went to and fro about our business at the Reproducer we moved between the Scylla and Charybdis of either tripping over something and breaking our necks or beheading ourselves as with a cheese-wire.

"You know, we'll have to put up a notice, 'Ancient Lights', if this gets any worse," remarked Dot one day.

I looked at her, and it occurred to me that it was the first joke I had heard from her that day. That realization started a train of reflection. Unconsciously, I found, I had acquired the ability over the last week or so to distinguish between Dot and Lena, whatever they wore. At first it was quite impossible, and they delighted to confuse me by pretending to be each other and inveigling me into talking absolute nonsense. One got into such a state that one dared hardly take the risk of trying to broach a serious subject with either of them. You would try to discuss Dot with Lena, and think you had really got somewhere and agreed about something, when you would find that you had been talking to Dot all the time, and she had been leading you up the garden path. Each was as mischievous and irresponsible as the other.

But now I noticed that without deliberate effort I had been picking Dot out as "the quieter one", and was making no more mistakes.

Definitely she had grown more serious; while Lena was still an unfailing stream of smooth wit, with odd and unexpected razor-blades sometimes concealed in it. Dot more often merely smiled instead of joining in Lena's insidious attack on us men.

Now, as I looked at her, it was borne in upon me that there were visible physical differences, too, which there certainly had not been. Very, very slight they were, and perhaps not immediately apparent to one not trained, like myself, to look for the smallest evidences of symptoms in the features. The palest of shadows under the eyes, which themselves appeared greyer than Lena's and were lacking now a little of that lustre. A certain compression of the lips, and the tiniest of frowns, as though daylight were too strong for the eyes. The brow was as smooth as ever, the hair had all its glorious sheen, there was no difference of complexion, for both girls were naturally pale, and she carried herself as erectly and easily as did Lena.

Yet I knew that there was something on Dot's mind, and she was worrying inwardly about it. Knowing how similar her outlook was to Lena's—Lena, who scarcely knew what worry was—I deduced that that something was no small thing, and moreover must be of an unprecedented nature. Lena had had her trials in her efforts to achieve artistic fulfilment, but she had faced and fought them. Only when it was inescapably apparent to her that she had lost on every front had she taken the one course which seemed plain and logical to her.

But fighting and worry are two different things.

Worry is the stress caused in the mind (and eventually affecting the body) by the inability to choose between two or more different courses, and through revolving the merits and demerits of each endlessly around a circle, getting to no place of rest to ease the strain. Such a procedure was so alien to the Lena-Dot mind, which always took the direct route, however painful or unpleasant it was, that for a moment I doubted myself. But the symptoms were unmistakable: in this nerve-racked world I had learned enough to know the mark of worry when I saw it.

All this passed through my mind during my brief regard of her, before I answered with some foolish rejoinder about our territorial rights, at which she smiled and became absent-minded again.

Since the days when Lena was my patient I had adopted a sort of guardian attitude towards her, and felt, I suppose with presumption, that to help her in any trouble was my responsibility. I knew she sensed this, and, indeed, did value my advice and asked for it, even though in the final analysis she herself formed her decisions. But since her marriage with Rob I felt the prime onus of responsibility had shifted, and I should not have dreamed of butting in with inquiries that would now assume the aspect of undisciplined curiosity.

Instead, my godfatherly regard had swung itself on to Dot. I could not think of my foster-son as a steady and reliable counsellor, as I thought of Rob. True, since his marriage Bill's switchback emotions had noticeably smoothed and quietened. He was more reliable than he had been, and certainly much more even-tempered. But he was no less impatient, and I could not trust his hasty and sometimes superficial conclusions in matters not directly concerned with himself. His darting intelligence was too aerial to descend often into the slow courses of wisdom.

Therefore, when I perceived the evidences of something that was disturbing Dot's happiness, I told myself that I must get her alone at the first presentable chance and endeavour to discover what it was. Subtly, if possible; and if that failed, then brutally. Which latter method, I thought wryly, was even more certain failure than an attempt at wiliness. The plain fact was that I had to abide by Dot's decision whether to tell me or not. But seek that decision I would.

The opportunity came quickly, and in a quite unexpected manner, that very afternoon.

The day's work was concerned with some fairly hefty broken slabs of ancient Greek bas-relief, and carrying them around as they came out of the Reproducer was tiring enough. Lena and Dot were carrying one between them, when Dot, her face paler than usual, slowed and swayed, her eyes closing, and began to crumple.

"Doc!" called Lena, quietly but urgently.

I had seen, however, and my supporting arm reached Dot just in time. Lena changed her two-handed grip to her left hand only, swung adroitly around and caught Dot's slipping end of the slab with her right hand and took the whole weight of the heavy piece of sculpture herself. She lifted it straightway on to an adjacent bench with a strength I never guessed was in her slim arms (afterwards I remembered her regular swimming), and next moment was helping me get the now unconscious Dot to a chair.

Bill and Rob were deep in the entrails of one of their new machines, and only now noticed that something was wrong. Bill came stumbling over in lively alarm, with Rob behind.

"What happened?" jerked Bill, threatening to overset everything in the vicinity in his agitation. Lena took his arm and drew him aside, explaining quietly, while I attended to Dot.

Superficially it was no more serious than a fainting fit. A cold douche on the forehead brought a responsive twitching of the eyelids, but they remained closed. I put my ear at her breast to check on heart and breathing, and a faint husky whisper, intended for that ear alone and only just reaching it, came from her scarce-moving lips: "Put me to bed, Doc. I want to talk to you alone."

I gave no signs of having heard. I straightened up again, pursed my lips, and said at large: "I don't think it's serious, but I'm not entirely satisfied. I'm going to give her a more thorough examination. I want no one in the room, not even you, Bill."

Bill looked shocked.

"Surely—" he began, but I cut him short.

"I know what I'm doing, Bill. Don't ask questions. Open the bedroom door, please."

Dumbly he obeyed. I lifted Dot—she was surprisingly light— and then carried her through into the room which had been mine and was now Bill's and hers. I laid her on the bed. Bill had followed me in, and now knelt and clasped Dot's hand as if he would never let go, gazing at her ashen face with unshielded anxiety.

"Please, Bill," I said firmly. He rose slowly and made as if to protest, but I shepherded him to the door.

"I shan't be long," I said, and as I was closing the door after him I noticed Lena, standing beside Rob, looking straight into my eyes with an enigmatic regard. I endeavoured to remain as enigmatic myself, but I was glad to interpose the door between us before she had drawn my thoughts and intentions from my head. Though, lord knows, they were vague enough.

I turned back towards the bed. I was irresistibly reminded of my first sight of Lena, for Dot lay sprawled in much the same attitude, her hair spilling over the pillow like an arrested flow of gold mixed with some darker metal.

I sat beside her. Without looking up, she reached out a hand and gripped my forearm. It was a dumb appeal for help that cut me to the heart. I laid my hand comfortingly on top of hers, and spoke as one soothing a frightened child.

"What do you want to tell me, Dot?"

The next moment her head was on my lap, her arms holding tightly on to me, as if I were the last hope in a darkened world from which every other gleam had been shut out. And my arm was about her shaking shoulders as she strove, with little shuddering gasps, like an animal in pain, not to give way to tears. Those dry sobs were quite the most pitiful sound I had heard in a lifetime spent amid human distress of all kinds and degrees. The more so because I thought so much of this girl, and because I knew that whatever had broken her steely spirit must have been a more killing torture than any the Inquisition had seen fit to use.

She was trembling uncontrollably from head to foot, and I realized that for some time now she must have been teetering on the brink of a nervous breakdown. Only her extraordinary self-discipline had kept most of the traces of her plight concealed from us until now. But the strongest constitution must cry out for respite sometime when the strain never ceases for a second, and when Dot had been forced to give an inch the whole burden crushed down inexorably, flattening thought and will into non-existence.

Presently she quietened down and became comparatively still, although I was aware that every one of her nerves was stretched like thin wire under tensile stress. And she began talking, at first in muffled, hesitant sentences, her face still buried in my lap. Soon she sat up, and I saw the grey depths of unhappiness in her eyes as she told of this first real grip of that unholy monster of circumstance, the four-sided triangle.

"I'm afraid I've been very stupid," she murmured. "Not only now, but... way back, when I was Lena... I suppose none of us, for a group of intelligent people, has been very bright. But the fault is mainly mine. I didn't use my imagination. I, above all people, should have known better. My error, our common error, was the assumption that I was to be born again, to start, as it were, from scratch, and to be able to make different choices from those Lena had made. What we overlooked was that who we were bringing into the world was not a *new* Lena, with a freedom to take a different path, but the same old one, dominated by the same memories and desires that Lena had at the moment of the duplication.

"I was born crazy with love for Rob!..."

Here I suddenly stood up as if someone had shot an electric current through my chair, and exclaimed at this revelation of my incredible, incurable blindness in the matter of seeing consequences that should have been obvious from the start.

"What an utter fool I am!" I stormed.

Gently she drew me down again.

"Never mind, Doc. The past is the past. It is the present that is... so terrible. I have never known anything like this. Rob is like the fruit that hung over Tantalus's head. So near, apparently in easy reach, and yet... light-years away. You know, sometimes with him I forget my role of Dot. I begin, without thinking, to talk and laugh about some little episode that happened to us—to Lena and him, rather—on the honeymoon in Cornwall. It seems so real to me. I've always managed to check myself in time, and I don't think he noticed. But some day I'm going to give myself away. I've not been used to watching myself; it comes as a strain to me, and spoils what there is that I could make of this life.

"As much as my hopeless love, it is the conflict of trying to keep up an act all the time against my natural inclination to be just what I am, and be accepted as that. Greatest of all, this awful hypocrisy of pretending to love Bill when my whole being cries aloud for Rob."

Here a fit of trembling overcame her again, and her grip on me tightened until she had once more composed herself. I confined my comments to the unspoken consolation of stroking her hand gently. It was best to let her get all this out of her system in her own way.

"I shall always remember that sickening moment when I came to consciousness after the... process. I opened my eyes to see that glass cover hanging above me, drawn up and away, when my last memory had been of it descending to extinguish me like a candle-snuffer. I could not think where I was at first, and then I remembered and wondered whether the experiment had been a success. And all at once a horrid doubt struck me: was I Lena, *or was I the other one?*"

I started. For a memory flashed before my mental eyes. The awakening of Lena after the duplication, when I had been massaging the cramp from her. There had been a flicker of strange expression in her eyes, and now I realized it was that very same doubt. How relieved she must have been when Rob immediately called her "Lena"!

But for Dot it had not turned out so happily.

"Then I saw Bill bending over me," she resumed. "The expression on the poor boy's face! He was pale and sweating, and he gazed at me with big round eyes full of an agonized mixture of doubt and hope, and couldn't say a word. I tried to sit up. My body was still semi-rigid with cramp—Bill had been much too agitated to make a good masseur. I got half-way, with Bill helping me, and pain shooting through every twisted muscle, and that was enough to see that the lab was empty. You and Rob were gone, and the twin case alongside, which was the one I remembered getting into, was vacant. The ends of the wires stuck up loosely, unattached. Lena was gone. I tried to absorb that. Lena was gone. And yet I, Lena, was left here. The immediate realization following on that was: Lena was gone—with Rob.

"A sense of unbearable desolation swept across me. There was an aching emptiness where something real and wonderful had been. The pain in my body was nothing at all to the pain that burned in my soul now. I felt physically sick with disappointment. And it came to me that from that very moment I was to begin a life of sham. Yet I was in this world for a purpose. It was to save Bill from that very same desolation of spirit which comes from loving another who has no need of you. I knew now how he had felt. I realized how he had suffered. And there he was, trembling in hope that I would be his rescuer at last, staring at me in fearful dumb questioning.

"So I had to make an effort. It was no good dwelling upon this pain, this tearing sense of loss, which was almost as if Rob had been killed. I had to form and act upon a philosophy, and it amounted to this: I am only a mirror image. Somewhere the real me is living and having Rob. The knowledge of that must be sufficient. I have a task and a mission of my own: to make Bill happy.

"Somehow I managed to smile, and reached out a hand to Bill. He seized it like a drowning man.

"He said stumblingly: 'I'd like to call you Dorothy. I've always liked that name.'

"'I am Dorothy,' I said, still smiling.

"And so the play began. At all costs I had to keep the truth, which would have broken him up, from him. It may seem queer that he never expected or suspected such a situation. But his mental processes regarding this whole affair were not normal. From the beginning he had been acting from feeling, not reasoning. He was blinded by his longings. His thinking was wishful thinking, and held the bar against any 'dangerous thought' that might spoil his dream.

"To begin with, I felt I must escape from the Dump and all its memories. I ached to set eyes on Rob again, but I knew that just yet, anyway, I could not count on controlling my reactions to his presence. The best thing of all would be to go away with Bill, far away, and never see any of you again. The immediate excuse was, of course, the wedding and honeymoon, and almost before I could stand properly again I was pressing Bill to leave with me as soon as possible.

"He was as pleased as Punch. He took my eagerness for an unqualified desire to 'make a go of it' for the pair of us. And, indeed, I did my best to enter into that spirit, in a hope as irrational as his, that I might in time begin to feel it in reality. For I am very fond indeed of Bill, as you know, and I couldn't—and cannot—bear to hurt him. If I had never met Rob it is most likely that I should have fallen in love with Bill. But I *had* met Rob, and I know now in my heart that my love for him can never lessen nor be supplanted...

"Well, we made preparations to leave for Eastbourne the next morning. As you know, Lena had left quite a wardrobe for me. Bill 'phoned up Rob and told him we were off. He wanted me to speak to Rob on the 'phone. I got out of it somehow—if I had heard Rob's voice when I was in that condition I—don't know what I should have said or done. And so we went.

"The whole of that fortnight was one long struggle to readjust myself and accept the circumstances, and yet never let a sign of that struggle show on the surface. It was a queer sort of purgatory. Modern scientists scoff at the ancient idea that the seat of love is the heart. All emotions take place in the mind, they say. It is they who are ignorant, not the ancients. None of them can ever have been 'that way'. 'That way' *is* a physical experience, Doc, a very real, tangible ache in the region of the heart. It tears and nags, and is relieved only by the presence of the person you love. My longing to be with Rob never ceased to gnaw.

"But I managed to keep this agony subterranean. I threw myself into every sort of foolery with Bill, tried to make our affairs occupy the whole of my attention. And there were times, you know, when I did find myself laughing unforcedly—Bill is the best of company when he's in good spirits—and at such times I had hopes that my heartache would mend.

"It is because of those hopes that I want your help, Doc. So long as I see Rob every day, as I do now, so long as he is easily accessible, then I have no chance of winning my fight. If I can separate from him altogether, and go and live far away with Bill, there's a chance that my fondness for Bill may grow into something greater. Although I can never hope to forget Rob, I may not have to remember him all the time when he is not there, but Bill is.

"Trying to live as we do now is no longer possible. I am at the end of my tether. I dread every evening when, after the day's work, the moment comes when Rob and Lena leave arm-in-arm for *their* home. That dreadful forsaken loneliness comes on me each time. I can stand no more of it. I can't fight this overwhelming longing for Rob and keep up a false front with Bill any more. It's all so unnatural. The strain… Sometimes I have felt I must blurt out the whole truth and get it off my chest or burst. At other times I have felt like running away from it all and from everybody. I would do that, were it not my duty to stay with Bill and fulfil my promise.

"Well, I've got to solve my own problems, and there's only one clear thing to do—as I said, cut away from Rob and Lena and the Dump and all this old life altogether, and start anew with Bill, preferably somewhere out of this country. I can't, obviously, tell Bill my reasons for wanting to do such a thing. But I must supply *some* reason—it seems such a mad thing to want to do: to cut our best friends out of our life, abandon our work with the Reproducer, drop this new atomic research Bill is working on with Rob—he's so keen about that, too. All without an explanation. I can't think of any false one to offer. I'm sick of trying to deal with falsity, anyway. But you can truthfully and reasonably order me away for my health's sake, Doc—God knows I shall break down altogether if I have to stand many more days of this. What you can say I'll have to leave to you. You've more imagination. Can you do that, Doc? Or can you think of any other way out?"

She looked at me with uncertain hope. I had got my subconscious wish. Here was Lena (or Dot—it made no difference) defeated, and looking up to me as her only source of help in this world. Seeking me out, indeed, in desperation.

I would that the wisdom of Solomon had descended upon me, and I could have seen in a flash a way to satisfy all parties. But I do believe that that learned one himself would have been helpless in the toils of the unprecedented tangle of human relationships which I named the four-sided triangle. For science had added a fourth side to the eternal triangle of two men and one woman by the bewildering move of doubling the one feminine side. And as yet, although we knew it not, we were only in the outer meshes of the formidable web.

So, in the moment that should have set the crown on my petty personal triumph, I failed. At as much a loss as Dot herself, I sat biting my nails, my mind darting all over and around the chains of current circumstances, seeking a direction and finding nothing but obstruction.

Presently I said: "I'm sorry, Dot, but I can't see any other course but the one you suggest. But I can't order you away for keeps, can I? I think perhaps a couple of months on, say, the Riviera, and then see how things are. Time and separation may tone down this feeling for Rob. At any rate, it'll give Bill a chance."

Dot looked away, gazed absently at the square of window which held a prospect of distant, tight-curled and very white cumulus clouds, apparently as stationary as though carven in ivory, yet imperceptibly climbing upon each other's backs up into the blue.

"Very well, Doc. We'll try that. I wish I could believe that it would succeed."

"You doubt it?"

"Well… I remember rather too poignantly how long the days were on my last trip away. Especially the last few. How I wished the hours away until I could get back and set eyes on Rob! And then the day I came he was away, in London. Remember? And when he did come…"

There was a little catch in her voice, and she paused a moment, still looking at that sky picture.

"When he did come," she resumed, "that evening at dinner, I was on edge with anticipation. I was managing myself better than I am now. It was as well. I don't think I could remain outwardly composed now under such a blow as that meeting was. From the outset he treated me as a stranger. I had to be introduced! To my own hus— No, I must not say that. But that polite, reserved way he behaved towards me—it was though an icicle was stabbing into my heart."

"He's more used to the idea now," I commented. "He ribs you as much as he does Lena."

"Yes, but I always get the idea of something being forced. He *has* erected a barrier between us—it's not my imagination. It was never there in… the old days. It's not there between Lena and him."

"H'm. Lena," I said, and rubbed my nose reflectively. "What do you imagine she thinks of the situation? Does she suspect your plight? You should know, if anyone does. What *did* you discuss that first day you went out together?"

"Very ordinary things. We didn't discuss Rob," answered Dot slowly. "You may think it strange, but I'm very little better at guessing what goes on in Lena's mind than you are. And no doubt that works both ways. For, you see, we're that improvident type of person who can't be bothered to wonder how we'll react to any change. We think of a thing only when we get to it. We're not so very good at putting ourselves mentally in other people's places, and less good at foreseeing our own mental states. I can't tell you whether this experiment of separation from Rob will succeed or not: I shan't know until it's been tried. But I can't imagine that Lena has, up to now, been aware of my feelings. Because she would have come straight to me and faced the problem—that I do know."

"Why don't you speak to *her*?"

"Why should I burden her with my trouble? It would not solve anything."

"The pair of you together might. You might come to some arrangement."

I left it suggestively at that.

She turned her wide grey eyes on me.

"Not without more play-acting, Doc. She would let me have Rob as much as herself—I know that, too. But as I've said, I've done with falsity. I could never be happy that way, with deceit. It breaks my heart to have to deceive Bill. I could never bring myself to deceive Rob. No, I must go away—it's all that can be done."

"Very well, Dot," I said, and rose. "Now, you just lie back for a bit and rest while I straighten this out with the others."

"You'll not tell them the real truth? Please, for Bill's sake, don't even hint at it."

"I'll see," I said. "But don't worry—I'll go carefully."

Bill was pacing up and down outside the door. He grabbed me.

"How is she? Can I see her now? What's the matter with her?"

"Hold on just a minute," I adjured. I wanted a private talk with him, but to manage one with any appearance of decency I had to dispose of Lena and Rob.

I seized a piece of paper and pencilled a prescription on it.

"Rob—Lena," I said. "Would you mind popping along to the dispensary and getting that made up straight away?"

"Of course not," replied Rob, taking the paper slip and reaching for his hat.

"You get it, Rob," said Lena. "I'm going in to see Dot."

"Excuse me, old girl, not yet," I said. "I can't allow even her husband in for the moment. There's a good reason."

"I have a good reason, too, Doc," said Lena. "Would you like me to tell you it?"

She looked at me very straightly, and I knew at once she had divined the real trouble. Probably, judging from her previous demeanour, she had suspected it as soon as Dot had collapsed.

I did not answer, and she walked calmly past me, let herself into the bedroom, and closed the door behind her.

Bill looked after her blankly.

"I say—" he began, but I cut him short.

"It's all right, she can't do any harm. But I've got to talk to you first."

"I'm away," said Rob, and went out.

"Now, Doc, for heaven's sake, what's it all about?" asked Bill, anxious to a degree.

"It's simply this, Bill. Dot's suffering from a delayed physical reaction to that rather unpleasant process of being—born. I had suspected such a thing might catch up with her, and it has." (I had started lying without reserve, and I thought I might as well make a thorough job of it.) "Her nerves have never been properly relaxed from the tension caused in them by the electrical current. Unlike Lena, whom we treated right away, she was left too long in that tensed state. I have an idea, too, that despite my tutelage you didn't make a very good job of easing her condition with massage. In addition, there were the shocks of your special process of resuscitation, which were spared Lena. Being the type who won't complain or rest, she's been doing all this heavy work here in the lab in a far from adequate condition, and now it's suddenly knocked her out."

"It's all my fault," said Bill miserably. "I was too eager to have her on her feet. I did rush everything. Gosh, I wouldn't have caused her this for the world! She must rest. She must stay in bed."

I was gratified that my hasty improvisation was accepted without question, even though Bill was too upset to think of doubting it.

"Knowing her, do you expect her to stay in bed *here*?" I asked. "With us talking and working in the next room to her? Lord, I could never manage to make her—I mean Lena—stay in bed that time she had been at death's door!"

"We'll have to shut the lab down, that's all," decided Bill.

"We have contracts to fulfil by certain dates," I warned him.

"Damn *them*!" he said.

"Don't you think it would be better if you took her right away from here, to some place where she couldn't get at any work, some place with an enervating climate? I suggest the French or Italian Riviera—Menton would be ideal: the warmest and most relaxing place on the coast. Have a second honeymoon, quietly."

"Do you think she would agree to that?"

"I'll make her," I said.

He gave a weak sort of smile at my confidence, not suspecting that for once I did boast with assurance.

"I hope so," he said.

"There's one thing," I remarked. "What about your new research here with Rob? You'll have to shelve it for a bit, you know."

"When it comes to Dot's health, such things as that don't matter a tinker's curse."

"You still… feel the same way about her as ever?" I ventured, playing idly with my pencil on the desk.

"I always shall, Doc," he said fervently. "She's everything in the world to me. I feel a new man altogether. I've got a squarer outlook on things now. She—do you know what William James said of his wife? He said, 'She saved me from my *Zerrissenheit'*—that is, literally, 'torn-to-pieces-ness'—'and gave me back to myself all in one piece.' That's what Dot has done for me. I couldn't do without her for any length of time."

"I'm glad," I said, and ruminated a moment. It was plain that to tell him the real truth would cause untold damage and still solve no one else's problems. I should have to keep Dot's secret, after all. And Lena would have to, too. That reminded me—she was still in there with Dot, and I must ensure that she did indeed keep her peace and not lay the affair frankly, as was her manner, before Rob and Bill.

"Can I go in and see her now?" Bill broke in on my reflections. I started.

"Er—I would rather you waited till Rob comes back with that nerve sedative," I said. "She'd be in a better state to discuss this trip with you then. I'll tell her that I'm ordering her a complete change and rest, and then you must do the sales-talk afterwards. Meanwhile, I'm going in to get Lena out of there. She's had long enough with the patient. Excuse me."

I went in. Lena was sitting on the bed with her arm round Dot like a protective big sister, and saying something quietly to her. She looked up at my entry. I closed the door and advanced.

"I suppose you've come to throw me out, Doc," said Lena. "All right, I'll go quietly. I just had to let Dot know that I am with her all the way."

"I'm glad to hear that. How did you suspect?"

"How *didn't* I suspect?" returned Lena soberly. "The awful thought which occurred to me, that I might have lost Rob, must naturally have occurred to Dot also. Why ever did I stupidly assume that it hadn't? Dot *is* me, every particle of me, as I was that day in the lab. I'm wholly responsible for her."

"The only person who is responsible for me is myself," murmured Dot. "I don't intend, if I can help it, to make any calls upon anyone else. This is my battle."

Lena just squeezed her hand.

"What do you intend to do?" I asked of Lena.

"Anything that is required of me, Doc."

"All that is required of you is your silence, Lena," I said. "Or do you think you *ought* to tell Bill and Rob?"

"My inclination is, I admit, to tell them. I believe it is only laying up treasure in hell to let things run underground. Much better to have everything out in the light of day, and thrash the matter out openly among ourselves. It does concern all of us."

"And what do you expect Rob to do? What *can* he do? As for Bill—he'd never get over it."

"Perhaps he would get over it now, Doc, in the early stages, as it were. If it were to come out later on, the blow would likely be even harder to get over. We have to think of him. I know what an awful shock it would be to him, but our lives are the withstanding of the thousand natural shocks the flesh is heir to. You've just got to muster up the required resistance."

"Could *you* withstand a comparable shock?"

She must have been surprised, but she didn't show it.

"Well... One never knows, of course, until one's had the experience. But I should try to adjust myself to it."

I merely let my gaze drop indicatively on to Dot's lowered golden-brown head. Lena followed my eyes, and then looked quickly up at me again. She smiled wryly.

"Your point, Doc?"

"You must realize, Lena, that your position is not what it was, nor are you the same girl that once you were. You used to be utterly independent and self-sufficient, but now you've allowed your life to get tangled up with other people's. You may imagine you're independent, but these other people are dependent on you—as I believe you're dependent on Rob."

"Of course, Doc. Things are changed, and they *have* changed me. I was wrong. I'll not say another word, I promise you."

After which we discussed for a time the plan of Dot and Bill going away.

We were interrupted by the door being flung open and Bill rushing wildly through as if he were bringing a last-minute pardon to the gallows. Rob was somewhere in the background.

"Here's the prescription!" exclaimed Bill breathlessly, holding out a bottle.

"You'll make an ideal travelling companion for a nerve case," I said severely. "I don't know that I ought to allow you anywhere near Dot."

He thrust the bottle into my hand and plumped down beside Dot, silent through sheer incoherence of thought. For all his impetuosity, there was a tender anxiety in his bearing which touched me deeply.

Lena gently relinquished Dot to him, and cast a thoughtful glance across at Rob, who stood rather uncertainly in the doorway.

With becoming gravity I measured out a small glass of the prescribed liquid, which was really very good stuff indeed *qua* cough mixture.

CHAPTER NINE

From time to time we got postcards from one or other of the pair. First a view along the front of Boulogne-sur-Mer—*La digue Ste.-Beuve*—and on the back:

> *Awful smell of fish here.—Bill.*

Later, a photograph taken from the sea of the Ponte San Luigi, which spans the gorge dividing the French and Italian Rivieras. Comment:

> *Nice place, but the pebbles on the beach are too big for my tender feet. Also, the rocks in the sea have thorny growths on them as well as seaweed. Trod on one an hour ago; still pulling the thorns out. Of course, Dot doesn't care a damn. She's swimming miles out. Gone over the horizon, I believe. She'll probably bring me back some dates from Tunis.—Bill.*

A view of San Remo. Dot's handwriting:

> *Writing this on top of Monte Bignone—Bill suffering from* mal de mer, *through coming up on the* Funivia. *Rest cure doing me good. We're going to slide back down the cable without holding.—Dot.*

Back to Menton: *Vue prise du Cap Martin.* Dot again.

Sailed to Bordighera and back. Nearly arrested for smuggling.
Sun turning Bill a horrible colour. Like a frightened Red
Indian. But his face is peeling right off now, so relief is in
sight. Do you think he'll grow a better one?—Dot.

On to Monte Carlo: the usual coloured view of the Casino and
gardens. Bill's writing:

We vowed not to gamble more than we could afford. We broke
our promise. We didn't break the bank. They broke our hearts.
Send a lotta money quick before the proprietor breaks our
necks. Hotel ——, Menton.

We cabled cash. A few days later, a reply cable:

Thanks doubled our capital this time leaving for Paris to
spend it—Bill Dot.

I groaned. "Enervating climate. Rest. Relaxation. No excitement.
And they're behaving like a pair of jitterbugs!"

"Well, what's the use of a holiday if you don't go places and
do things?" commented Lena. "Arrest is as good as a change of
occupation, as the cat burglar said when they caught him. I'm glad
they didn't let the tables beat them."

Presently a letter from Bill, in Paris.

… Dot's been showing me around, especially the Louvre. I think
Mona Lisa overdid plucking her eyebrows. Ran into some old
acquaintances of Lena's there—Janie and Edmond—whom
she knew at the École des Beaux Arts. Anyway, that's what

they call themselves—I don't think they have any surname(s).
But Lena might tell you. Naturally, they thought Dot was
Lena, and we didn't disillusion them: just a bit too much
of a mouthful to explain in casual conversation, you know.
Dot, of course, remembered them and behaved as if she were
Lena, and we had a mild drinking bout. By the way, Dot's
going to a nursing home here for a couple of days. A very
minor ailment, of no consequence. After that, we're going
out to Versailles to hang around in the vicinity of the Petit
Trianon in the hopes of getting a trip backwards in Time,
like Miss Moberley and friend in An Adventure. *If you*
don't hear from us for a week, you'll know we're back in the
eighteenth century...

"Nursing home?" I queried, raising an eyebrow.

"Don't worry over that," said Lena. "She's probably been laid
out with an empty bottle or a chair or some such blunt instrument
in a café in Montmartre. I know Janie and Ed and their mild drinking bouts. Most probably it's galloping D.T.s. *Crème de menthe* and
vermouth and champagne mixed in buckets and taken with a ladle
does make the flowers step down from the wallpaper and remark
that it's going to be a nice day if it doesn't snow and do you like
spinach? I've seen and heard 'em."

"You must tell me more of your early struggles in Paris, darling," said Rob, with an almost imperceptible wink at me.

"Oh, it was fun in a way, and all experience," meditated Lena.
"But they were almost all frustrated souls like myself, trying to
forget their disappointments in drink and horseplay. I wonder how
many of them were in actuality trying to find what I was seeking
too—and what I *have* found, thank heavens!"

And she slipped her arm through the crook of Rob's elbow and held herself close to him, as if a gust of wind might suddenly spring up and waft him from her.

The weeks passed, and the cards came less frequently. It was almost always Bill who wrote. I remember a certain vague disappointment because Dot never wrote me a letter: I thought she might have sent me a report of how things were working out.

At last a view of the Dôme des Invalides, and a scrawled inscription:

Coming home. Expect us Tuesday.—Bill & Dot.

When Tuesday came I was so restless that I could not give my mind to anything. It was corralled in the question: Has Dot become reconciled to the loss of Rob or is the desire for him still consuming her? Shortly, has the experiment succeeded or not?

I went for a walk along the lanes and over the fields hoping that the pair would have arrived by the time I came back.

They had not. It was not until I was finishing supper in my room that the landlady of the "Pheasant" came heavily up the stairs to inform me that I was wanted on the telephone. I went down.

It was Rob, 'phoning from "Hawthorns".

"That you, Doc? Bill and Dot have just arrived here. They're staying for supper. Can you come over and join us?"

"I've just had supper," I said. "But if Lena is making any of that milk cocoa—"

"She is."

"Then I'll be over right away."

"Good."

"How are Bill and Dot?" I ventured.

"Oh, fine, fine. Brown as berries, to coin a phrase."

"That's all right, then," I said. "'Bye, Rob. See you anon."

"So long."

Half an hour later I was standing outside the front door of "Hawthorns" with a queer feeling as though my stomach sac had detached itself from the intestines and was floating like a balloon inside a body that had become hollow. No doubt many a soul in the past had waited in my waiting-room for me with just that feeling, in suspense for my verdict. Now it was not I who was to give the verdict. It was something independent of all of us, a dispassionate and heedless fate.

A faculty quite other than reason informed me that this was the crux of all these fantastic events. That unless Dot's passion had been subdued by time, we were all of us committed to become non-self-governing parts in a machine over which no one had any degree of control, and its pistons would move ever faster until they became flails of their own substance, unseating the balance of the mind. And our very spirits would writhe to the frictional screeching of overheated bearings until we were flung apart in the final catastrophe of disintegration. At any rate, that was the image from a sort of mechanist Inferno which haunted my mind at that moment. Thus, waking or sleeping, in dreams or nightmares, do we apprehend the looming form of the future.

The maid opened the door.

In a matter of seconds I stood in the doorway of the dining-room and surveyed my companions in this drama. They were at the table, in the middle of supper.

My eyes sought Dot first, distinguishing her from Lena by the light tan she had acquired in her travels. She smiled at me. I thought she looked much brighter than she had, and my heart leapt with hope. But she conveyed nothing, neither by bearing nor expression. Her thoughts were as unreadable as those of Lena at our first encounter.

My gaze passed on to Lena herself. She, too, smiled, as she caught my eye, but again it was the smile of the sphinx. Rob had that almost studied casualness about him, his habitual façade, which might have concealed anything or nothing. Only Bill's red and sun-roughened face looked as open as the day, and he was grinning a welcome, tinged with a faint puzzlement at my deliberate regard.

"Hullo, Doc," he called. "Why so serious? *Entrez! Avanti!* In other words, come in. We haven't been converted to cannibalism in 'furrin parts'. Anyway, I bet this cold beef is tastier than your salty carcase. Come and try some."

I still hesitated irrationally at the door, so Bill thrust his chair back and almost leapt over to me and hauled me in.

"No supper, thanks," I said. "I'll just sit by the fire till you've finished."

"I know what he wants," said Lena. She poured out a steaming cup of milk cocoa and brought it to me.

"Thankee, child."

As she bent to place it on the wide arm of my chair, thick strands of her shining hair escaped from behind her shoulders and swept across the cream of her cheek. From her downturned face her eyes gazed widely up at mine. It was like looking into the azure distances of an August sky. There was an indefinable loveliness, but it was just as empty of intent as the sky. I could only draw the negative conclusion that no red imp of mischief was evident this time. Yet she was smiling. That sensitive mouth, those red lips and small, regular white teeth, reminiscent in some way of an infant's first set, lit again that cherished image of my boyhood's romantic dreams, with the strange ache that accompanies the regard of wonderful things far off in space or time.

"She walks in beauty like…"

Like the morning, I thought. Lena's was not the dark loveliness of the night. She reminded you of the sun. She was one of those people remarked on by Stevenson who seem to light a gloomy room when they come into it.

In a moment I shall be slobbering about angels, I thought, and put on my own armour against insidious sentiment—a crust of that wit that I liked to believe was caustic.

"Is the milk in that of human kindness, Lena, or the usual curdled stuff you reserve for me?"

"It's milk of magnesia for your obviously bad stomach," returned Lena solicitously, not a whit taken aback by this uncalled-for slap in the face. "I think your digestive troubles arise from not chewing people's heads properly when you bite them off. Remember, masticate thirty-two times before swallowing, rest after meals, and your disposition will improve with your digestion."

"Something *is* wrong with the old bear," sang out Bill, from the table. "Let's all psycho-analyse him after supper, and strew the bits around the carpet."

I took refuge in sipping my cocoa.

Presently they joined me around the fire.

"How are you feeling now, Dot?" I probed.

"As well as can be expected under the circumstances," she replied. "The circumstances being a mad husband, a malicious twin sister, and an unmannerly family doctor."

"What about your affectionate brother-in-law?" said Rob, a shade heavily.

I was watching Dot intently at this moment, and I could have sworn her eyes misted a little.

"You—you're so good that you're a nonentity," she said calmly, and became interested in extracting a cigarette from the box on the occasional table.

To divert any possible attention from her, I said quickly: "What I like about my friends is their openness. They are open-hearted, open-minded, open-handed, and I'm sure that if I stood on the gallows they'd open the trap for me."

There was a laugh at that, and the conversation became general.

Bill and Dot gave a most amusing account of their doings on the Riviera and in Paris, especially with the modern bohemians.

"Your decision to return seemed a bit sudden," remarked Rob.

"Oh, I don't know," said Bill. "I enjoyed it all, of course, but there came a time when I'd had enough of playing and was itching to get back and into this new atomic stunt. And Dot found she had rather grown away from that set—"

"I had lost the urge for creativeness—at least, in paint—which I used to share with them," meditated Dot. "And somehow they hadn't, it was apparent, learned anything new about life since I had been away, and I have."

She paused as if she were about to say more, but she did not add anything, and Bill took it up again.

"Dot was looking much better and seemed quite O.K. again— but I'd like you to vet her, Doc, and make sure—so one morning I suggested we eased up on the gay life and tried the old country again. Dot said we might just as well go home—she didn't fancy spa-water, especially after so much absinth—and of course I seized on that. We were off within the hour."

"I see," I said. "But I didn't prescribe absinth and late nights and gambling and brawling with eccentrics. Nor anything like your 'Around the World in Eighty Days' methods of travelling. I'm going to vet Dot all right, and see if she's got any system left to examine."

"I think you'll find her all there," said Bill with an airy gesture.

"Which is more than a psychiatrist might find her husband," I retorted.

"I'll give you the chance to withdraw that, if you like," said Bill. "It's not up to standard."

Lena, Dot and Rob all laughed at this impudence.

At a loss, I grabbed Dot, who was still laughing, and pushing her ahead of me, left the room, pausing at the door to threaten, "I'll be back!"

In the privacy of the bedroom I faced Dot squarely and said, "Now, girl, tell me how it has worked out."

The traces of her amusement faded. Her face went as passive and inscrutable as that of a cat sitting before the fire and gazing at the secret pictures of its mind. She sat on the edge of the bed.

"Well... if you must know why we returned so quickly, it was I who forced it on Bill. Oh, not directly—more in the manner in which a conjurer doing a card trick forces the choice of a particular card upon a person. By certain remarks, 'unconscious' revelations of inclination—I think I'm making quite a success of this subtle, if unpleasant, business of acting. My hunger to see Rob again was becoming an obsession."

"Oh, lord!" I said glumly.

"There's no need to worry, Doc—I am not myself worrying any more. Things are under control. I've reached a point of balance.

Rather like a rocking stone, I admit, but at least I have a foundation, and don't feel that I am walking over thin ice which is breaking up beneath me, as it seemed before."

"What foundation?"

"Just an arrangement: that I see Rob every day, and live with Bill. I've settled, as I say, at a point of balance between the two. I really have become attached to Bill, but that affection alone isn't enough. If I can fill my eyes and my ears and my memory with Rob each day, then in the evenings and nights I can transfer my love of him to Bill. It's a trick of imagination, of course—I never thought I could come so much under the sway of self-delusion. It's like living in a dream, but not wholly an unpleasant one. It's bearable, anyway."

"It's a pretty poor sort of life," I said dubiously.

"It's the best I can do for Bill," she said.

A sudden wave of compassion almost overwhelmed me. Any woman thrust into such a position as hers had every right to rail at a fate which had cheated her of the heart and meaning of her life, and left her but a sorry, make-believe imitation of it.

I sat down beside her, and put my arm about her shoulders in a sad attempt to comfort.

"You poor child! It's not fair. We're all to blame for causing you this—I more than anyone. A man of my experience should have had the sense to see—"

"Don't blame yourself, Doc. I brought this on myself. You forget—I was Lena. I walked into it voluntarily. I would do it again. It has saved Bill all this sort of suffering. I'm more able to bear it than he. It would have broken him up, and science and mankind and ourselves would have been the losers. Now he's free to get on with his research again. I myself am of no account. I can produce nothing for humanity. This is the only way I can help."

"Thank you, Dot," was all I could manage. And presently: "What you do for Bill... is shared by me. It makes me happy to see him happy. As for humanity, you give it an example it may learn of one day, if I can ever tell the story."

She smiled.

"You're a romanticist, Doc. Just now you'll have to go down and tell the others another story—that you've vetted me, and I'm as fit as a batch of Swedish-drill instructors."

"You really do feel all right, do you?"

"Of course. I'll stand on my head if you like."

I had to restrain her. But I was glad to see that the chirpiness was coming back again. I might have been wrong, but I think she got some sense of relief in being able to confide in me when she chose to do so.

It was strange how when I was alone with either Lena or Dot I looked upon them as one and the same person, a girl about whom I was growing steadily more fatherly and fond. I was disposed to regard them both as my daughter-in-law, and wished vaguely that somehow they were my own daughter. And in a detached way I was amused at this late-flowering paternal instinct.

So we went down and delivered the report, and everybody seemed cheered by it. There followed spontaneously a typical session of animated talk and badinage, wild flights of fancy from Bill, sometimes brought suddenly to earth by a dry observation from Rob, while Lena and Dot provided the feminine constitu-ent, varying from that knowing exchange of glances meaning "All-men-are-really-little-boys" to the insertion of comments like claws emerging from and slyly retiring between cats' pads. I was "in the chair", but rarely felt master of the situation.

In the end the company divided into two portions: Bill and

Rob, who got deep into technicalities about the continuation of the new research; and the remaining three of us, who discussed the future of the Reproducer Company.

The talk went far into the night.

We thought we were on top of things again. But actually the machine was gathering speed, and the next clash and confusion of opposing parts and forces was drawing near.

For the next few weeks new apparatus was arriving daily at the Dump—enormous installations, some of them, requiring whole trucks to themselves. As fast as it came, Bill and Rob fitted it into their fresh brain-child, another intricate monster, lever-horned, gleamingly dial-eyed, steel-legged, breathing electricity and alive with power, only tenuously bound, it seemed, by the wires and cables lashed round it.

Our power supply was, indeed, trebled, new cables being run underground to us.

Bill explained something about the experiments needing a much greater voltage than the Reproducer, because the latter machine only made use of an existing force. Whereas this new apparatus had to build up its own force, an alternating current of terrifically high voltage.

This machine, I gathered, was not to be a product nor even a maker of products. It was purely an experimental concatenation to verify in practice the novel theories of Bill, which held that the cumbersome carbon piles which surrounded atomic engines and made their weight out of all proportion to the actual power-producing system were unnecessary.

Instead of thus clumsily absorbing the flying electrons which had missed targets in the disintegrating element, Bill meant (again, so far as I was able to understand what he meant) his machine to "unwind" these loose electrons and dissolve them from hard, penetrating "balls" into free but harmless energy, by a sort of reversal of the principle of the Reproducer. Which transformation, he insisted, could be brought about by a piece of apparatus no larger than a pencil box—if his theory could only first be checked and tried out and the effect measured on this latest contraption.

Rob had gone over the mathematics of the business, and checked and re-checked them.

Privately I asked his opinion of it all.

"Well, as usual with Bill's ideas, it's sound enough in theory," he said. "There's nothing you can think of to prove it impossible or unworkable. But you can't base much of an opinion on that. It's when you start trying to put theory into practice that all the things you couldn't think of show up. Sometimes things—brand-new effects—you couldn't possibly have known of beforehand. Occasionally these subsidiary effects, like Fraunhofer's lines in the spectrum, turn out to be of more value than the original aim of the experiment. More often, being inseparably bound up with the sequence of events, they either nullify the aim altogether or else remain as a perpetual fly in the ointment and minimize the value of the experiment. That's the way of science. Prediction in science is largely guessing and hoping. I'm afraid that doesn't enlighten you much, Doc, but that's how it is. It's a great idea, and I hope it works. But it appears to me a particularly tricky procedure. We'll have to go very delicately. We're trying a new sort of harness on the most violent animal known to mankind. We've got to be careful the harness doesn't slip and that the animal can't kick out in an unsuspected direction."

*

Three months passed. Three months of grace, though we did not know that, working happily together towards our own destruction.

I think, little as I really knew of the subtleties of Dot's feelings beneath the surface, I could include her in that "happily". She recovered the old straight-faced mischief peculiar to Lena and the inimitable way of doing exactly as she pleased without offending anyone, seemed just as impervious to surprise or discomfort, and was quite unpredictable.

The intimacy between us during that period of suffering had given place to a sort of wordless affection. We smiled understandingly at one another sometimes, but she never vouchsafed any more confidences and I never sought them. So long as she retained her health and cheerfulness—and she had so far recovered them as to be absolutely indistinguishable from Lena in appearance and manner—I judged she was also maintaining that emotional balance she had spoken of, and was content to leave well alone.

Hindered though we were by the wide-flung activities of Bill and Rob in the Dump, eternally tinkering with their machine and its ubiquitous outcroppings, we nevertheless maintained the standard and quantity of products of the Reproducer Company. The work never really lost its fascination for me. How Lena and Dot continued to regard it I don't know, but certainly they never displayed any slackening of effort or loss of interest.

But our labour was interrupted by the day when Rob and Bill planned to carry out their first full-scale experiment with the Absorber, as Bill had by now named it.

It was Rob who was insistent on clearing us out of the Dump.

"You'll all have to retire to a safe distance. We're going to light the blue paper," he said. "My idea of a safe distance is to the village at least. Go home, the lot of you."

"It's all quite unnecessary," said Bill. "My ideas never go wrong. You would be as safe holding my coat-tails as you would be in the deepest vault of the Bank of England. But you know Rob's methods of excessive caution where there's no need for it, and a glorious fools-rush-in act where there is need to go carefully—in rugger, for example."

"Yes, I know his methods, but they don't apply to me," said Dot. "You're my husband, and you instigated this dinky little machine, and I want to stay and watch it pop."

"My place is beside my husband, too," said Lena. "Let's have a 'stay put' pact, Dot."

Solemnly they shook hands.

"Irresistible force, immovable objects," I remarked, amused. "I should like to see how this turns out."

"The result is quite logical and inevitable, Doc," said Rob determinedly. "The force wins. Sad as it may be, it isn't mental or moral force but always brute physical force which settles little problems like this."

He made a swift dart and grab at Lena. Swift as he was, she was quicker and eluded him effortlessly, laughingly gaily. But he reached after her, and just managed to catch her by her flying hair. It pulled her up with a jerk which made me wince. But she was still laughing as he hauled her steadily back to him. Even then he had to fight to subdue her. He got her arms pinned to her sides, but I saw by his tense jaw muscles what an effort it cost him to hold that grip. As I had noticed before, Lena possessed a physical strength one would never have suspected from her slightness and grace. And she would fight back with every bit of that strength so long as she believed there was the slightest chance of success.

As they stood in deadlock, I could not but observe also the masculine strength of Rob. His mouth was set and tight-drawn, his strong brows frowning, his body rigid in his domination. You might have thought he had his mortal enemy by the throat. Lena's laughing eyes looked straight up into his serious face. And all of a sudden his expression relaxed and became tender. He bent his head to kiss her, but she met him half-way with a Latin eagerness. That kiss was so passionate that I should have felt an embarrassed onlooker, only somehow it seemed the most natural thing in the world, and I was no more aware of myself than if I were watching a close-up in a film.

I was full of a wonder that the quiet, reserved, typical Englishman I knew as Rob could possess such intensity of love. I had always realized that I had never met Rob as he really was under that top layer of socially correct behaviour. I should also have realized that all men share the same emotions. It's the different ways they find outlet, or are denied outlet, by that top stratum of habitual social behaviour that make our apparent differences, that make this man seem heartless and that man an indulgent fool, one man frigid and another amoral.

"They like being handled that way," commented Bill, a trifle wistfully. "I wish I could push Dot around like that."

"You're welcome to try, my love," said Dot with an ominous sweetness.

"Not today, thank you," said Bill. "I should like to be able to see out of my eyes to carry out this experiment."

"Are you going to be good?" asked Rob, still holding Lena tightly.

"I'm always good," she breathed.

"I mean, will you promise to go quietly?"

"Of course not. I'm bound by a pact."

"In that case, we'll make sure you're properly bound," said Rob, with a return of grimness. He wrenched Lena's hands behind her back, gripped both her thumbs together in his right hand, and with the other reached out for one of the many spare lengths of wire which lay around the lab. Then he began to tie her wrists tightly together.

"Below the belt, old man," said Lena, with an assumption of the public-school accent. And in her normal voice: "Isn't anyone going to rescue me? Are you all going to stand around and allow this sadism? Doc!"

"Neutral," I said.

"Bill, then."

"Sorry, lass, but you *are* getting in the way of the proceedings."

"Dot, you're letting me down. What about our pact?"

"It was a 'stay-put' pact," pointed out Dot.

"Betrayed by my own flesh and blood now! A curse on all your houses! Very well, then—alone!"

Rob had finished tying her wrists and was selecting another length of wire. Lena began straining to break the wire that pinioned her, using all her strength. I could see the wire cutting ever more deeply into her wrists.

"Stop it, you silly girl," I said, with some concern. "You'll cut your hands off."

"Serve Rob right if I did," said Lena. "He'd have to go without any more of my cooking."

"Not a bad idea," said Rob. "It might save my life."

As he spoke, he thrust Lena face downwards across an upturned packing-case, in which some of the new apparatus had arrived, and tried to secure her ankles. She did her best to prevent him, kicking her legs with vigour, but he got her hobbled at last.

"Phew!" he sighed, standing up and taking out his handkerchief to wipe his brow.

Lena was impotent to do anything but roll. So of course she rolled. Right off the packing-case, to land with a thud on her side on the floor.

In an instant Rob was kneeling beside her, his face alive with concern. He lifted her head.

"Darling, are you all right?"

For answer, she tried to bite his hand.

"It would take a steam-hammer to finish her," said Bill. He glanced uneasily at Dot, and muttered in a stage whisper to me, "Got a steam-hammer on you, Doc?"

Rob picked up the helpless Lena and flung her over his shoulder. As he strode out of the door, Lena managed, just before they disappeared, to raise her bobbing head, look back at us and remark mildly, "I wish everyone a very good day."

Through the window we watched Rob stowing her into the car.

"Nothing to it when you know how, is there?" said Bill.

"I thought she gave in too easily," remarked Dot casually.

Bill coughed, and I smiled. Rob returned.

"Would you like to join Lena in the car, Dot?" he asked politely. "I'll get the Doc to drive you both up to the house."

"Sorry," smiled Dot. "I'm staying here."

Rob looked at Bill inquiringly.

"Don't look at me," said Bill. "I know who'd get hog-tied if I started anything, and it wouldn't be Dot."

"Look here," said Rob. "You want us to carry out this trial today?"

"Nothing more," returned Bill.

"Then the girls must be well away from here, or I shall not permit the trial. I mean that."

"You have my permission to remove my wife in any way you see fit."

"Do you still refuse?" asked Rob, looking straight at Dot.

She met his gaze levelly, still smiling, and folded her arms.

"I'm sorry, this may be ridiculous, but it's necessary," said Rob, and seized hold of her. She struggled to escape, and, indeed, wrenched one hand free, and he was forced to encircle her completely with his arms, crushing her. And suddenly her smile faded, a queer expression came over her face, and she ceased to resist.

Rob almost snatched his hands away from her, and stepped back a pace.

"I—um—sorry. Did I hurt you?"

She lowered her head and shook it gently.

"No. It's quite all right. I'll go," she said very quietly.

She turned and walked slowly out to the car. Rob was left standing and staring oddly after her.

Bill did not know what to make of this.

He glanced at me, glanced at Dot's retreating back, looked at Rob, and turned to me again.

"Strange, giving in like that. What's that—a moral victory, Doc?"

"Blessed if I know," I said, though I was beginning to understand.

"I'll see if she's all right," muttered Bill, and went after her.

Rob looked at me and quickly averted his gaze again, pretending to turn his attention to the nearest part of the Absorber. Still appearing to have his mind on the machine, he said: "Drive them away from here, Doc. Better go to 'Hawthorns'—I'll 'phone you and give you the word when it's all right to come down here again."

"Right," I said. "Good luck."

"Thanks."

I went out to the car.

Dot was patiently assuring Bill that she was feeling as well as she ever had been.

"Stop worrying about nothing, boy. I was suddenly smitten with the merits of pacifism, that's all. Good-bye—and be careful, love."

She kissed him warmly on the lips. He became cheerful again, and returned the action.

"So long," he said. "You'll be hearing from us soon."

"You'll be hearing from me soon if you don't let me out of this," broke out Lena, still sitting bound and helpless. "All of you."

"Later," I said heartlessly, assisted Dot into the car, got in myself and drove off towards the village.

Presently, from behind me, a soft, concerned voice, which might have been either Lena's or Dot's: "You're trembling, darling. Is anything wrong?"

I looked round. Dot was trying to untie Lena and not, apparently, making much of a success of it, and Lena was watching her wonderingly. I stopped the car, and went to assist.

Dot was trembling, surely enough, and obviously trying not to cry. I unloosed Lena, and immediately she put her arm around her twin, who bowed her head on Lena's breast and began to cry almost silently.

Lena raised her eyes to me inquiringly.

"Rob put his arms around her. It seemed to upset her," I said gloomily, foreseeing a reopening of old wounds.

Lena made a little consoling noise, and held Dot the tighter.

"Of course it would," she said.

I gazed round rather helplessly, and was glad only that we had stopped in a deserted part of the lane. I did not want to parade in an open car before the public this act of love trouble, especially as I felt part and parcel of it myself.

But soon Dot, with Lena's help, regained control of herself.

"I'm sorry, Doc," she sniffed. "Drive on."

When we were in the sitting-room at "Hawthorns" Lena made Dot sit in one of the comfortable armchairs, while she herself began to pace up and down the room, frowning.

"We've got to work out some arrangement about this," she pronounced.

"There's no need," said Dot, recovered now. "I did that and it was working quite well. It was merely an accident that upset the balance today. When Rob embraced me, squeezed me—the feel of him, which had become only a memory to me—it was too much to withstand. I felt a fierce urge to respond, and then suddenly went as weak as water. That awful hopelessness swept over me again. It's a wonder I didn't throw myself beseechingly at him. If he could only understand, I thought. But I managed to turn and walk away."

"You were great, Dot," I said.

"She's great all right," said Lena. "And she doesn't deserve this. We *must* change this situation somehow."

I sighed.

"It's a blind alley, Lena," I said. "We've explored it thoroughly. Bill is the blank wall at the end of the alley."

"You mustn't talk like that, Doc," said Dot. "Bill is the reason of my existence, the cause of my existence. For what I do get out of life—and there are real pleasures, when I forget the heartache—I must thank him. No one, not even Rob, could be kinder or more loving than he. I can never let him down in any way. I should—kill myself first."

"And *you* mustn't talk like that," I reproved, with uneasy memories.

"What is this arrangement you spoke of, Dot?" asked Lena.

Dot rather haltingly explained, while Lena listened intently and sympathetically and at the end was silent in consideration.

Then she murmured: "There, but for the grace of God… You don't think, Dot, that time may shift this balance? That you might tend more and more towards one or the other?"

Dot answered: "I might learn to love Bill more than I do. I'm sure that with every day he means more to me. But I know that never in all my life will he mean anything like so much as Rob. I love that man with all my heart. My great fear is that one day he might suspect it."

"He already more than suspects it," said a voice—Rob's voice.

We turned sharply. Rob stood just inside the room, by the door. How long he had been there we didn't know. Certainly we had not heard him come in—in our absorption we hadn't even marked the arrival of a car.

He advanced to the centre of the room, while we watched him, dumb.

"It's all very awkward, isn't it?" he said. He thrust his hands deep into his trouser pockets, looking worried and depressed.

"A bit of an understatement," I said. "It's very nearly intolerable. How long have you known?"

"For certain, about an hour. When—well, you know what happened back there."

He nodded towards the window and the prospect of the distant Dump, small, sharp and clear in the bright morning sunlight.

"But I've feared it for a long time," he went on. "How the devil I overlooked such a possibility in the first place I can't understand. Later, in that period we made Bill wait to see if he were really sure of what he wanted, it occurred to me that it was the logical conclusion to things."

"Then, for heaven's sake, why didn't you tell us, or warn Bill at least?" I cried.

He made the slightest of shrugs.

"Principally because I had given my word to Bill to see it through. And, I suppose, because I hate backing out of a promise, I thought and thought upon it, and thought myself out of it, so to speak. I magnified irrational hopes and clung to them. I thought such an eventuality must have occurred to Bill and he had good reasons for ignoring it. I remembered what he said about Lena's twin living a different life from the moment of her creation and growing into quite a different person. I thought it likely that the new Lena could soon learn to do without me and appreciate more the very real qualities of Bill."

There was a faint sigh from Dot.

I recalled the times I had happened upon Rob and noted the signs of anxious preoccupation and wondered about them. Now I understood. I also understood his initial reserve with Dot, why he had kept her at arm's length and insisted on treating her as a new acquaintance: he was in fear of any embarrassing advances from her.

"Another thing," went on Rob, "was the hope that the experiment would fail. That Bill would not succeed in bringing life to the copy of Lena. The thing still seemed incredible to me. I trusted in some divine intervention. I see now I should have been the instrument of intervention, and I failed. I am the most to blame of anybody."

"I think we have all made that claim in turn," I said. "It's time we all accepted the blame and forgot it. What we have to do is try to square things up. I think Bill should be told and come in on this."

"No!" exclaimed Dot.

"No," echoed Rob. "I can't see that that would get any of us anywhere. It would only cause unnecessary unhappiness to Bill."

"Then," I said, "it's an impasse."

There fell a silence, in which each was busy with his or her thoughts.

The telephone rang. Rob answered it.

"Hullo… Oh yes… No, I'm having trouble finding the damned thing… No, I can't just now… Yes, of course it matters… All right, I'll be as quick as I can… 'Bye."

I looked at him interrogatively.

"Bill," he said briefly.

"Bill? You haven't explained why you came back like this. I thought—"

"Oh, things didn't go right. The moment the current started going through there was a backlash effect that wasn't in the programme. I didn't like it. Bill said it didn't matter a damn and wouldn't affect the main issue at all. That was just his careless way. But I like to know what I'm doing. I remembered that somewhere Fermi had described an effect similar to this, and I had made a note of it at the time. My note-books are here in the study, so I told Bill to hold everything while I borrowed his car and went to find that particular reference: we might get a bearing on how to eliminate the interference. But now he's fretting, and wants to know what's delaying me. Says he can see the car standing outside the house here, but where am I?"

"You'd better get the book and go back before he does something foolish," I said. "He's not the waiting sort."

"Yes…" He paused irresolutely, looking at Dot, still reclining rather listlessly in her chair, and then at his wife, leaning thoughtfully against the edge of the table—she had not said a word since his irruption. "But all this..." he said, trailing off.

"It seems there's nothing we can do about all this," I said, moving slowly over to the window and gazing unseeingly out. "Things will just have to go on as they are."

He made a husky noise in his throat that might have meant assent or protest or almost anything. Out of the corner of my eye I saw him go to Lena and kiss her lightly, then cross to Dot and kiss her still damp cheek, and then he vanished behind me, going towards the door.

At which instant it happened.

There was a flash of white light that obliterated everything visible. It was as if the sun had fallen suddenly to earth. It was so dazzlingly overbright that one had no sense at all of the direction of the source of it. It seemed to come at you all ways, and stab and pierce to the very vision centres of the brain. It had come and gone before I could shield my eyes from it, but the numbing effect of its transit still remained as actual as its presence had been. We cowered under a nerve-memory of intolerable effulgence, dazed, blinded, confused, fearful of the unexpected and unknown.

I had a fleeting impression of the window-frame, a bright square hole cut in solid darkness. Outside it hung a fantastic etching: a mushroom of white smoke, with, stuck lightly in its upper surface like a row of tin-tacks with only their points embedded, the line of giant oaks which had stood along the lane outside the Dump. Only now their roots were some three hundred feet above the earth which had nourished them.

And then the blast reached us. I went flying backwards to the noise of a smash like someone dropping a great crystal ball on an adamantine surface. Rushing to overtake that sound, so it seemed, came a clap of thunder so loud that I felt rather than heard it: it ground through me, shaking me to my bones. I turned in the air, landing sprawling on hands and knees by the farther wall in a hailstorm of hurtling, falling and bouncing objects.

I lay for a little while with my eyes tightly shut, trembling and gasping and trying to stabilize my reeling mind, and the thunder passed over me and went rolling into the distances, and presently passed from earshot.

There was an almost blissful silence, interrupted only by the occasional light thud of a laggard piece of plaster falling from the ceiling or the tinkle of another shred of glass dropping away from the shattered window.

I opened my eyes; but for an age, it seemed, I could not see anything. The deadly fear of blindness closed on my soul.

Then, to my infinite relief, the outlines of a wild disorder emerged from the darkness and spread and grew in my vision, like the forming of something in the receiver dome of the Reproducer. I still had to try to perceive between the shapes of floating black patches which the violent assault of the light had impressed upon my retinae, but now I could make out Rob lying by the door under a smother of broken ceiling plaster, with the carpet stuck fantastically up against the wall like a sagging tapestry, the occasional table smashed into firewood in the corner, and diamonds and daggers of broken glass glinting over everything.

My fear for myself changed to a fear for him, and then, memory returning, for Lena and Dot also. I sat up and gazed around, and as I did so colour returned to things: at first everything had appeared only in black and white to me.

I beheld Lena, or Dot, rising slowly to her feet, her dress torn, her whole person daubed with grey plaster dust. As she rose, she

automatically brushed some of it from her, and I saw by the
dress that it was Lena. Dot was sitting up with much the same
expression of returning apprehension that I must have been
wearing.

"Are you all right, Doc?" asked Lena, walking over and pausing beside me.

"Yes," I said, and she helped me to my feet.

I cast another glance at Dot, and saw that she was already on
hers. She assured me that she was unhurt.

The three of us went to Rob.

He groaned and stirred even as we bent over him. Blood ran
slowly from a gash somewhere under the black, disarranged hair.
He had been thrown headlong against the door.

The couch had managed to retain its four legs, though not
to remain upon them. We stood it up, and lifted Rob on to it.
Dot brought water, and Lena hunted out some rolls of bandage,
and I attended to the scalp wound. It was long but not deep. We
had none of us said a word as we worked, but done what was
necessary as quickly as we were able. He was conscious before
we had finished, but also silent.

Dot and I left him with Lena. I felt that what had happened
was too stunning to comment on until I had properly absorbed
and accepted it. I think we all felt that way.

I went to the window again. Beyond the village stood a wall,
still spreading slowly laterally, of white-brown smoke, hundreds
of feet high. Through rifts here and there one glimpsed little
segments of the countryside which lay on its farther side. There
was no sign of the Dump. The area of it lay well inside the
smoke wall. I doubted whether any trace of the place remained,
anyway.

And then the little pain which lay at the back of my mind, and which I had barred from my conscious thought because I was afraid of the growth attention would give it, overcame my defence and entered into realization with all its anguish.

I should never see Bill, my foster-son, again.

His vitality, his humour, his restless intelligence, his sensitivity, his boyish affection, his appreciation and knowledge, and all those endearing faults and quirks, were dissolved utterly away in that blank wall of smoke. Nothing of him remained even as substantive as that smoke. Where his bright, eager life had moved but a few minutes ago there was now—non-existence.

I thought of a fly swatted on a window-pane.

That impersonal fate had expunged him.

Yet he had in a way brought it on himself, perhaps as unconsciously as a bluebottle does not realize that its buzzing restlessness and interference with the *status quo* is suicidal. He had been impulsive beyond discretion, beyond sanity even. In his cocksureness and impatience he had taken too great a chance with what Rob had styled "the most violent animal known to mankind". And the harness had slipped.

What design, what purpose, in a young life of promise truncated so abruptly by accident? I wondered. Yet Bill himself had maintained that the very stuff of science was chance and accident, that all scientific experiments are taking chances, and that some of the greatest discoveries of science had been made by accident.

By "accident" he meant an effect not deliberately sought by the person involved. "An accident is not something that comes up and happens to us," I remembered him once saying. "It's a consequence we blunder into through ignorance of how to avoid it. But, after all, we're only human—not Omniscience itself."

He would not have complained at his own premature finish. He would have shrugged his shoulders, laughed and commented, "That's how it is."

A warm hand gently closed about mine. I looked and saw Dot standing at my side. There was sympathy in her eyes, and grief lay behind it.

"We've lost him, Doc," she whispered, and pressed my hand. I put my arm about her shoulders, a gesture of solace that was now becoming almost automatic in her presence, and together we stared out at the screen of smoke, each seeing the projections of their own mind upon its drifting surface.

"But I'm glad he went in ignorance and happiness," she went on presently. "It may not have lasted much longer."

That awakened me to an awareness of complications I had not considered under the initial impact of the loss of Bill. And I heard, almost as though it were a material actuality, the wheels of that devilish machine whirring faster and rising to a shriller note as a greater strain fell upon the remaining parts.

The metaphors in which we had pictured relationships had to be amended.

The blocking wall of the impasse was down. Now the road led on. Where?

Dot's balance between Rob and Bill was overset. Now Rob would wholly dominate her.

The geometrical absurdity of the four-sided triangle had changed into another absurdity: a triangle with three sides, two of which were one and the same. Or were they?

I gazed back over my shoulder at Lena and the recumbent Rob. Lena was adjusting cushions at her husband's back, and she paused a moment to kiss the lobe of the one ear that was not covered by his bandages. I felt Dot's hand twitch as she noted my regard and guessed my thoughts, and pity stole into my heart for every one of my companions in that room.

Pity and foreboding.

CHAPTER TEN

I WAS WALKING THE LANES ALONE AND THINKING OF LIFE AND of Bill.

For days now he had lived on in my mind. More exactly, he relived old scenes for me.

Sometimes he was a small boy asking my interpretation of Omar Khayyám, and thinking deeply, and then saying something that gave me to review my own assumptions about determinism. Again, he was in his teens and trying to get me to share his struggles with the Principle of Uncertainty.

And then he was at the time when he laid aside the last volume of *War and Peace,* and sighed, and said: "Yes, a truly great novel. Probably the greatest yet. But it could have been greater. It's a complete picture of how war came to the aristocracy of the Russia of the Tsars. But only to that aristocracy, the educated. How did it appear to the peasant, the serf, the conscripted soldier? How did it affect *their* lives, relationships, outlook? Tolstoy had an amazingly wide sympathy, but it didn't extend beyond his experience. He was a born aristocrat. He could not look through the eyes of the poor and humble. He had no experience to base that vision upon."

"He realized that lack," I said. "Later he tried to acquire the experience artificially."

"I know," said Bill. "But any way of life not shaped by necessity remains artificial. *War and Peace* is incomplete. It does not embrace all humanity."

"A rather tall order," I smiled.

"Shakespeare fulfilled it," said Bill seriously.

"Was Shakespeare a real philosopher? Did he achieve a con-clusion beyond *'As flies to wanton boys, are we to the gods, They kill us for their sport…'*? What do you think of Tolstoy's interminable arguments for determinism in that book?"

"Whoa, one at a time!" adjured Bill. "Shakespeare. He was near to it with Hamlet's *'There's a divinity that shapes our ends, Rough-hew them how we will…'* But I think he got it backwards. Something other than us rough-hews the general shapes of our lives. We our-selves impose pattern on them, as best we may. We are not wholly the prey of destiny. He was nearer to it, I think, with that line of Cassius's: *'Men at some time are masters of their fate.'*"

"*Fates,*" I corrected. "How do you expect me to take your judgments seriously if you can't even bother to quote properly?"

"The sentiment is right," he rejoined. "Damn unimpor-tant details. Intuition's the thing—to be roughly right. All the sages of all the ages have striven by reason to disprove either Determinism in favour of Free Will, or *vice versa*. And still neither is disproved. Intuition tells me, therefore, that there is truth in both, both exist, else they could not have withstood the cen-turies of assault."

"Both?"

"I don't want to bring the physicists—Bohr, Planck, Schrödinger, Eddington and all those—into this. Let's stick to the analogies of literature. Tolstoy's view of a predetermined life is a man wedged helplessly in a crowd. Because every separate impulse of every person in the crowd totals into a resultant force which pushes him in a certain direction, this man imagines he is moving in that direction of his own free will."

"Like Napoleon invading Russia," I said.

"Yes. But Tolstoy makes every man a negative. A mere recipient and conveyor of impulse, a middle-man. But somebody starts that chain of impulse, and it is a positive action; somebody who knows where he wants to go. I believe that all people to greater and lesser degrees possess that positive power to *start* where they want to go. But only single-mindedness and continuity of purpose will get a man anywhere near the goal he has fixed his eyes upon. He has to push constantly, seize every advantage of a gap, perhaps tack around obstinately immovable people. Perhaps he will be swept far off course by surges of the crowd; but if he never gives up, the chances are for his getting there eventually. I say 'chances' deliberately, for he is up against chance panics or enthusiasms of the crowd that he could not have foreseen. Accidents, too—he may step in ignorance in a slippery place, and fall and be trampled, with his ambition, beneath the crowd's feet."

"Such a view gives a meaning to human life, at any rate," I said. "An end, a purpose, and the stimulation of a fight. I wish I thought it more than a theory."

"I know it's so," he said. "Only, of course, I can't communicate that knowing. In the ultimate analysis everything can be resolved into the opposing forces of positive and negative. Resistance and non-resistance. Plan and *laissez-faire*. Ambition and apathy. Or, if you wish, Free Will and Determinism."

And so I rambled on, going over these memory conversations with Bill.

It was the best I could do towards an actual consultation with him. Never before had I so desired the active help of his intelligence. Always when I had been in a quandary I had turned to him. A discussion with him seemed to light up a whole situation and show a path to take which had been hidden in darkness before.

That apprehension of being part of a machine out of control and inevitably bent for disaster had made me in my very helplessness seek the ghost of Bill.

How could we fight this destiny? What positive action could we take?

Must I walk in a squirrel's cage until the next predetermined event came at its place in time?

I turned a high-hedged corner of the lane and almost walked into Lena.

"Why don't you sound your horn on bends?" she asked.

I made apologetic noises, and inquired where she was going.

"Oh, nowhere in particular. Just taking my thoughts for an airing, as Bill used to say."

It seemed that I was not to escape from the memory of Bill. Yet to exchange thoughts with Lena might be more profitable than to pursue any longer the full circle of my own introspection.

"Will it interfere if I accompany you?" I asked.

"But you've just come from that direction."

"It makes no odds. I've been doing nothing but getting back to my starting-point for some time now."

She smiled sympathetically, but made no inquiry. We began to walk slowly back along the lane together.

"Where's Dot?" I asked presently. Since the tragedy, Lena and Dot had been practically inseparable. The Dump being destroyed, Dot was homeless, and Lena had insisted that she stay with her and Rob at "Hawthorns". I had not until now seen them apart. They even, I learned, went swimming together in the river early every morning, continuing Lena's old custom. Just how Rob came into this new relationship was something I could only wonder about. But in case my own presence should be an added embarrassment,

I had kept away from "Hawthorns" lately as far as politeness permitted.

"Dot?" echoed Lena absently. "Oh, she's paying further consolatory visits to the Ferguson and Matt families, trying to give any assistance she can. She's pretty cut up about it. Insisted on going alone."

When Bill went, he did not go alone. He took with him two agricultural labourers working in a neighbouring field, named Ferguson and Matt. It was extraordinary, in view of the violence of the eruption, that the casualty list was not much longer than that. Rob had assured me that it would have been had not the Absorber muffled the greater part of the disintegrating effect. Had the explosion been entirely naked, there would have been no living thing left within a radius of miles.

As the wife of the man responsible for those two innocent deaths, Dot had gone directly to the men's relatives and dependants and involved herself in their welfare and comfort. From all accounts, she was as much distressed about the unfortunate men's decease as were the two widows.

"I see," I said, and then dared to voice my thoughts. "You were rather taking the bull by the horns, weren't you, Lena, to have her come and live with you and Rob? I mean, it's asking for trouble. You can't expect her…"

I trailed away to silence under the sudden direct and almost accusatory stare she gave me with eyes like grey granite and glinting like that stone. The hardness passed almost immediately, but the grip she took of my wrist, as she halted me, was intense.

We had stopped by a stile set in the hedge, and a lately trodden footpath led from it across the brown waves of the ploughed field behind that hedge.

She half pulled and half impelled me to the stile.

"Let us sit down and get a few things clear," she said.

We sat, backs to the field.

"As you were about to say," she began, "I can't expect Dot to sit and watch Rob's and my married life at close quarters and purr like the cat on the hearthrug. I know what I should feel like in her place. On the other hand, if I let her out of my sight, if she has to live apart and alone and hardly ever see Rob at all, I also know what I should feel like in her place. And I would do it, too, just as she would."

"You mean…" I hesitated at the word I had come to hate.

She nodded.

"Suicide," she said bluntly. "We had the same grandmother, you know."

"I was afraid of that," I said.

"I don't think there's an immediate danger of it," she went on. "I've given her hope to go on living for a while yet."

"How?" I inquired eagerly.

"I told her that in time another Reproducer could be built. And then we could solve the whole problem in a way we couldn't while Bill was alive."

She paused.

"Go on," I said urgently.

"I said Rob must have a duplicate made of himself for her."

"Good God!"

My mind grappled with this further twist to things. It seemed at first fantastic—almost comically so, the development of an idea into the absurd. A fairy-story gone mad. But I could not see that it was impossible. Indeed, it fitted flawlessly like the last piece of a jigsaw puzzle, a perfect rounding off of the whole business. And everyone should be satisfied. An immense relief flooded over me.

"You wonderful girl!" I said warmly. "Why couldn't I have thought of that? Here have I been racking my brains…"

I faded again as I saw no response of enthusiasm in her eyes, only a strange sadness.

"A red herring, Doc," she said. "No more. Just a way of gaining time."

"Why?" I exploded. "What on earth's wrong? Do you mean Rob would refuse to be a party to any more sacrilege, as he calls it? Does he think all this trouble is punishment by a jealous God for the copying of you? It's ridiculous. Why, Dot's very life depends—"

"It isn't that, Doc. I don't say that for those reasons he doesn't feel very keen on building another Reproducer. But the fact is, his feelings quite apart, he can't."

"Can't?"

"There can't be another Reproducer. I tackled him about it. He said there was a lot about the machine and its function he didn't understand—in fact, was quite incapable of understanding. It was almost wholly a product of Bill's incomparable mind. The principle lay in realms beyond Rob's complete comprehension. He said that in effect he played little but the mechanic to Bill's designer. Even so, the most vital part of the machine was built and adjusted by Bill alone, and he alone knew what he was doing. Rob said he would scarcely know where to begin if he had to design another machine. He said he knew definitely he never could in a thousand years."

My heart sank.

"Isn't there anyone else capable of it?" I asked, not very hopefully.

"Rob didn't seem to think so. He said the discovery of the principle was one of Bill's 'accidents of science'. It was unlikely to be repeated, even for a deliberate seeker.

"Another thing," she went on. "Even if another Reproducer were possible, we still don't know the secret of how Bill animated those copies from life."

"I know something of that," I said. "But not all. Not enough to be successful, I'm afraid."

"You see how hopeless it is, then."

"And what about when Dot also sees it?"

She made no answer.

"Why give her false hope?" I persisted. "To gain time for what?"

"For the leopard to change his spots. For a born monogamist to become an unnatural polygamist. I mean, for Rob to accept us both on equal terms."

I whistled softly.

"That would be a strain on the nature of any normal man," I said. "But for Rob, of all people…!"

"I know. He finds it impossible."

"You've had it out with him?"

"Yes."

And then she recounted the scene with him in their bedroom on the night following that day of disaster, the first night of Dot's stay with them. I narrate it as closely as I can remember it.

Rob, in his dressing-gown, was sitting in the basket chair by the fire when she went in. She had just seen Dot to her lone bedroom.

She walked slowly across to him, and sat herself on the rug at his feet, also facing the fire. He put an arm about her, drew her to him, and pressed his cheek against her ear. Together they gazed into the unresting flames.

Presently she asked, in her straightforward manner, "What do you propose to do about Dot, Rob?"

A pause.

"What *can* I do?" he said.

"You can—you must—accept both of us. It's the only solution. You mustn't look on us as rivals. I hope we shall never be that. I think we'll be able to keep clear of jealousy. One can never be certain of one's future feelings, of course, but I don't think you need worry about that. We'll not get in each other's way. After all, we're one and the same person—there's no getting away from it."

"But I don't look upon you as one and the same person!" exclaimed Rob. "I don't know how far it's an illusion, but to me Dot seems quite a different person. It's *you* I love. It's you I married. It was you who came to Cornwall with me—Dot didn't—she never even existed then. It's we two who have lived together in this house, in this room. I feel Dot is making claims on me that—well…"

"Dot has made no claims," she said. "I'm making them for her. Rob, don't you understand that all those experiences—on our honeymoon, in this house, in this room—are as real to Dot as they are to me? They exist only as memories now, even to us—*and Dot has those memories.* To her it must seem that she lived that life and was suddenly cut out of it and forced to go and live with Bill. And who is responsible for that cutting out? We are. You and I. We never stopped to think. We owe her something, you and I. The only way to square things is for the three of us to share our lives. Unstintedly."

"But, Lena—" He stopped, struggling with a viewpoint he did not know how to put to her.

She divined something of the causes of his mental distress. Quite aside from his own personal scruples in the matter, how could he carry on such a life in the face of his parents and friends?

They knew nothing of the complicated origins of Dot. To them she was Lena's sister—and Bill's widow.

He would feel an out-and-out-cad. Yet he would be helpless to explain the truth to anyone, even if they were likely to believe him. To do so would reveal one of the last things he wished to be common knowledge: that the Reproducer had the power to create life—indeed, had done so—and that he had taken a hand in this sacrilegious procedure.

All around he was hemmed in by social disapproval of any course of action he took, and he was of his nature supersensitive about breaking the social code.

But was ever a man so caught in a snare of rights and wrongs?

By all his standards of decency it was wrong to shut Dot out of his life. Yet by the same standards it was wrong to receive her into it.

"Darling," she said, "I know how hard it is for you. But no one need know how we live here. 'Hawthorns' is our castle. There's nothing strange in my sister continuing to live with us—my bereaved twin sister, above all. Even the servants needn't suspect anything. Dot and I are alike enough to change identities whenever we wish. Or, if you prefer it, we can give up the house and go and live abroad in seclusion."

She felt the damp of sweat on his face.

"Being surreptitious about it won't change the nature of it," he muttered. "I—I can't live with two women. I just can't. It wouldn't work. I want only you. I couldn't avoid distinctions. I couldn't satisfy Dot. I can't divide my love. Monogamy is in my very blood. I can't conceive of any other way of living. It's no good. None of us would be happy."

"Very well, darling. But we can't go on living like this, either. I couldn't enjoy our love knowing that Dot was suffering—outside. Just as she is outside now, at this moment. Can you imagine her thoughts as she lies alone in that room now, Rob? I tell you she must not be left alone overlong with those thoughts, or the consequence is inevitable. I'm afraid we'll have to separate, Rob. Dot and I will go away together and cease being such a worry to you."

"No, no!" he cried. "Please, Lena. I couldn't go on without you."

He was in a state of frightful unhappiness.

Lena slipped her arms around him and kissed him over and over again. He held on to her, and she could feel him trembling in his fear and misery. The rare tears came to her eyes.

"Dearest, don't think it wouldn't be hell for us, too, not to have you. We—I love you with all my heart and always shall."

"Don't leave me," he pleaded. "Give me time—give me time, and perhaps—"

She stroked his hair gently.

"All right, darling. We'll stay. But after tonight I sleep with Dot in her room. I can't leave her alone in it another night."

He made no answer at first. He just sat looking in utter depression into the fire.

"All right," he got out at last, in an uncertain undertone.

And then he tightened his arms about her, almost as though it were their last embrace.

They clung together awhile, and presently went to bed.

Next day Lena moved into Dot's room. Dot apostrophized her, tried to bar her.

"There's no sense in our both being miserable," she pointed out. "It doesn't help me, and it certainly doesn't help you or Rob."

"It's only for a while," Lena told her. "And it may turn out better for all of us. If Rob is left alone, I think he might come to a change of opinion. It can only come in solitude. If I stay with him, he'll never change."

*

"You were gambling on his 'Give me time, and perhaps…'?" I asked.

"I was," said Lena. "But I saw Dot had about as much real faith in that as I had—which was very little indeed. So I tried to give her some more solid-seeming hope with the idea of another Reproducer—and another Rob. She clung to that. I'll tell her anything to keep her from thinking herself superfluous and taking the obvious course. Once, she had to do all the lying and deceiving, to Bill. Now it's my turn, to her. I hate it, but… Oh, Rob *must* break out of it! I'm hanging on foolishly to that hope, and yet I know it's as baseless as that I gave Dot."

"One of the most damnable parts of this whole set-up is how you are forced to hurt one another although you would give worlds not to," I said. "Rob hurts Dot, but doesn't want to. You hurt Rob, but don't want to. You are forced to give false hope to Dot, which will hurt her horribly when she finds out the truth."

"Yes," she said. "Life only appears to give you a choice, doesn't it?"

An echo of my musings on that subject.

"We have to keep trying to get what we want," I said, with a sudden resolve. "I'm going to have a go at Rob myself, and see if I can't get him to see sense."

"You think it's sense?"

"The only convention I'm a stickler for is the Christian one of loving thy neighbour as thyself—Bill once said it was the difference between religion and Christianity. Rob has missed understanding that, somehow."

"Thanks, Doc. I'll take some hope from you."

"Don't count on it. The trouble isn't that Rob is unreasonable: it's that he's *too* reasonable. He might argue my beliefs away."

I was glad to see that she smiled.

"I'll have to be getting back," she said, slipping from the bar of the stile. "Are you going my way?"

"No, it's a bit too early for dinner. I'll hang on a bit and see the sunset."

"Good-bye, then," she said.

"'Bye."

I watched her until she had vanished round the distant curve of the lane, and then fell to my thoughts again. They centred around Rob. I recalled Bill's analysis of him: the analogy of the 'Long-heads', the illustration of the way his outlook had been conditioned almost from the cradle.

It was a Jesuit priest who said, "Let me have a boy until he is seven, and he is mine for ever."

Could any argument persuade Rob to disobey his conscience, which he thought was the still, small voice of the Divine, and which, according to Bill, was but an unconscious memory of the current social code drummed into his mind in childhood?

It was not likely. The Jesuit knew his psychology. The really long-standing unconscious bias is almost always too deep-rooted to be overthrown by the fresh winds of reason. It is the great fault in the design of the instrument known as the human mind. The unconscious bias of nationalism alone might well bring mankind to self-destruction, one of Nature's failures.

Here I wandered right off the point and into profundities about the inherent stupidity of man. Two or three people had passed me as I sat there, and I had not even taken note of whom they were, returning their salutations mechanically. But now one of them had stopped by me and insisted on being noticed.

She didn't have to insist very strongly. Almost any man, how-ever absent-minded, would have his attention caught when a pair of almost lyrically shaped feminine ankles appear and stop in the centre of his downcast vision. My gaze ran up a figure proportionately as shapely as the ankles, and met the inquiring eyes of Dot.

"Turn again, Dick Whittington," she said. "Where's the cat?"

"About two feet away and standing on two feet and very nice ankles," I said.

"Insults, compliments, I take 'em as they come," she said. "Actually, the verb 'to insult' is meaningless. One can't be insulted: one can only choose to feel insulted. It's psychology really. Or something."

"I'm getting a little tired of psychology," I said. "You have to think such a lot. And it never seems to work out in the end according to the rules, anyway."

She took the place beside me lately occupied by Lena.

"I can see you've been thinking, Doc—you've got that worried look. Now, what's the trouble?"

It occurred to me that I had to be careful what I said. There were things of which she mustn't be told. Yet.

I shifted the onus of discussion.

"Nothing that you could do anything about, Dot," I said. "How are Mrs. Ferguson and Mrs. Matt?"

That sobered her.

"Mrs. Ferguson was out. I'm calling back later this evening," she said. "Mrs. Matt is bearing up pretty well. They're both over the shock of it. The sense of their loss is really setting in now. It's a damned shame. I feel so helpless. Money just doesn't seem to count as recompense, though I've forced it on them. I don't think they blame me. They sympathize and accept me as a widow in fellowship with them. But I feel that they blame Bill, not as a person, but as one of those crazy scientists who wouldn't care if they blew

up the world so long as it proved something or other. Yet I know
Bill would have smashed the thing first if he had thought there was
any real risk of causing people injury. He was just over-confident.
Oh, Doc, why do people have to hurt others like this, when it's the
last thing they'd choose to do?"

"You're asking me!" I said, rather bitterly. "I've asked myself it
so often that I can tell you straight away the answer I always get—'I
don't know.' Circumstances always seem to be forcing people to
hurt one another against their wills. Sometimes I think we're all
caught up in a mad machine."

I described to her that waking dream I had of our little circle
as being maltreated parts of some robot run amok, and how each
subsequent breakdown led to conditions of further intolerable
stress and another inevitable breakdown, and so on, until in the
end... I did not describe the end: I did not know the end.

"A pretty fancy," she commented. "Well, Doc, one never knows.
My faith is that there's a way out of this if one can only stick it
long enough. The next turn of the wheel may put us all straight."

She looked as though she were about to enlarge upon this, but
apparently thought better of it. I was expecting an exposition of
the idea of creating a copy of Rob for her, and dreading the false
surprise and enthusiasm I should have to display. I didn't trust
myself as an actor, especially before an audience so perceptive and
intelligent as Dot.

She stood down from the stile and laid a hand on my shoulder.

"Don't let it worry you, Doc. I give you my word, there'll be
another turn to events, and it will all straighten out."

"I hope you're right," I said, and knew she was not.

"What a beautiful sunset!" she exclaimed, gazing at the sky
behind me. I looked back over my shoulder.

From the zenith sweeping down with increasing brightness to the fierce red fire on the horizon was a study in chromatics. The clouds had lost any aspect of separate existence: they had become the transcendent brushmarks of a master painter, a greater Turner, elements of gold, coral pink, arterial crimson, made with faultless taste to merge into the whole colour scheme of a hundred shades.

But it was a painting that lived, moved, changed. Even as I watched, the last visible portion of the centre and source of this glory modestly sank from beneath the flux of light, and disappeared with a final unexpected touch of pale green fire, a transient flicker like summer lightning.

With this departure came a change of mood. The scene so like the panorama of hell in Berlioz' *Damnation of Faust* gave place to the ethereal. The angry flush faded from many patches and mauves and greys infiltrated and spread over them. And, all at once, immensely long beams of a misty whiteness smote radially up and out from the hidden sun, lancing through and through the clouds and restoring their third dimension with a startlingly stereoscopic effect. Thus revealed, the clouds became solid pieces, bars and twists of metal, some grey and red, like a poker in the hot coals, others shining strips of silver or of the bright straw colour of steel at the tempering point, and others again were just lumps of effulgence, passing white heat. Isolated flecks and flakes of gleaming gold were set, mounted and fixed in an unknown constellation.

"It's poetry," I said. "'*Brightness falls from the air…*'"

"'*The incomparable pomp of eve…*','" said Dot.

"'*The clouds that gather round the setting sun…*' I think that's the greatest of them all," I said.

"Does that give you intimations of immortality, Doc?" asked Dot, nodding towards the dying splendour with its crude foreground of ploughed earth.

I mused a while.

"At some moments like these I do get uplifted and enraptured, in a fine vein of mysticism. I can get roughly the same effect from a bottle of whisky, too. Is there any great distinction between the two forms of intoxication? Is it not just the imagination on the loose?"

"I wouldn't know," she answered. "What is imagination, anyway? Why disparage it with that 'just'? Imagination is the parent of reality. All existing inventions existed first in imagination. The trick is to bring them from the world of the unreal into actuality. The secret is to have the faith to make the positive effort."

I got down heavily from the stile, and by an unspoken understanding we began to walk side by side up the lane.

"Imponderables," I said presently. "Argue as you like, you come round eventually to the conclusion that you can't know anything. Bill backed his intuition. In the end it let him down. And where is Bill now?"

"Gone for ever, you think?"

I shrugged.

"I look at things from the medical viewpoint, of course. That abstract one calls 'personality' is a manifestation of our physical body. A poor liver, and you have a grouchy nature. A malformation of the skull, and you think and talk crazily. Over-active sexual glands, and you can't leave women alone. Bill had a hyper-thyroid gland. It gave him his drive, restlessness, impatience. That gland was blown into a thousand pieces. Obviously it doesn't function now. How can Bill function now, in any world, without it? Has he got, instead, a 'perfect' gland? Then he won't be impatient and restless. He won't be Bill. He'll have lost his personality. Can you imagine a patient, serene Bill?"

She shook her head, smiling.

"All the same, I think you're being unduly magisterial, Doc. For all you know, you might be talking Irish. On what grounds do you judge where to plant cause and effect? Supposing the truth is that a restless nature causes the hyper-thyroid gland, that an obsession with women overstimulates the sexual glands? That the personality causes the physical characteristics, and might cause them again— somewhere? As a doctor, you should know the indisputable fact that the mind—the imagination—can and does create bodily changes, symptoms, abnormalities."

"I don't know whether you're pulling a Shaw on me or talking Christian Science," I said. "It makes no odds. We can't solve or prove the question of survival. I merely tell you what I believe. What do *you* believe?"

"I haven't any beliefs about the future," she said. "Because I rarely think of it. I'm a creature of the present."

As she was speaking, she was looking past me at the western sky, and her eyes were clouded with unuttered thoughts.

I looked, too. All the life had drained away from that lately vivid scene. It was black and grey, like a burnt-out log fire. The real horizon had lost itself in layers of illusory mountain ranges of dark clouds, the forbidding frontiers of a strange, chill, unknown land revealing itself only transiently among the mists at the close of day, before the blackness of night descended over real and unreal alike.

We did not speak much after that, and parted with common-places at the "Pheasant", where I went in for dinner, and she con-tinued her lone walk back to "Hawthorns".

CHAPTER ELEVEN

IT WAS ABOUT EIGHT O'CLOCK THAT EVENING THAT I DECIDED, as Lena had before me, to take the bull by the horns and go and see Rob without further delay.

My inclination towards procrastination sought me to leave it, as I had planned, till the morning. I argued that in the present state of things at "Hawthorns" Rob would be in no mood to entertain visitors. Perhaps it were better if I left him to thrash out his problem alone.

But I had promised Lena I would try to influence him, and a sense of urgency began to nag me more and more. It might have been an after-effect of that rather sombre talk with Dot, but thoughts of death haunted me. A horrible fey feeling that it lay somewhere near to us kept chilling my soul, and I felt I had to fight somehow to stay its hand or I should get no sleep that night. And tomorrow might be too late.

So I climbed through the darkness to "Hawthorns".

The maid let me in with, I thought, a somewhat worried expression. She said nothing, but I understood the expression when I saw Rob.

He was lounging in an armchair with his feet resting on a pouffe. A tray of bottles, a siphon, and some glasses reposed on the table at his elbow. His pipe lay amid them, cold, black and abandoned. A cigarette canted up from his wry lips. A tumbler half full of amber liquid stood on the arm of his chair. His face was flushed. His eyes had the fixed bright gaze of the alcoholic at zenith. With difficulty he focused them on me.

"Come right in, Doc, and have a drink. I'm getting morbid, drinking alone." His voice was unnaturally thick.

I shut the door carefully behind me, pulled up a chair opposite him, poured a straight Scotch, and sat and regarded him.

"Don't look at me like that, Doc. I don't do this sort of thing often. I'm entitled to one wet night a year, surely?"

There was almost a question in the statement.

"It's all right, Rob," I said. "It's not for me to sit in judgment. Sometimes I feel I'm being driven to drink myself."

"And what have *you* got to worry about?"

"You," I said, "for one thing. Lena and Dot for two more."

"Listen, Doc, there's nothing you can do. It doesn't concern you. It's all up to me. You understand?—*me!*"

There was an unmistakable tone of hysteria in this.

"Well, I wouldn't say it wasn't," I said. "As I see it, you are the pivot on which everything turns."

"And you, like the girls, think I won't play my part?"

"That's what I really called to find out."

"When you do, let me know, will you?" he said, almost carelessly. His gaze slid from me and fell upon the tumbler on his chairarm. Deliberately he reached for it, and as deliberately drained it. He poured himself another glassful, full to the brim. He sipped a little off the surface.

"It isn't 'won't', Doc," he said, setting the tumbler down again. "It's 'can't'. I can't... play that sort of part."

"There's one thing that overrides both your and my idea of morals, Rob," I said. "That's a matter of life and death. And that is what I believe this to be."

"There's no life about it," he said. "No life at all. You can't call that sort of existence life. God, it would be the death of love, the extinction of all intimacy between Lena and me, the end of everything that made life worth living! For all of us."

"I think you're taking this all much too seriously."

"You think it's not serious? That I ought to give a gay, light laugh, and change my whole nature with a wave of the wand, and become a sort of flagrant Casanova and be damned to everybody and everything—my parents, my friends, my memory of my best friend, poor old Bill? Not to be content with my own wife alone, but seduce his widow and think nothing of it? You think I *can* do that?"

"If you were big enough."

"Big?" he repeated incredulously. "Big? You have a strange idea of sizes, Doc. I can think of nothing smaller and meaner than that."

I sighed and sipped my whisky. He took a gulp of his.

"Where are the girls?" I said quietly.

"Oh, Dot's calling back at Mrs. Ferguson's—she was out, I believe. She's taking things seriously if you like. She's taken up the burden of unhappiness of those two women—can't do enough for them. She doesn't think of herself enough. As for Lena, she went up to her room. I don't see much of her now, you know. She's almost always with Dot. It's as though we've quarrelled, but we haven't really: she's just leaving me to myself. She, too, thinks it all depends on me and I've got to undergo a sea-change. Does no one understand me?"

"One person did," I said.

"Who?"

"Bill."

He finished his glass.

"I'd give a million pounds to have him back with us now, if only for an hour," he said, resting his head on his hand and staring at nothing. "He could get to the heart of things."

"Well, I'm trying to be his mouthpiece. He would say what I am saying. And I'll tell you what he said about you one evening when *he* was drunk."

I repeated Bill's analysis of Rob; the root of the fear of the opinion of the community; the unthinking acceptance of the public-school conventional beliefs; the confusion of "the decent thing" and indecency; the kind of religion pumped purposefully into his child-mind, overlaid now with strata of experience and reflection, but still buried there in the subconscious, still influencing him as "feeling". And the rest of it.

He struggled to comprehend it through the whisky-induced muzziness of his thinking centres.

"No, no," he protested at last. "I know my own mind. It isn't that simple. Even Bill can't explain my feelings away like that. A man must have standards! Mine might be those of my parents and my school, but my reason backs them. It's civilization. Civilized society is built on that mutual faith and trust and adherence to the law. If you fail to play your part, you're letting everyone down. If everyone made their own rules, the world would soon collapse in a chaos of lust and greed and spite. I know I'm right, I tell you!"

I stood up.

"Rob," I said, "you would make a good soldier. Perhaps that's what your training is designed to do for England, anyway. The playing-fields of Eton, and all that. The men you officered would call you 'regimental'. Probably you would never quite understand what they meant by that. I would describe it as a sense of duty exaggerated almost to the neurotic stage. I suppose you think that attitude would be highly logical and efficient. But you would get closer to the men, and get more out of them in both work and respect, if you showed one or two little human failings, like tolerance—if, in fact, now and then you could turn a blind eye to your idea of duty."

I showed my own attribute of tolerance by not giving him a chance to reply. I turned about and marched out of the room.

I was angry through the vain effort of arguing with the blind who will not see. Especially as I was fretting with the urgency of getting my convictions through to him.

It never occurred to me to reflect that I was as self-righteous as he was, and that I must appear just as obtuse to him. If one sane man and one lunatic are the only inhabitants of a world, then who sets the standards of civilized behaviour? One man's notion of them is as good as the other's.

In the hall I sought my hat, and then hesitated. It struck me that I had accomplished nothing at all through my mission. I was being weak, and accepting defeat too easily. Yet—what could I say or do?

I teetered indecisively, and then climbed slowly up the stairs. There was one little thing I felt I ought to do.

I paused outside the door of the room Lena and Dot were now sharing. No sound. Possibly Lena was asleep already? I pushed the door open gently.

The electric light was on, throwing unshaded beams out through the wide-open windows into the cold dark night. Lena, in a brown dressing-gown, sat at a small desk, writing busily. She looked up, saw me, then deliberately blotted the sheet of paper she was writing on and left the blotting-paper on it, covering it.

"Good evening, Doc," she said. "What now?"

"That, indeed, is the question," I said. "What now?"

"Oh, I see, it's a riddle," she said, pretending to look bright. "Why is a raven like a writing-desk?"

"Very apposite, Alice," I said. "Riddles without answers. Dot, for instance."

"What about her?"

"I met her this afternoon, in the lane, after you had gone. I didn't like the tone of the conversation at all. Not so much what she said, as her manner. Rather... spiritual. I'm afraid she's thinking of doing something noble, like stepping out of this affair, and leaving a clear field for Rob and you."

"No doubt she has considered that. It looks a pretty obvious solution to me."

"It would," I said bitterly. "This damned suicide complex of yours, Lena! Can't you see—it's wrong? One must continue to fight. It's heartless, too—you forget how you hurt those who are left behind, who love and miss you."

"I don't," she said. "Anyway, we're talking about Dot. Who can she leave behind who loves her and would miss her? Rob doesn't love her. And Bill has gone before her. One must continue to fight, yes—while there's hope. But you and I know that as things are she hasn't a hope in the world."

"This doesn't sound like you, Lena. It appears almost as if you wish her to go."

"It's my nature to face the facts, Doc."

"Lena—sometimes you're inhuman!"

I paced up and down the rug by the fireplace, running my fingers through my hair, at my wits' end, and she watched me with a Gioconda smile.

Abruptly, a little gust of chill wind spurted in through the wide windows, caught up the papers on her desk and spun them in my direction. Some fell at my feet. I bent to recover them, and in the act I glanced up and found that in a swift, smooth movement she had come to be standing over me, her hand extended to take them from me. I thought such eagerness odd, and could not forbear to glance at the topmost sheet in my hand. What I glimpsed made me retain the sheets tighter. I put them behind my back, out of her reach.

"Back to your seat, Lena," I ordered.

"You're not intended to read it yet. Give it me."

"When I've read it and not before," I said firmly, and she saw my mind was made up, shrugged, then sat on the edge of the bed and lit a cigarette.

"Much good may it do you," she murmured.

Keeping one wary eye on her, I read this letter addressed to *"Dear Doc"*.

> *I don't really know why I should bother to write this at all. It were better, no doubt, if no one ever knew the truth. But you ever had a suspicious nature, Doc, and I don't think you would be wholly taken in by my accidental demise. Of all people, you know the most about me, and my grandma, and our funny little ways. So to forestall any investigations of yours which might make public the fact that I don't want known—least of all to Rob—I want to tell you the good reasons why I have chosen this way, and why you must do your best to influence the coroner that it was "Accidental Death" and not that nasty word beginning with "s" and ending with "e" which you use much too freely.*

Here I paused and glowered at the girl on the bed, who now lay comfortably on her back, trying to blow smoke rings into the air above her.

I read on.

It is plain that if I don't do this thing now, Dot will beat me to it. I have tried to delay her by raising false hopes, but they cannot fool her much longer. She already feels that the reason for her existence died with Bill, and she has no right to exist any longer as the fly in the ointment. She feels she is an unwanted intruder. I know what I'd do if I were in her shoes, therefore it follows that I know what she'll do—the moment she knows there's no hope.

I ask you, has she had a square deal in this life? Every moment of her existence has been anguish: that unsatisfied, gnawing longing for Rob. Who was responsible for bringing her into this? I was, as much as anyone. Allowing my duplicate to be born, not realizing nor caring how she must live and endure a life quite apart from me. I was all right—I had lived with, and been loved by, Rob. I had had my fun, my halcyon days. She'd had none, none at all. Made to suffer the more by being forced to act love to another man—you may talk about rubbing salt in the wound!

I feel responsible for my alter ego. She's due her fun, and I'm going to see she gets it.

I know Rob will miss me at first. I hate terribly to have to hurt him. But it will pass. He will grow to see that I am not dead, that I live on in Dot. You must see that he understands that, Doc. Get them together all you can, and make him see. The need for me will pass to her, I am sure.

You, too, must look upon her as me, Doc. Sometimes, perhaps, in lonely places you may remember she who was Lena, and feel pity. You'll be wasting your pity, Doc. I treasure what

I've had, and feel grateful. Regrets are nonsense. Although sometimes I think it might have been better for all concerned if you hadn't been so handy with a stomach-pump on a certain occasion. But you can leave your pump behind this time, my dear Doctor, for there'll be no coming back

It ended where I had interrupted the writing of it.

I found my eyes were unduly moist, and turned away from Lena, who was still idly smoking, and began feeding the sheets to the fire.

"Well, it's saved me a stamp, anyway," murmured Lena.

I rounded on her.

"You—you wretch!" I stammered. "You heartless hussy! You—"

Realization of the ludicrousness of calling her heartless, just as I had previously labelled her inhuman, stifled my fear-impelled outburst. And to be regarded with that now perceptible cherry smile, as I was, was no help.

I went and sat beside her.

"Listen, child, I'm speaking the dead straight truth now. This is the most useless thing you could do. So far from clearing up anything, it would make matters even worse. I've been talking with Rob down there tonight. It's plain that he regards you and Dot as two entirely different people and always will. He has a horror of 'seducing Bill's widow', as he persists in putting it. If you go, he will cherish the memory of you always, jealously. You were *his*. Dot was Bill's. That's how he looks at it. Now, he is not one to change his views about such things. They're set. They're part of him. You should know that. And if you go, you'll give him a life of lonely grief. And you'll not save poor Dot, the unwanted, at all."

She was not smiling now.

"He's been drinking," she said slowly. "You can't put any value on what he said."

"*In vino veritas*," I said. "That's the rock-bottom truth, and I guarantee it. You'll never get more of the real Rob than now, with all the inhibitions off that will come off."

"We'll go down and see him," she said, getting up. "I must make absolutely certain of this."

"One moment," I said. "If you are satisfied, will you promise me two things? Firstly, that you will not—*never*—do what you were intending? And secondly, that you will watch and guard Dot carefully, and prevent her from attempting anything on those lines?"

"If I'm satisfied, I'll promise the first. As for the second—why do you think I have been going around with Dot like her shadow lately? Why do you think I told her those white lies? It was for that reason, to stop her doing that very thing. I don't like her going out alone to see Mrs. Ferguson like this, but she refused to let me go with her. I'll not let her go alone again. I'm beginning to wonder what she's doing now."

"If she's not back soon I'll go and look for her," I said. "We'll give her another twenty minutes."

And I had called Lena inhuman, I reflected, as we went down the stairs. Was I never to fathom her correctly?

Lena went boldly ahead of me, walking without pause straight into the sitting-room. Rob lay sprawled in the same armchair, his chin digging into his chest, his eyes shut, his arms trailing listlessly to the floor. Lena, first removing an empty tumbler, seated herself on the arm of the chair and lifted his head, so that it lay against her breast. Gently she began to stroke his forehead, smooth his dishevelled dark hair, and run her hand round his cheek.

Presently he started to murmur, and half opened his eyes.

From the effort one would have thought his eyelids were made of lead.

"What's marrer?" he mumbled. "Who's zat?"

"It's Lena," she whispered. "Listen, darling. I'm Lena, but I'm Dot too. And Dot is me. You've got to understand that. If one of us goes, the one that remains is always Lena. You can't lose Lena. She loves you too much."

He tried to screw his head round to look up into her face, but he was too far gone even to manage that.

"I'm drunk," he said thickly. "I'm awful drunk. D'you know why I got drunk? I thought… if I got drunk… wouldn't matter if you were Dot. Thought… would… drink myself into not caring. But I *do* care!"

His voice grew louder. He struggled up half-way to sitting, and tried to bang the chair-arm with a fist for emphasis, but missed it altogether. He fell back.

"I do care!" he repeated in a blurred shout. "Even if you went away, Lena, Dot would… still mean nothing to me. She's Bill's. Can't you see? Without Bill… I can do nothing. I don't know how… build Rep'ducer. No idea… in the world. Oh, lord… what have I done… deserve this? I only want to… to live decently… with my wife. Don't leave me, Lena… please don't…"

He shut his eyes again, breathing heavily.

Lena looked up and across at me, and then immediately past and behind me. I turned.

Dot stood in the open doorway, still wearing her hat and coat, obviously just having let herself in through the front entrance.

She looked very pale, but was composed. There was even a faint smile on her lips. She came in, removing her hat, and the silken hair tumbled across her cheeks; she juggled it into place with a toss and shake of her head.

"Nothing like knowing where you are," she remarked, with studied casualness, and my heart bled for her.

I found a whisky bottle with some spirit still left in it, and poured three drinks. Rob had passed out again, and Lena was still holding him closely, but her eyes were on Dot, and I thought they veiled an infinite compassion.

"Have your drink, Dot, my girl," she said quietly. "Then we'll go to bed and have a little talk."

We drank.

Lena stood up.

"Doc, I'll leave you to see to Rob. You might as well leave him here—he seems quite comfortable. Come on, Dot."

"Yes, Mummy," murmured Dot. "Can I kiss Daddy good night first?"

She came over to me, kissed me lightly on the cheek.

"Good night, Doc," she said.

"Good night, Dot." I pressed her hand. It was ice-cold.

She turned and walked slowly, but with head up, towards the door.

As Lena passed me in following, I whispered urgently, "Your promises?"

"You have them," she whispered back. "Both of them."

I watched them go up the stairs.

Then I covered Rob with some coats which were hanging in the hall. He was snoring gently. I made up the fire, and settled in the armchair opposite him. I had left the sitting-room door ajar, so that I might hear any unusual noise. I was not going to leave this house tonight, nor even sleep if I could help it.

What Dot had overheard must have sounded like a sentence of death to her. At all events she must be prevented from seeing to it herself that it was carried out, and the immediate future was the danger period.

I remember hearing five o'clock strike.

It must have been shortly after that that I slipped from a light doze into sleep.

The thing which awakened me was the swish and rattle of the heavy curtains being drawn back, and the sudden influx of sunlight striking my eyes. I blinked and sat up. The maid was bustling about the room, clearing up the confusion of empty bottles and dirty glasses.

"What time is it?" I yawned.

"Half past seven, sir."

I looked at Rob. He lay in his chair exactly as I had left him last night, except that his mouth had dropped open.

"Are Mrs. Heath or Mrs. Leggett up yet?" I asked the maid.

"Oh yes, sir. They always get up at the first light and go swimming together. I saw them from my window this morning, walking down towards the river."

Disquiet came upon my soul like a physical reaction.

"At what time was that?" I asked, and cleared my throat.

"About six, sir."

"Are they usually as late returning as this?"

"Well, it's a tidy walk to the river, sir, at least to the place where they bathe. But they're generally back round about a quarter past seven. I don't know what's keeping them this morning."

"Thank you."

A quarter of an hour late. It wasn't much, but in the circumstances I didn't like it.

I took the layers of coats from Rob and shook him. I had to

shake him violently before there was any response. At last he sat up, licking dry lips and holding his forehead.

"Hades, my head!" he muttered.

I generally carried aspirins with me. I fizzed a glass of soda-water from the siphon and gave it to him with three aspirins.

"Swallow those and lie back a moment," I instructed.

I went to the window, and peered as far down the riverward slopes as I could see. There seemed to be not a soul about.

I paced fretfully up and down for a short while.

"What's up, Doc?" asked Rob, regarding me vaguely.

I halted. "I'm going to get the car out," I said decisively. "Get ready to come with me."

In a few minutes he joined me, just as I was turning his car into the drive from the garage. I drove rapidly down towards Howdean. The rush of cool air cleared Rob's head.

"Will you explain what we're up to, Doc?" he asked.

"You were probably too drunk last night to realize what you said, or remember it if you did," I said, and told him concisely what had happened, and why we were investigating the delay. He became worried. I tried to reassure him to some extent.

"Mind you," I said, "we're probably going on a wild-goose chase. It's a fine morning, and maybe they're extending their swim. But I just want to make sure."

We had paralleled the river for a way, and now came to a bend in the lane which was the nearest point to that high bluff which I knew to be Lena's regular swimming spot. We left the car, and hurried across the field and through the trees which screened the bluff and gave it privacy. We ran to the top. Two little heaps of feminine clothes reposed there, unattended. I recognized Lena's red sandals and Dot's pale yellow frock.

I gazed down into the deep pool below, with its twin spurs of rock, which Bill had described, and its surface was unbroken by any human head. My eye lanced right and left up and down the river length, scanned the bare shelving slopes of the farther bank, sought to pierce the trees which stood thick on this side. And saw no living thing. Apart from the gurgling of the waters, there was silence.

"Let's shout," said Rob. His voice was trembling.

We shouted their names. The echoes flew and persisted till we cursed them, lest they prevent any answering call from reaching our ears. But there were no answering calls. We made sure of that.

"Rob, you search the bank on that side," I said urgently, pointing to the left side of the bluff. "I'll take the right. Shout if you discover anything. Come back up here in a quarter of an hour if you don't."

"Right," he jerked, and went plunging down the left slope. I went the other way.

Something over fifty yards away I pushed through some thick bushes at the water's edge and came upon a spit of a sandbank reaching out into a miniature bay. White, naked, on her back, caught on this spit, lay either Lena or Dot, her head, shoulders, and the firm mounds of her breasts motionless, but the rest of her body trailing away under the gently moving water and seeming to undulate and her legs to kick slowly, swayingly. Her eyes were fast shut. Her wet bright hair was thick with blood, like pirates' gold; a halo of crimson stained the sand around her head.

In a moment I had her under the armpits and was drawing her carefully from the water. She was breathing faintly with little bubbling noises. I turned her face-downwards, and a trickle of water ran from her nose and mouth. There was some—not much—in her lungs. I got it out.

I kneaded, pressed, and rubbed her vigorously, and her heart-beats grew stronger and her breathing deeper. These efforts made the gash in her scalp bleed the more, but before I attended to it, I stood up and hallooed for Rob.

I had to keep shouting as I worked to give him a bearing on where I was. Soon he broke breathlessly through the bushes beside me.

He fell on his knees beside the girl, peering at her face.

"Is—she alive?" he gasped.

"Yes," I said. "But we must be quick. Now, did you discover anything on your side of the bluff?"

He wasn't listening to me. He was still peering, taut-faced, tense, at the girl's countenance.

"Is it Lena?" he burst out, with a certain shrillness. "Is it Lena?"

"I don't know," I said brusquely. "We'll find that out later. Listen to me, for God's sake—did you discover anything on your side?"

"Eh?" He jerked his head up like a startled wild thing. "Oh no. I went over the ground thoroughly. It's pretty open. There's no one there."

"Right," I said. "Now carry Lena—if it is her—to the car: you're stronger, more able to do it than I. Wrap her in the travelling-rug in the back. Keep her head up. I'm going to have a quick scout round here. I'll catch you up."

I helped him lift her, and held the bushes apart so that he could get through with his burden. He stumbled towards the open.

I careered around the area in desperate haste, nevertheless omitting no corner where another body might be concealed. I found nothing, gave it up and ran across the field to the car.

Rob already had the girl wrapped up in the back seat, and had his arms around her. He sought my eyes anxiously.

"No luck," I said briefly, and took the wheel and drove like mad to the cottage hospital. She was in Hake's hands within ten minutes, and I was straightway on the 'phone to the police.

Rob was pacing up and down outside the door of the examination room, in an agony of indecision whether to wait for Hake's verdict or to go back to the river and search further for the missing twin.

I told him to wait where he was. The police and I would do all the searching.

When we found her, I was glad I had told Rob to stay.

She had been entangled in the strong weeds in the pool below the shoulder of the bluff. Persistent torn tentacles of them still clung greenly round her arms and ankles as she lay limply in the drag-net like some captured sleeping water-nymph. The rough cords of the net sawed harshly and insensately at her fine body as they hauled her in.

Apart from the white weals thus caused, there was not a mark on her. Her face was as peaceful as that of St. Catherine of Siena. I could not, for the moment, bring myself to believe that she was not merely sleeping. I felt that if I touched her she would open those unfathomable blue eyes and murmur in her lazy way, "Hullo, Doc."

But she was dead, and past all our efforts.

And when the realization of that had sunk in, I felt as though my heart were breaking.

"Said the Rose: 'To punish, I die...'"

Now I felt the true poignancy of that line, as Bill had before me.

CHAPTER TWELVE

HAKE ASSURED US THAT THE GIRL IN THE HOSPITAL HAD A good chance of pulling through.

The skull was definitely fractured, but by no means need it be fatal.

"It depends largely upon the effort she makes herself, of course," he said. "I don't think we had better tell her of the death of her sister. It wouldn't help. They were very fond of each other, weren't they?"

"Yes," I said. "You know how it is with twins. They're part of each other's life."

"Um. What do you think happened?"

I had my answer ready for the inevitable question.

"They were fond of diving off that bluff into the pool. It was risky because of the rocks, but they got excitement from the risk. They were like that. One of them must have dived too deep and got caught in the weeds. When she didn't come up, the other must have dived to her rescue, but in her haste misjudged and caught her head a glancing blow on a spur of rock. A freak of current washed her up on that sandbank, unconscious. It's a miracle she didn't drown."

"Yes, indeed. I wonder which one she is? Is there no way of telling? They didn't wear bathing costumes, did they?"

"No. I don't suppose it would have told us much if they had. Dot lost her entire wardrobe when the laboratory went up. She was still borrowing most of her clothes from Lena. If she had worn a costume it would have been Lena's. We should still be stymied."

"What a situation!" he said. "I've never heard of anything like it. However, it'll be cleared up when she comes to."

"Are there any signs of it yet?"

"No. But I don't think it will be long now. Mr. Heath is with her. He won't leave the bedside. He's been there ten hours now."

"I know. I've just left him. Well, I'm going out for some dinner. I'll be back in an hour or so."

But I didn't feel very much like facing food. I had a few biscuits and a cup of tea, and then I was walking off my restlessness along the lanes, and revolving over and over again, as I had done all day, my surmises as to what had happened.

Firstly, I decided, relative to the events of last night, it was too much a coincidence to be the sheer accident I had made it appear to Hake. It was part and parcel of the whole black chain of events which had bound us all this time. Another turn of the wheel of that mad machine, which must be near the final break-up now.

Bill had gone. One of the girls had gone, and the other was on the brink of it. Rob was going to pieces, and approaching a nervous breakdown. I myself was being driven to distraction by the urge to *do* something to stop this awful sequence, yet the killing thing was to find anything that one possibly could do. My attempts to influence events were like a man, barehanded, trying to divert a runaway tank.

This tragedy which had befallen the girls, coming so soon after the loss of Bill, had about knocked me endwise. I felt numbed and dazed by the shock of it. What sort of life was this, that such things could happen to decent, well-meaning people? Even the most heartless man would recoil from tormenting animals so long and so devilishly ingeniously as this. "God is love," I thought with bitterness. And again, "God helps those who help themselves." Help ourselves!

And yet, I reflected, this latest twist of things in all probability resulted from an attempt by Dot to help us. I felt sure of it.

"I give you my word, there'll be another turn to events, and it will all straighten out."

If the girl at the hospital recovered, and if she turned out to be Lena, then the ending would be well, at the cost of Dot's self-sacrifice.

But if the attempted martyrdom had gone awry, and the survivor proved to be Dot and the victim Lena, then the situation would be, incredibly, worse than ever. So far from Rob being able to accept Dot as a substitute, he would probably never be able fully to forgive her for causing the death of Lena.

For the affair at the river had not been a suicide pact. Lena had given me a definite promise not to seek that solution, and also to do her best to stop Dot choosing that way out. I knew I could count on those promises.

But Dot had promised nothing but a new turn to events. It was pretty certain that she had attempted suicide, as I had feared she would. There were two ways in which she might have done it, and either could appear, as she meant it to appear, an accident.

She had, of course, all Lena's indifference to death and manner of dying, and a cold courage and determination far beyond the ordinary.

It was certainly not past her to dive from that bluff and deliberately appear to misjudge, and strike her head on one of those twin spurs of rock instead of going between them. If so, she reckoned to be killed outright. Had she dived with that intent, and misjudged indeed, so that she had struck the rocks only a glancing blow and fallen unconscious into the pool? And had Lena, seeking to save her, gone swimming and searching in the depths of the pool after her, and got entangled in the weeds and drowned, while, in fact, Dot's body, still with life in it, had been swept away by an undercurrent and washed up in that hidden inlet?

One was always seeing such ironies in the newspapers: the would-be suicide saved, and the would-be rescuer drowned.

Or had the suicide been successful? Dot's nature was also equal to swimming to the bottom of the pool and deliberately enmeshing herself in those all too willing weeds, and thus drowning apparently by accident. If she did that, then no doubt Lena, realizing when Dot did not reappear that something was wrong, had dived too hastily to the rescue and genuinely misjudged, in the manner I had described to Hake.

All of which settled nothing, of course. We could only contain our patience until the survivor recovered her senses and her identity was revealed.

I found I had, without thinking where I was going, arrived at that same stile where I had sat the previous evening speaking with Lena and Dot in turn, about Rob and his foibles, and life and sunsets and immortality.

But it was later now than yesterday. The sun had given its wondrous show and I hadn't even noticed it. It had gone now, leaving that same grey cloud-country of yesterday covering and camouflaging its exit. I remembered how Dot had gazed upon it with that strange, far look in her eyes.

She must have known then that she was going to set forth, a lone traveller, into just such an unknown hinterland, a place of mist on the edge of darkness, cut off irretrievably from the warm human world. She certainly knew it when she made the unusual gesture of kissing me good night a few hours later. God, what a great soul she had, I thought.

All man's virtues stand in doubt at some time or other, except courage.

Love might be a payment for returned love. Humour might be an escape from, a way of laughing off, responsibility. Generosity might be a bid for a reward in heaven, *quid pro quo*. Humility and resignation could be weakness. But courage stood like a rock, and no cynicism could shake it.

I marvelled at the spirit in that slight, young girl, which nerved her to walk up the Valley of the Shadow, alone, without a tremor or thought of withdrawal.

I was becoming an old man, and had lost much of that fear of death which haunted my adolescence and early life. But I still wished to die easily, in bed, and shrank from the thought of a physically violent end. Never could I take it, as Dot had taken it, as a matter of course.

Whether Dot was alive or dead in this world, existed or was nothing in the next, I paid tribute to her unquailing heart.

The temporary glow of feeling died down, and that heavy sadness blanketed things again.

Besides that haunting line by an unidentified poet, some equally persistent tune, lugubrious and sweet, had moved in its slow way at the back of my mind all day. Involuntarily now I found myself humming it dolefully, and for the first time consciously took note of it.

Ravel's *"Pavane pour Une Infante Defunte"*.

I could imagine Dot's unaffected chuckle of amusement had she been able to know of it.

Suddenly I swore, and tore myself roughly out of that mood of near-unbearable sentiment, and hurried back to the hospital.

There were no new developments there. It was three days before the patient recovered consciousness.

It happened in one of my rare absences from the bedside vigil, and when I heard of it I made all speed back.

Rob was waiting for me outside the closed door of the private room in which she lay.

"Don't go in, Doc, just yet. There's something you must know first."

He was beginning to look almost old and haggard these days. The strain of waiting for the decision of life or death, as well as the decision of Lena or Dot, had a marked physical effect. But now I sensed in his manner a new onset of worry.

"What's the matter? She's been talking, hasn't she? She's not—delirious?"

He brushed the back of his hand wearily across his brow, and motioned me to the window-seat in the corridor.

"No, she's not delirious," he said heavily. "But she's lost her memory."

"What?"

I stared at him.

"She doesn't know who you are?" I ventured.

"Oh, she knows me all right. She remembers you, Bill, every-thing—up to a point. The point is when she was lying drugged in the Reproducer, waiting for the experiment of copying her to begin. The last thing she remembers is that cover of the container descending over her 'like the glass cover over a railway-station buffet ham sandwich', as she described it."

"She made that remark before, when she came out of the drug," I said. "Lord, she's got this spell of unconsciousness identified with that one! How could it have happened?"

"You know the accepted theory of the cause of loss of memory," said Rob slowly. "She's unconsciously repressing the whole unpleasant sequence of events which she doesn't want to remember, which caused her so much mental pain, and which began for her with the creation of Dot."

"That would be it." I nodded. "Well, it doesn't matter much so long as she's well in other respects."

"Doesn't matter?" he echoed. "Don't you see that that effect probably means it's Dot? She was the one who suffered the more and the longer of the two, and she would feel the need to forget much more than Lena."

"I think you underestimate just how sympathetic Lena's nature was," I said, with some sharpness. "Anyway, if it were Dot, would she be likely to remember anything of the experiment at all?"

"She was created complete with all Lena's memories. She would seem to remember it. That may very well be Dot in there, remembering a life she never led in actuality and forgetting one she did."

"Well, if it is Dot, what then?"

"Then, Doc, we are at diametrical opposites. I remember the life she never led, and it wasn't hers—it was Lena's. I remember the life she did lead, and no part of it was mine—it was Bill's. I wish I could suffer loss of memory about the last part too, but I can't. I'd give worlds to really believe it was Lena, but one can't create faith where there's such a large element of doubt."

He looked miserably out of the window into the darkness.

I could only gape at this victim of rectitude. He must be a man in a hundred, I thought, and more was the pity.

"I suppose it's no use trying now to explain again how over-conscientiousness can lead to evil," I said. "I got tired of doing so last night. But I'm damned if I'll give up—I'll make you see yet.

Still, this loss of memory may be only temporary. Her memory may return of itself. If it doesn't, we can get a psycho-analyst to work on her: we can give him a good indication of the root of the trouble."

"We can't," Rob said abruptly. "Do you want to make public the fact that we have created human life—and look where it has led us!—and that others could do what we have done, and worse, with a Reproducer?"

"As there isn't a Reproducer any more, and no one knows how to make one, I don't think there's much to fear on that score. And we didn't create life—we only copied it. Anyway, a reputable psychiatrist is bound to secrecy in a client's case, just as us doctors are."

"It would get out," he said in a flat tone. "Psychiatrists have an itch for getting into print."

"Oh, damn this arguing!" I said, losing patience and jumping up. "I'm going in to see Lena."

The "Lena" was deliberate, and born of exasperation.

Hake was in there, and I sent him a silent message by my attitude that I wished to be alone with the girl.

"Go easy," he whispered cryptically, as he passed me going out.

The girl I had called Lena lay in bed propped up on a double pillow, such hair as the surgeon had not shorn from her quite concealed under the layers of plaster and bandages round her head. Only the pale oval of her face showed. It quite lit up at the sight of me, and I felt a sudden pang of joy at this real response from the composite being of Lena and Dot, for whom I had been grieving with such a devastating sense of loss.

She could not move her head much, so I sat where she could see me.

"How glad I am to see you, Doc," she murmured. "Perhaps we can get to the bottom of things now. Everyone's behaving so mysteriously, especially Rob. That doctor who just went out told me not to worry about my sister, because she's all right. My sister! Did the experiment go off all right, then? Where's Bill? Or did something go wrong with the apparatus? What's wrong with my head? For goodness' sake, Doc, don't be like the others—tell me these things."

I opened my mouth, but no words would come for the moment.

"There's so much to tell," I said finally, mentally cursing Hake for saying anything at all.

"Well, make a start, Doc."

"I have to think," I said, getting up and walking to the fireplace.

"I can't see you there," she complained.

I took no notice.

"Can I have a cigarette?"

"No. You're in no condition."

"No one will co-operate," she said, a little wistfully. "I feel awfully outside of things. Have I had a mad fit or something, and murdered someone? Everyone seems to be holding me off at arm's length, when they're not humouring me."

I came back and sat down.

"Can't you remember anything at all?" I asked seriously.

"Only what I told Rob. I was lying in the Reproducer—"

"He told me."

I fell again to wondering how much it would be wise to tell her.

"Remember me?" she ventured presently. "My name's Lena."

"I'm sorry, Lena," I said. "I—"

"That's the first time anyone's used it since I woke up, Doc. Even Rob never once called me by name. Nor did you till just now. It's very unusual."

Trust her quick perception to put its finger right on the spot!

"Tell me honestly," she continued. "Did the experiment come off, *and am I the other one?*"

Of course, it was natural that she would imagine that. I thought rapidly.

It seemed to me that sooner or later she would get some garbled idea of the truth by pumping the not over-astute Hake (my friend) and piecing that together with what she divined from the attitude and remarks of Rob and myself. Besides, the absence of Bill had to be explained sometime. And, moreover, I had an idea which might set everything right, if all were explained.

So swiftly, and yet missing nothing, and with a constant fear that I might be interrupted by the return of Rob, I told her the whole nigh-incredible story of events since the completion of the experiment.

She was very upset to learn of the death of Bill. The tragedy of Dot meant nothing to her. She could not imagine Dot at all. The existence of another person who was still oneself was beyond the conception of anyone who had not had, or did not remember, that bizarre experience. I made the scrupulous attitude of Rob plain, and why he hesitated to accept her as his wife.

"And now this is what I want you to do," I said, urgently. "Fake a return of memory, *and remember that you are Lena*! It's probably true enough, anyway. If you say that definitely, he'll believe you. He thinks you incapable of lying, and, indeed, he'll be only too willing to believe you. All he is seeking for is some base of fact to place his faith on. Give him it."

"Give him a lie for a base, not fact, you mean?"

"Heavens, are *you* going to display a New England conscience now?"

"I'm sorry to be awkward, Doc. I want Rob to accept me for what I am, not what I pretend to be. It's a fifty-fifty chance that I am Bill's wife, you know. I've not any misgivings about the morals of that—I know Bill would understand. But I don't think I can keep up a lie for a lifetime, especially to a man who believes—if your judgment of him is correct—that I couldn't lie to him."

"Look here," I said. "You don't realize that these last few months you, and you again in the form of Dot, acted a lie very successfully for the sake of Bill's happiness. Now it's Rob's happiness. You can do it again."

"Dot nearly broke under the strain, didn't she? Besides, how can Rob believe me incapable of lying when I've shown in that way that I can and have done so? Don't you think he might suspect I'm lying again? He has only to talk about any event we've shared—that Lena and he have shared, that is—since the experiment to realize from my total ignorance of it that my recovery of memory is not genuine."

"Oh, why must everyone argue so much?" I said, feeling near despair. "Is what I am trying to force on you both so unreasonable?"

"Can't you see, Doc, reason doesn't come into it? We can't reason our feelings away. I'm a nameless person without an identity, and I want Rob to accept me for whatever I may be, without pretence on either side. If he cannot feel that he can do that, very well then, it cannot be helped and he cannot be blamed."

At which point the door opened and a little crowd came in—Rob and Hake and a nurse.

The nurse took the girl's temperature, and at the same time Hake took the pulse. He tut-tutted.

"I'm afraid you must have been exciting our patient, Harvey. You at least should show more discretion."

Thus friend Hake. Certainly, now I looked at her, a tinge of colour had come, rarely, to the girl's cheeks.

"Before you tell me to go, Hake, I'll tell you I'm going anyway," I said. "You try to get some sleep, Lena—it's getting pretty late."

"I'm the doctor," said Hake testily. "I'm afraid you'll have to be getting along too, Mr. Heath. The nurse will be on duty here all night. You may come first thing in the morning. I'd rather the patient did no more talking tonight."

Then Rob surprised me. He bent over the girl in the bed, kissed her, and said, "Good night, Lena darling."

I saw her eyes following him as we left the room, but, as so often before, I could read nothing from them.

Rob and I walked slowly down the hospital drive.

"Would you care to sleep at 'Hawthorns' tonight?" he asked presently. "Somehow tonight, now the house is empty, I should be grateful for your company."

"Of course, Rob," I said, with more warmth than I had expressed towards him lately. Partly because I felt a twinge of pity for his loneliness, partly because of his unexpected action when parting from Lena.

"I noticed you insisted on calling her Lena," he said. "Do you really believe she is Lena?"

"I don't know who she is," I said frankly. "I just choose to believe she's Lena."

"How can one choose to believe? You may be quite wrong."

"It does not matter what a man believes so long as that belief makes him and others happy, and hurts no one. Being wrong in fact doesn't matter a damn. Being right in feeling, intention, and result matters. That's all the justification a belief needs. Truth is relative. Fact may well be fancy. You can't know anything absolutely. You may remember me describing how Bill and Lena and I thrashed all that out the first night we met together."

"Yes, I remember. But, Doc, you say being right in feeling matters. And it does. But I can't *feel* right about accepting this particular belief."

"Yet you called her Lena yourself just now. Why?"

"I was trying to force myself to believe it, Doc. But I can't conquer my doubts. She sensed it. She knows I hadn't really accepted her."

"I see," I said, and thought for a while about the type of which Rob was a specimen. How driving and persistent and single-minded they were when they were living within the framework of their code, knowing by precedent how they should react to each and every situation. The breed of Empire builders. Rob's mouth and chin could turn to granite when he knew what to do, and every obstacle would be attacked methodically with firm and sure hands. But place such a man in a totally unprecedented situation, where none of the rules of his code seem properly to fit, and he is lost and doubtful in a wilderness of insecurity.

They were so certain of their ideas of right and wrong, these people. They could be coldly logical in practical things, yet hopelessly illogical in things that touched their emotional springs. They would be aghast at the moral wrongness of using poison gas in warfare, but if the enemy used it just once they would, with a burning sense of righteousness, drench him and his family with it, with interest. Once there had been a precedent, the "wrongness" of using poison gas somehow vanished.

It was part of the code not to be cruel to animals, and to be indignant with those who did. It was also part of the code to hound stags to an unpleasant death, and to be indignant with anyone who said it was cruel.

They honestly believed they were Christians, and they made a parade of their belief in God and in Christ's teachings. Their reaction to the preaching of humility was that one white skin was worth an astronomical number of black ones. "Thou shalt not kill"—and they made war with vigour, even zest. "All men are brothers"—and they regarded Europe as necessarily an eternal patchwork of queer "foreigners".

They saw nothing incompatible in these attitudes. Nor could they be made to see.

They built the British Empire, these people, their pride and sense of duty both upheld it and fettered it, and they supplied the reasons for the belief abroad that the British were hypocrites.

"I know you believe I'm a slave to tradition," said Rob, breaking in on my thoughts as though I had been speaking them aloud. "But it isn't so. I do act according to my own judgment. For instance, when Dad wanted me to follow the family business, I broke away and chose to take up my own research."

"There's been plenty of precedence for that sort of thing, else you wouldn't have done it," I said. "It comes under the heading 'Pride' in your code, and sub-heading 'Independence'. Your sort used to run away to sea and found colonies. It's all part of the tradition."

"It's easy to be cynical, Doc," he answered, and there was a note of real pain in his voice. "I'm not posing. I'm being as sincere as I can be. You behave towards me with a sort of despairing superiority, as if you can see all the works that make me tick, and I'm beyond any change or improvement of design. But I don't think you really understand me at all."

"I really am sorry if I seem unsympathetic," I said. "I do think you're acting sincerely, according to your lights. But one can't feel over-sympathetic towards a steamroller which is crushing the life out of a person, and that is what your behaviour is doing to Lena."

"I can't help myself!" he cried, with something like a sob.

I laid my hand on his arm and patted it reassuringly.

"All right, all right, Rob. I know that. Let's forget about it."

"Forget!" he exclaimed muffledly. Then he made an effort to compose himself.

"Listen, Doc," he said in a strained voice. "This is my final attempt to make you see my point of view. You can't understand why Lena and Dot seem fundamentally different to me. Well, suppose the Reproducer had been large enough to make an exact replica of Westminster Abbey. And that the original Abbey was destroyed by some disaster. Could you fool yourself that the copy could take the place of the original?"

"I don't know," I said doubtfully.

"The actual material of the stones has no inherent value— it's the accumulated sentiment attached to them that affects us. It's the memories of the events which actually happened within those walls which make the place so dear to the Englishman. One walks into that building and the past envelops one like a tangible presence. The very air there is heavy with history. You feel an almost ecstatic affinity with the slow centuries that have passed in there; you are linked to them. You may touch the very same stones that Edward the Confessor touched nine hundred years ago. You may walk on the ground William the Conqueror walked on. Think of the history of the Coronation Stone!—even Cromwell had reverence for it. When Nelson went into the attack off Cape Trafalgar, his last thought of England was of the Abbey—they are the same... But in the spurious Abbey, would you get anything of this effect? You would know those stones were created only yesterday. They were not even as old as you were. Those great figures of the past knew nothing of them. You could have no illusions in a place like that. It would be quite interesting to look at, but you would *feel* nothing. You could not make yourself pretend to feel anything."

"I haven't all your reverence for the past," I said slowly. "But I can see what you're driving at."

"I cherished Lena—Lena herself," he went on. "Not the mere appearance of her. My memories are bound to her—the same girl who actually did spend that wonderful honeymoon with me in Cornwall, who raced me to drink first from St. Keyne's Well and bathed with me in Prussia Cove, and who has lived with me since. I can only look on Dot as a stranger—one who shared the marriage-bed of my friend, who went to the Continent with him, one with whom I've never had a heart-to-heart talk at any time. She was Bill's girl, never mine. She may even be with child by Bill, for all I know."

He paused a while, then went on: "I am trying not to be over-particular. I am trying to shut my eyes to certain possibilities, to accept that girl blindly. But I am without faith. If only I could *know* absolutely that it is Lena! Lord, if only I could know!"

It was then that I made my final drive at conviction by reason, remembering every word of Bill's arguments on the side of pragmatism that first night at Lena's cottage. Words, words, words! Intellectual distinctions are just meaningless to a man who cannot help thinking with his emotions.

I knew at last I was gaining no ground, nor ever would by these methods.

Rob told me as much himself. "It's no use, Doc. I know all those arguments. I've tried to reason with myself. But reason isn't a constituent of blind faith. You can't manufacture faith with the wrong materials."

"Yet you put your blind faith in God, in your country, and in your creed," I reproached.

"That isn't based on reason either. It was inculcated in me in early life. I didn't make it myself. Whatever puts faith into me must come from outside me. It is the gift of a greater Being than my own small mind."

"It's plain I can't give it you," I sighed. "Well, I've done all I can. What happens now depends upon your God."

He made no answer. We reached the house in silence, and he went to bed without having anything to eat. He had not eaten all day.

Lena's rise of temperature had been the first sign of a fever. We were rarely allowed in to see her for the next few days. Then suddenly it left her. She was near exhaustion point and very weak. Both her temperature and pulse now dropped to sub-normal.

She could only whisper. Her face looked thinner. Her eyes were of a flat greyness now: they had lost those inner lights which reflected her vitality and mischief.

Rob hardly ever left the hospital, even when he was not allowed to see her. He had so obviously committed himself to do his best for her that I had long ceased to feel any antagonism for him or impatience against him. I had that intuitive apprehension that the course of events was still out of our hands, and no effort of any of us could affect this immutability. We were like figures in a Greek drama or a Hardy novel.

"As flies to wanton boys, are we to the gods…"

That talk on determinism with Bill was often in my thoughts those days.

Hake took me aside.

"It's getting serious," he said. "That fever didn't help, but the real trouble is that she's making no effort to help herself. So far from having a will to live, I'd almost say she had a will to die. I can't understand the reason for that. You know more of her life than I—can you explain it?"

"Yes," I said. "All hope is dead in her. You know she lost her memory. Well, she doesn't really know who she is, but she thinks she's Mr. Heath's wife. But he can't be certain of that, and won't accept her wholeheartedly. She believes he never will. And so she's turning her face to the wall."

"It's a fantastic, pitiful situation. I don't see what we can do."

"I was thinking of bringing in a psycho-analyst to try to bring her memory back," I said, mentally setting aside Rob's objections to that.

Hake was against it too.

"You know the methods of psycho-analysis," he said. "Weeks, maybe months, of battering at her mind with questions. She's not got the strength left to stand that."

"As I see it, it makes little difference now. The end will come just as certainly if she is left alone. We could at least take this last chance."

"All right," he said reluctantly.

Rob surprised me by agreeing too.

"If it ends this awful uncertainty, if it lets me know, if it saves Lena, I don't care any longer what the world gets to know," he said.

But it came to nothing.

The psychiatrist was one of the most able and experienced men in his profession.

The sick girl was quite indifferent about his efforts. She answered his questions mechanically, but her replies were almost wholly negative. He attempted to get something positive proven from them by a process of elimination, but the element of uncertainty remained ineradicable.

He switched to hypnosis, and failed completely.

"I've never known a mind like hers," he said in puzzlement. "I can't seem to get in touch with it at all, let alone influence it. It seems to live an utterly independent existence."

"It always did," I said.

"Well, I defy anyone to get her under hypnosis. She doesn't resist, she just ignores me. I might as well try to hypnotize a lump of rock. I'm afraid, much as I hate to throw my hand in, I'll have to give this case up. If she were stronger in health, I'd peg away. But Dr. Hake thinks I'm beginning to do physical damage."

"All right," I said wearily. It was one more example of our complete inability to wrest the direction of things from the Fates. The machine had reached the last stages. The unknown girl was being broken in her turn, as inexorably as the other had been.

I was allowed in to see her that afternoon.

She lay as still as a carven knight on a Crusader's tomb. Her eyes gazed unseeingly at the ceiling.

"Hullo, Lena."

"Hullo," she whispered.

"My name is Doc."

Her gaze slid down to me. There was the faintest twitch at the corners of her mouth.

"Sorry—Doc."

"I'm getting very annoyed with you, Lena."

"Again?"

"Look, girl, make an effort, will you? For my sake."

"I can't live without Rob."

"But he'll never leave you. You know that. He would be at your side here even more than he is, if only Dr. Hake allowed it. He won't leave this building. We can't even persuade him to go and eat."

"His body is here. His love isn't. Doubt keeps it away. It always will."

"Rubbish!"

"You wouldn't know as I know, Doc. You remember that barrier Dot always felt that Rob set up between himself and her? It's between us now. I can't get to him. All hope of that old intimacy is finished. If we can't share our lives in the old way, then I can't go on. I can't live outside, any more than Dot could."

And she turned her face away.

I was baffled. I could think of nothing more to say. All argument was over, I knew. The end was determined, inescapably, now. Everything was changing to ashes. She was fading out of our lives, and when she was gone we faced unrelieved loneliness, pointless existence. I thought of Rob alone in that big house. I saw my own future—a steady passing into old age and immobility, with no occupation, laughter, friendly argument, nor anything of youth to brighten my days.

When we get old we seek the company of youth, to get again that precious taste of optimism, gaiety, freshness of outlook, and hope.

I recalled with incredible nostalgia those golden days when Bill and Dot and Lena and Rob and I had worked together daily at the Dump, the genuine interest of our work and the humour and fun as we went about it. I had begun every morning with anticipation for the day's work and play, the satisfying accomplishment and the vivacious conversation and the eager planning for tomorrow. Living in that atmosphere of zestful youth, I had become young again.

And now it had come to this. An old defeated man sitting and watching his last interest in life slowly dying of its own despair and defeat. And her case was much harder than mine, because she was so young.

"*To punish, I die...*"

"*To punish, I die...*"

The refrain throbbed in my mind.

I felt like breaking down and blubbering, but whether because of sorrow for myself, or for her, or for all of us, I did not know.

It was as well Rob came in at that moment and gave me a reason to get a hold on myself.

"A telephone call for you, Doc," he said quietly.

I nodded, and looked again at the girl. She seemed oblivious of our presence. I got up, and Rob took my place. I left them there, as silent and unmoving as figures in a photograph.

The call had come through to the superintendent's office, and I took it there.

"Hullo," I said.

"This is Inspector Downley," came a voice. "That Doctor Harvey?"

"Yes, Inspector."

"I'm speaking from a call-box near the scene of the explosion at Mr. Leggett's laboratory. You are aware that we are still investigating that?"

"Yes."

"Well, my men have dug a safe out from under the débris. We've managed to get it open. It was supposed to be a fireproof safe, but the heat of that explosion charred almost everything in it. But there are one or two things you might take charge of, Doctor, as you're Mr. Leggett's executor. They don't give us much of a line on anything. They're all private documents, letters, and so forth—pretty badly burned, I'm afraid."

"I'll come down and collect them right away," I promised.

I was on the spot in a few minutes, picking my way over the fine rubble—for the Dump had been reduced almost to powder.

Lying on its back half below ground, with a depression lately scooped out round it, was Bill's safe. Once it had been a neat green-and-cream affair. Now it was a grey-black bulging iron box, split at the corners and pitted all over through the ravages of intense heat. The door had become a clumsy, twisted lid, and lay open.

Beside it on the ground stood a little heap of blackened books and scorched letters.

Four or five men were poking round desultorily with picks, and Inspector Downley detached himself from them and greeted me.

"There they are, sir. Not many, I'm afraid, but they may mean something to you."

"Thank you."

I investigated the pile. The letters, which I riffled through casually, seemed to be mainly business ones. There were a number of old bills and receipts among them. I set them aside and concentrated on the books. There were three of these, odd non-consecutive volumes of Bill's personal journal.

The leaves were so badly scorched that it was often impossible to make out the loose undisciplined writing. Obviously he had regarded his scientific research as part of his personal life, for comments on its progress were constant—he even brought mathematical formulae into it. There were references here and there to me, always in affectionate terms, and sometimes I had to turn over quickly lest the memories prove too poignant for my already disturbed state of mind.

The pages referring to the coming of Lena into his life were so much cinder. The first decipherable reference began:

> *My love for her is tormenting me every hour of the day and night. If I could only pluck, up the courage to tell her, and take the consequences...*

Most of the account of the bringing to life of the rabbit was there. He was reticent in this narrative at least about the details. Near the end of the book (I wondered whether the Inspector had read it, and judged from his indifference that he had not) began the record of the duplication of Lena. It concentrated mainly on his lone achievement of changing Dot from a lifeless copy to a living and breathing one, by repeating the methods used on the rabbit.

The last page was, in fact, but half a page: its lower part had, in common with the back cover, been burnt right away. The account stopped abruptly part way through a sentence.

I read the last complete sentence again, and my stomach turned suddenly into a vacuum. I just stared dazedly at the page for a moment and then turned and literally ran to my car, clutching the book tightly. Lord knows what the men conjectured had bitten me.

I tore back to the hospital, and had difficulty in checking my speed on entering the private room. Rob and the sick girl were there alone, just as I had left them. I doubt whether they had exchanged a word.

"How is she?" I inquired urgently of Rob.

"She's sleeping," he said, a little surprised at my impetuosity.

I made sure that she was. Then I looked fully at Rob, and held the book up for him to see. My heart was thumping.

"You wanted definite knowledge about her, Rob. Whether she is Lena or Dot. And here it is, in this volume. Now you can *know*, absolutely."

He went rather pale.

"How?" he asked with hoarseness.

I let him examine the book.

"That is a volume of Bill's journal," I said. "You'll recognize the writing. You may have seen him writing in that very book. It's just been recovered from his safe by Inspector Downley and given me not ten minutes since. You can verify that."

"I can see it's genuine," he admitted. "I know he kept a journal like this. His writing is unmistakable."

I reached over and opened the book at the fragment of the last page.

"Then read that—especially *that* part," I said, stabbing at the relevant portion with my forefinger.

For the last words in that book were these:

> ...*The insertion of the tubes of the Autojector into Dot's veins, for this purpose of pumping the blood through her veins until her own heart pump began to work in sympathy, had caused two tiny wounds. These left two permanent scars at the base of her neck, the only blemishes on an otherwise perfect replica of Lena. I rather resented this...*

When I had first read those words I had an immediate vision of the rabbit Bill and I had brought to life that night, hopping about the lab with a ridiculous ruff of bandage about its neck.

Of course, Dot must have worn a similar bandage for the same reason, but Rob and I had seen her only briefly and at a far distance that first morning. She went straight away with Bill on their long honeymoon, and naturally when she returned her neck had healed and the traces of the small scars were not noticeable without fore-knowledge and a close scrutiny of them.

Rob put the book down with shaking hands.

"Would you rather I looked?" I asked.

He shook his head. He could not trust himself to speak. He stood up, and gently pulled the bedclothes down from the sleep-ing girl's shoulders.

He hesitated, and then (I could see him shudder with the effort, for fearfulness at the consequences of this certain knowledge was almost paralysing him) he bent over her and carefully scrutinized the base of her neck.

"Can't see any signs this side," he muttered presently, in his throat.

"Then move her."

Slowly, like an automaton, he lifted her head and shoulders from the pillow. Her eyelids flickered.

With a fearful care he completed his examination.

"Nothing... at all," he grated.

As he spoke, through jaws clenched in tension, she awoke. Her eyes gazed into his blankly at first, and then a faint trace of wonder showed.

And then, like the snapping of a steel cable, his tension broke, and he seized her roughly, holding her tightly and kissing her with passion, half crying, half laughing with hysteria, relief and joy.

"Lena darling, forgive me," he kept choking over and over again, pressing his cheek to hers.

Her fingers played about caressingly with his hair, but she was bewildered, and her eyes sought me.

I was beaming.

"It's all right," I kept burbling. "He knows! He knows!"

The genuineness of our uninhibited behaviour must have been apparent to her. Perhaps she sensed, too, that that barrier between her and Rob had vanished right away, for she gave a glad, warm little cry and embraced him.

I was striding elatedly up and down the room impatient to give her proof, but when I did get in with my story and my exhibit she listened with scarcely half an ear. She did not need any other proof than the manifest love of Rob.

Presently she said: "Take me out in the sunlight. Let me see the world again."

And so we pushed the bed on its castors out through the french windows on to the verandah and into the golden afternoon sunlight.

There was the Howdean valley spread out below us, and "Hawthorns" crowning the neighbouring hill. Lena looked across at her home with fondness. That which was lost was found again.

Once more the world was wonderful, and full of colour and promise. I was quite heady—I felt like singing.

Rob smiled at me.

"Perhaps we were not so foolish after all in leaving it to Whom we did," he said.

"No more arguments, Rob," I said. "I don't mean there's nothing to argue about. There will always be. But we'll not start that one again."

"Right, Doc," he said. "You're happy, we're happy—what more do we want?"

"A spell of privacy, I think," I said. "I'll leave you two to it."

They protested that they didn't want me to go.

"I must go," I said. "I came rushing up here in such a hurry I left the rest of Bill's journals and his letters lying open to everybody. With this sort of information in them! I'll have to do something about that. 'Bye! I'll be seeing you—we'll have a minor celebration tonight."

I drove back to the one-time site of the Dump, where the Inspector and his men were still picking about, but now on the far side. They looked across at me curiously, but left me alone.

From where I was I could see the hospital clearly, set on the hill in the midst of firs. I could just make out the white-bandaged head of Lena—she must have been sitting up in bed—and the dark one beside it that was Rob's, showing over the verandah rail.

Obviously they could mark me also, for they waved. I waved back.

Then I turned again to the pile of burned documents.

The two remaining volumes of Bill's diary were in such a piecemeal state that they were not worth saving. Most of the pages looked like torn sheets of black carbon paper. Besides, the legible portions contained personal matter that I thought should go no further. Most of the letters were valueless, though I selected two or three to keep for sentiment's sake.

The receipts were obviously finished business. In a little hollow I started a fire with them then and there, put the journals on it, and began feeding the remaining letters one by one to the blaze.

I paused at a typewritten one that I had glanced at only cursorily first time and dismissed as a business letter of no importance. It was the printed heading that caught my eye, a name: K. F. R. HUDSON.

I remembered him now, Ken Hudson, who had been a student with me at St. Thomas's. He'd taken up plastic surgery, and was, I had heard, doing very well as a beauty surgeon in Paris.

What had Bill to do with him?

I glanced through the letter:

...Removal of the small scars on Mrs. Leggett's neck... quite successful... in a few weeks no trace... fee, at your convenience...

Everything around me appeared to become dim and ghostly, and sounds faded as though large wads of cotton wool had been pressed over my ears. It was as though I had fallen out of the material world which had been so hard and real and alive but a moment ago. I seemed to be gazing with unfocused eyes into a grey mist, and from the mist came throbbing the wild racketing beat of that horrible machine of my imaginings.

Somewhere in the depths of my memory a voice was speaking. It was Bill's. It was quoting from that letter he had written from Paris:

"...By the way, Dot's going to a nursing home here for a couple of days..."

I tried to suppress that voice in my mind. But it persisted, and now it was saying something else. I recognized the very intonation this time.

Very distant, but very clear, Bill's voice came through the nerve-tearing clamour of the machine, speaking Cassius's line:

"Men at some time are masters of their fates..."

The moment I recorded that, the machine noise stopped like a radio that is switched off. A glad glow of realization enveloped me, and by its light and in its comforting warmth I came back from the shadow of impending chaos to the present. This moment in time was mine, all mine, and for its duration I was the *deus ex machina*. At last.

I dropped the letter into the flames, and watched it until it was quite consumed.

I raised my eyes to the hospital on its hill. Lena—the "Lena" is still deliberate—and Rob were yet sitting there as close as a pair of love-birds.

I turned to go, but paused to wave a farewell for the present. They waved in answer. They were still ten years of shared happiness away from the train smash which killed them and their two small daughters, and made the publication of this chronicle possible.

I like to remember I gave them those ten years in my brief authority.